THE GHOSTS OF THE EIGHTH ATTACK

THE GHOSTS OF
THE EIGHTH
ATTACK

David Beaty

SOUVENIR PRESS

The right of David Beaty to be identified as author of
this work has been asserted by him in accordance with the
Copyright, Designs and Patents Act 1988.

First published 1998 by Souvenir Press Ltd,
43 Great Russell Street, London WC1B 3PA

ISBN 0 285 63423 2

Printed and bound in Great Britain by
Creative Print & Design Group (Wales), Ebbw Vale

*Despite every effort, it has proved impossible to trace the copyright owner of
the poem by J.L. Hitchings which is quoted in this book and which inspired
its title and story. In future printings, such acknowledgement as may be
necessary or desirable in consequence of our use of this material will willingly
be made.*

To, for, and with B

And I sometimes think, when the night winds howl

And never a ship is out,

That I hear the roar of a DH 4,

And the wail of wires in doubt;

And I think I see in a spectre ship

Spirits that must come back;

And I hail them then, who have died like *men* —

The Ghosts of the Eighth Attack!

J.L. Hitchings

THE PRESENT

22nd December

Flight Sergeant Jack Horner

'Happy Christmas!'

The voice came through the letter flap, now being held open by two blue fingers.

I unlocked my front door. Fractionally I opened it.

A new postman, smiling, cap rimmed with frost, stamping his feet on the mat. In his right hand my sister's traditional rye from Chicago and a letter, his left opening like an oyster for his tip.

As I groped in my trouser pocket, a shaft of sunshine bored through the overcast onto the left side of my face.

I dropped my head.

Too late!

Hastily, 'Well, I'll be off, then!'

Quickly bottle and letter passed through the crack in the door.

Hurriedly, the mist ate him.

Footsteps muffled in snow.

Silence.

Slowly I unwrapped the whisky, studied the label. Indian Chief as usual. Eighty per cent proof. My sister still thought I was on the alcohol, that the only thing she had to do to fulfil her sisterly duty was to send me a bottle every Christmas. Alcohol, drugs, music, literature, religion, doctors, art, counselling, psychology — I had tried all the walking-sticks designed to help the human being along the rocky road of life, and given all of them up years ago. Here I lived, a tortoise under the shell of my bungalow roof, every now and again putting my neck out to take a quick squint at the decaying world outside before hastily withdrawing it.

I was on my own. Nothing and nobody was going to help me now. Nobody cares.

'Nobody cares, Horner!' Over the lonely years I have developed the habit of talking to myself because there isn't anyone else worth talking to. 'Nobody cares, Horner? You tell a lie! Boots cares. Securicor cares. On your last excursion to buy food, you saw that poster: Harpic cares!'

I put the rye down unopened on the hall table. Slowly I studied the handwriting on the letter.

Flight Sergeant Jack Horner, RAF.

A silly name I've always thought, redolent of the old rhyme, 'Little Jack Horner sat in a corner . . . He put in his thumb and pulled out a plum'. Fat chance of that for me!

My eyes slipped downwards to the next line on the envelope.

23 Railton Road,
Walsall.

I knew that handwriting. Large 'O's like his spectacles. Flight Lieutenant the Reverend Simon Wetherby, padre at RAF Marshfield, dunning me yet again for a subscription for the memorial window he was organising for St Michael and All Angels, the Marshfield village church.

I didn't even bother to open it. As if I'd give a farthing! As if I'd ever go near the bloody place after more than half a century of trying to forget it. Marshfield, where it all started to go wrong. Where my face had been replaced by a burned mask. Where my life had come apart into two separate pieces, and the RAF allowed me to depart with the piece it hadn't broken.

Funny chap, Wetherby. Hair the colour of a dead mouse, drooping shoulders, flat feet, face as ugly as sin. Probably a bit of a pansy. OK perhaps for holding the

4

hands of Waafs who'd lost their boyfriends, but hardly man enough to minister to bomber boys.

Aircrew didn't go to church. Wetherby had been known to pray for the Germans, for God's sake! Got on Wing Commander Cavendish's wick because he wouldn't lead the Waafs cheering our Blenheims taking off. If that bastard had spent less time trying to get rid of him, and more time kicking our boy captain back to elementary flying school, things would have been a helluva lot different, and a window in memory of kamikaze 13 Squadron would never have been dreamed up.

I stared out of the window at the grimy snow and the grey overcast, my mind suddenly flooded with memories of faces as fresh as yesterday.

Like many other boys in the mid-Thirties Depression, all I wanted was to get away from my unemployed father, away from my snivelling sister, away from the smell of washing which my overworked mother took in, away from the Walsall back street in which we lived, even away from my headmaster's pressure to try for a university scholarship.

Fired by flying films like *The Dawn Patrol* and *Hell's Angels*, I looked up into the sky and ached to be up there, way above the Black Country smoke and the grinding poverty. My mother died when I was sixteen, so there was no longer anything to stay for.

And off I went to the Birmingham RAF recruiting office.

Best education you could ever have, they told me. Taught a trade! See the world! Cheap beer and cigarettes! Good pay! Bags of promotion!

In August 1937 I signed like a shot. Found myself in a dormitory at Halton, the RAF Apprentice School. Next bed to mine, Ginger Johnson, grocer-cum-lay preacher's son — butcher-boy hands, rosy face, red hair — who'd done the same thing as I had.

5

We reckoned we were on the pig's back — taking to pieces American Liberty engines from the DH 4s flown by the Yanks in the last war, putting them together again, and listening raptly to the sweet sewing-machine sounds they made on the test bed. Promoted to corporals, we were sent for aircrew training — Ginger on a W/Op A/G course at Yatesbury, me to the Navigation School at Blackpool — then both of us posted to 13 Squadron.

Thirteen Squadron was equipped with the best aircraft in the world, they told us — the Mighty Battle, the first all-metal monoplane in the RAF, mainstay of Bomber Command.

Six months after we arrived on the squadron, the war started. But it was called the Phony War because nothing much happened. We went on patrols from our Norfolk base into the North Sea, but there was very little activity.

And then, in the Spring of 1940, the Phony War abruptly ended and the German Blitzkrieg overran Holland, Belgium, Norway and Denmark.

When the Germans penetrated into France, we were sent to Arras to stop an overwhelming invasion by bombing bridges and columns of tanks.

Strafing the German columns, we ran into solid blocks of anti-aircraft guns. The sky was full of Me 109s and Heinkels. The French put up little resistance. Our squadron lost six aircraft on our first sortie. Mighty Battle, eh? Too slow, armed with .303 pea-shooters against 20mm cannon, with Me 109s running rings round us.

Thirteen Squadron was decimated. The little Lysanders operating with us on reconnaissance were shot down like flies. Within seven weeks the RAF had lost the cream of its regular aircrew, together with 1,000 aircraft, more than in the whole of the Battle of Britain.

Nevertheless, Ginger and I were in the thick of it, completed twenty-six operations against the advancing Germans, seeing Battles, Lysanders and Hurricanes disintegrating, blazing, spinning and exploding all around us. We were only saved by the masterly flying of our pilot, Squadron Leader Rutherford.

France capitulated. The British Army left via Dunkirk. And the Germans marched triumphantly towards Paris.

Outclassed and defeated, all RAF aircraft were withdrawn from France. On 22nd June, 1940, the three remaining Battles of the squadron, piloted by Rutherford, MacGregor and Slade, flew to Abingdon where we were all sent on leave while 13 Squadron was re-formed.

The RAF had to decide what to do with us. With Rutherford it was simple. He had finished his tour of thirty operations and went off to command a flying training school. Ginger and I had four more operations to do. All we could hope for was that we would get as good a captain as Rutherford to see us safely through.

I had six weeks' leave in Walsall. Unemployment had dried up, and my father was working at a factory making Spitfires. My sister was in her last year at school.

Now Britain stood alone against the victorious Nazis. So it was not exactly a morale-building leave, while Hitler assembled an armada of invasion barges against us, and the Battle of Britain began. My leave was terminated by a telegram ordering me to proceed to an operational training unit at Bicester, where once again I met up with Ginger Johnson.

The Blenheim was originally a commercial aircraft financed by the *Daily Mail*, converted to a medium bomber. Powered by two nine-cylinder Mercury engines, it was slow. It was underpowered. The propellers could not be feathered, which made flying on one engine almost impossible. The tanks were not self-sealing so the petrol could be ignited by one bullet hit. The wireless was located behind the turret and was difficult to get to, while the T1083/R1082 transmitter/receiver was cumbersome and complicated. A back-up R/T set had only a

7

small range. There was a front gun, fired by the pilot by a button on the control column beside the bomb firing button. The turret was equipped with two .303 Brownings, hydraulically operated by foot pump and twist-grip handles. Should the controlling wire snap, the heavy turret would immediately descend, on occasion breaking the air gunner's neck. Against its German counterpart, the formidable cannon-firing Ju 88, the Blenheim could not compete.

But at least the Blenheim was better than the Battle, and at least we were together again. There we stayed at Bicester, with the RAF apparently forgetting all about us till the end of September when we were again posted to 13 Squadron, now based at an airfield called Marshfield on the south coast of Kent.

Ginger and I met up in London. The Luftwaffe had recently turned its attention on the capital, bombing the docks and Woolwich Arsenal and all stations in between. There was a helluva raid going on when we left London Bridge station, and the outlook on the other fronts wasn't brilliant. U-boats were sinking more ships than we could build. Food and fuel supplies were dangerously low, strict rationing had been imposed and, to our shame, the Eyeties had advanced from Abyssinia into British Somaliland and were streaming across the Libyan border into Egypt.

But on the way down through Kent we neither talked nor thought of the war situation except in so far as it affected us — our tour of thirty operations and completing those four still outstanding. And most important, who we would get as our skipper.

'We won't get some sprog straight out of OTU?' Ginger asked me. 'The RAF wouldn't do that to us, surely?'

Ginger was always the optimist. He went on, 'It'll be some second-tour chap, I bet.'

All I said, as the intermittent sunshine gave way to a

sudden heavy shower, was, 'I hope Marshfield doesn't live up to its name.'

Marshfield. Even then, I knew I would never forget that name.

Freud said you forget what you want to forget. Certainly forgetting was what I wanted most. I wanted to forget everything about Marshfield,

But up came memories — a few words, disjointed incidents, faces. And the face that came up most, the face I most wanted to forget, returned with such a vivid intensity that my whole body shook and trembled every time I thought of her.

I tried to turn my mind to other things. But in spite of all my efforts, the pictures, the voices, the sounds, kept breaking through the ruins of my memory.

Where did they come from? How did they appear, like now suddenly into my brain, in the air all round me? All mixed up, jumbled, flashes of light disappearing into darkness. But too small, too brief, too muzzy, too quick adequately to be placed and understood.

A feeling of being lost in a wet something — was it cloud? Of bending over photographs with the Intelligence Officer shaking his head at me silently and sadly. Another too quick exposure. A Wing Commander shouting about a court-martial. The Navigation Leader retracing on a fresh dead reckoning sheet the plot on my chart and putting my fix in a totally different position. Sounds of heavy gunfire, the smell of cordite, Me 109s so close I could see the pilots' faces. A quick shot of an enormous ship belching fire. Mosquitoes that turned into German fighters. A pool of blood glueing my boot in the cockpit. Trying to unclench dead hands. The ground rushing up to meet us.

Then suddenly feeling burned by yellow and red fire, choking in smoke — just seeing Ginger's face looking down at me, his arms coming towards me.

9

Each one of those visions must have happened to me, the ones I wanted to forget — operations from Marshfield, broken pieces which desperately I tried to put together again and understand. I even tried talking to a psychologist beside my bed, but he didn't answer, simply went on asking his own questions. What can you expect, he said, after thirteen months in a coma?

So the jumbled pattern continued, sometimes just one frame, next a whole blurred cine film, going first forwards, then backwards.

And all the time, echoing in my ears, Blenheim engines were revving up to take-off power . . .

Now, sitting by the frost-flecked window, still holding the whisky bottle and the padre's letter, I watched a robin with one leg shivering on a holly tree, all very seasonal and Christmassy.

And suddenly I heard her voice.

From way back on that last walk along the military canal that I could remember, words from decades ago came over to me — sweet, sharp and crystal-clear.

'Look round, Jack! Slowly, slowly! A robin with one leg is on a bough observing you.'

I could see that robin again as clearly as I could see this robin. And just as that robin had chirruped, so did this robin, opening its beak and singing to the snow.

And that wasn't the only sound. Suddenly from the sky came a song equally sweet. Not the raucous macho roar of a jet engine, but the feminine sound of a sewing-machine. Now it was the Halton engine shop that came back to me. Listening to the sound of the First World War Liberty engine from a DH 4 that Ginger and I had both been working on.

Quickly I opened the window, put my head out, stared upwards.

Nothing. Just cloud flecked with falling snowflakes.

10

But it had been there. A DH 4 had been in the sky, calling to me.

I sat back. Well, it wasn't there now. Neither were the pictures, the sounds, the voices.

One picture alone now obsessed me. The picture of lying in bed and an orderly pointing out to me a man in a long white coat talking to a nurse by the door of a ward and saying, 'Doctor Stainthorpe saved your life.'

And I was saying, 'What life?'

What life indeed? I'd got a job in a big, anonymous Manchester home for the disabled, teaching them carpentry and elementary engineering, a job I kept till I retired. And then I disappeared into my Walsall tortoiseshell.

She had never written to me. None of 13 Squadron had ever been near me. Only my sister had visited me in hospital, when finally I was conscious, to tell me excitedly that she was engaged to an American naval lieutenant with whom she left after the war as a GI bride.

Boots, Securicor and maybe Harpic cared about me. Nobody else did. And here was the padre's letter in my hand, inviting me to go back to a life I never wanted to remember.

I opened it. Sure enough, an invitation to all RAF and WAAF who had served at Marshfield, to the unveiling of the memorial window in St Michael and All Angels church (I always thought it a laugh that St Michael was the patron saint of airmen) in four days' time.

December 22nd.

That was a date to remember, not that I could. But I knew from my medical records which I'd pinched when the nurse wasn't looking, the true significance of 22nd December, 1940.

That was the day I was first admitted to the first of the five hospitals to which I went, still unconscious. So that was the day I collected all those physical insults to my body.

Something memorable must have happened on that day, in which I had taken part. Something worthy to be commemorated. That date had been carefully chosen.

There had been times, as I walked with her along the military canals, thinking about the future, when I dreamed the dream which the poet brought to life:

> . . . ere I descend to the grave,
> May I a small house and large garden have . . .
> A Mistress moderately fair,
> And good as guardian angels are,
>   Only beloved and loving me.

Well, I certainly got the small house, but the garden is small. As for the mistress 'good as guardian angels are', I'd given up all hope of finding her again when I emerged from the coma and saw my face.

It was the sort that would make children run squealing to their mothers.

McIndoe and his East Grinstead Hospital Guinea Pig Unit had done their best, but . . .

What do I do with my time? I spend most of it alone, reading a lot, listening to music and Radio 4. I have an old Austin that I maintain myself, which is gradually turning into a valuable antique. In it I go for trips over Britain, taking my food and a sleeping-bag with me and kipping down on the back seat because I don't fancy strange beds.

Now and again, out of my wounded memory come words . . .

'Look round, Jack! Slowly, slowly! A robin with one leg is on a bough observing you.'

After all those decades, again those same words came over to me — again sweet, sharp and crystal-clear.

And suddenly the robin with the one leg flew up and perched itself on the holly bush just outside my window.

I read the padre's letter over and over again, rolling it round my hand, wondering what I should do.

Should I go?

'The Past is another country,' a wise man had written. 'They did things differently then.'

Did they? I didn't know my past, the most important parts of my past. I'd always said I didn't want to know it either. But now I studied that date in the padre's letter, 22nd December, and thought to myself, that date had been chosen for some reason. And that date was the date I'd been put to sleep in a coma for thirteen months.

If I didn't go back to Marshfield, I'd never know what happened.

My eyes went out again to my tag end of garden. Now it was snowing hard. But the one-legged robin was still there, shaking itself and chirruping.

'Why not?' I said to myself. 'Why not?'

So here I was after all, back into the icy ectoplasm of a Marshfield mist, vowing to head back to Walsall straight after the service, pushing the creaking lych-gate open, and walking up a slushy path to St Michael and All Angels.

A line of white RAF headstones, carved with wings and *per ardua ad astra* (standard issue, always kept handily ready in Stores), stopped me in my tracks. They were too far away for me to read the names. But I stopped. Out of respect, I suppose, even though I didn't know whose they were.

I groped helplessly within the mists of my moribund memory.

I was still standing there, looking across at the graves, when I felt a clap on my back.

'Jack!'

I turned to the right.

13

Ginger Johnson himself! With Pam from the Parachute Section!

And immediately he was telling me all about himself and how he'd stayed in the RAF and married Parachute Pam and they had a family, while all the time I kept my head turned away from them.

'Now it's your turn, Jack! What've you been up to?'

'Nothing much, Ginger. A real stay-at-home, that's me.'

And then I had to move to let a couple past. I saw tears in Pam's eyes as she looked at me, and Ginger was saying hurriedly, 'Hadn't we better be going in?'

So I led the way into the porch. It was swathed in garlands of ivy and Christmas roses. And then into the soft shadowy glow of the candlelit nave. More Christmas roses, twisted here with hop-bines. Regiments of candles along all the beams and on every ledge, their flames smoking and dancing in the draught from the open doors. A decorated Christmas tree stood in one side-chapel, in the other — the Lady Chapel, I suppose — a huge sheaf of virginal white lilies.

The smell of warm candlewax mixed dizzily with the scent of flowers and hops and pine, and the smell of people close together. The pews were almost full, taken up by a congregation of oldsters and boys in uniform. Had I not met up with Ginger and Pam, I might have turned on my heel and gone before it ever began.

But I didn't. I led the way towards the darkest corner and ushered Pam and Ginger into a couple of spare seats, while I took one where I could have the protective shadow of a Norman pillar over me.

Suddenly, a fanfare of trumpets. We were on our feet for the congressional hymn and in came the Colour Party — the 13 Squadron standard held by a white-gloved flight sergeant of the present 13 Squadron. And then of all things (and that was something my memory certainly

14

couldn't explain) in came the Stars and Stripes carried by a master sergeant in USAF uniform.

They moved slowly to the altar where a doddery, over-dressed cleric, an RAF retired Chaplain-General according to the printed Order of Service, received both standards, which were angled to each other beside him.

As the 13 Squadron standard unfurled, I saw its phoenix badge and underneath its motto, 'Out of the Fire'.

What a load of old cobblers, I thought, putting up my hand to shield my face. That's what rose from the fire — burned flesh, burned bones, a nightmare face. I kept my hand over my face as the organ groaned into silence and we all sat down again on those ancient oak pews.

Then the retired Chaplain-General spread his pale hands and quavered, 'Welcome back to Marshfield!'

THE PAST

29th September, 1940
to 22nd December, 1940

1

'Marshfield . . . Marshfield . . .'

An old man in a peaked cap stamped his feet in front of the two beheaded poles where the station name had once been, intoning sonorously, 'Marshfield! Alight here for Marshfield!' before disappearing in a ghostly white cloud as the engine blew off its steam.

'This is it, Ginger!'

Jack Horner, a tall gaunt-faced flight sergeant, wearing the navigator's half wing, dragged his battered suitcase from the rack, slung his respirator and tin hat over his shoulder and picked up his kitbag.

'You heard what the man said. Alight here.' He shoved his head through the open window to turn the carriage door handle. 'Jesus! What a dump! And Christ, it's raining again!'

'Certainly clouded over,' Ginger said cheerfully. 'Mebbe a good thing.' He turned his small bright blue eyes skywards. 'With all them up there.'

'Typical Johnsonian understatement,' Jack Horner scowled. 'Hellfire corner! That's what we've come to.'

And in confirmation of his gloomy prediction, as they stepped out onto the platform an air raid siren on top of the railway station suddenly began to howl.

The city had been in the middle of an air raid when they pulled out of London Bridge. Their noses had been filled with dust and the acrid stench of burning. Sirens were howling, ambulance and fire bells ringing, the crump of bombs, the boom of ack-ack fire. Looking down

19

as the train clanked over the bridge they'd seen buses upended, office blocks and houses turned to rubble, the streets awash with burst hydrants. A right busman's holiday, as Ginger had remarked. And down through the glistening garden of England, with its hop-bines heavy and ripe in the intermittent September sun, the blue and white sky had been crisscrossed with vapour trails, spattered with wheeling, diving, warring aircraft. They had seen five separate aircraft, fire bursting out of their bellies, nose-dive to the ground.

'Ker-rump!' Ginger had said cheerfully each time, licking his finger and chalking up an imaginary tally on the dirty compartment window. 'One of theirs.'

'Never knew the Huns flew Spitfires,' Jack Horner had said with his daunting adherence to truth and reality.

'They weren't Spits!'

'You know bloody well they were!'

They had argued mildly to pass the time. Twice they had ducked as first an Me 109 and then a Hurricane had screeched inches above the carriage roof. Ginger had brought the *Daily Sketch* out of his pocket, but had tossed it away when he saw an item about Hitler's latest boast that barges would be landing on the Romney Marsh coast of Kent. Ginger Johnson hadn't a nerve in his stocky body, but he never liked taking on board irrelevant information. Skilled gunner that he was, he kept his eyes dead ahead on the target and nothing else.

But several times during the journey he had remarked with rare feeling, 'Hope we get a decent Skipper.'

'I'm going to make bloody sure we do!'

Aerial combat had continued fiercely above them. Then, just after Ashford, the clouds had rolled in from the south-west, and now a light, mizzling rain had begun to fall, shrinking the daylight.

'Any RAF transport waiting out there?' Jack asked the porter, as they handed over their railway warrants.

'You'd be lucky!' the railwayman said, waving off the train. 'Just a tractor out there and a beet lorry.'

'Going towards the airfield?'

'No, matey! Hard luck! The other way. You want that-away!' He jerked his thumb to the west. 'Coupla miles, no turnings. Can't miss it. And the best of British luck!'

As they humped their kit-bags on their shoulders, there was a muffled explosion, followed in rapid succession by two more.

'D'you lads want the shelter? It's just down here,' the railwayman called after them, making for the direction in which he was pointing.

'No, thanks,' Horner called back. 'Claustrophobics, us!'

'Oh! Well, you better put your tin hats on!'

He waved them off down a country road, thin as an eel, which wriggling round the reeds and rivulets of Romney Marsh connected the railway station with the village.

Now, above the low cloud, they could hear the desynchronised grind of enemy aircraft.

'More Spits,' Jack Horner remarked sarcastically.

Ginger smiled unconcernedly. 'The Huns are lousy shots.'

'Yeah! But they might get us while they're aiming for Buckingham Palace. Or the Short's factory.'

'Or the Liverpool Docks.' Ginger drew in his breath. 'I can smell the sea.'

'Too bloody close. Listen! Stop a minute! I can hear the bloody sea, never mind smell it! Waves breaking.'

'I can't hear then!'

'It's the guns. Made you deaf, Ginger! Sea can't be more than a few hundred yards away. Just beyond that bloody dreary-looking marsh.'

He pointed to the south of the road where flat mar-shland, covered in short, tussocky sheep-grazed grass, was intersected with the old Napoleonic canals left over from

21

that previous invasion threat a hundred and twenty-five years ago.

Twenty miles across the Channel, a thousand enemy barges had been assembled in Calais, in Boulogne, and in Dutch and Belgian ports. Three times as many tanks, four times as many guns, twice as many aircraft as Britain then possessed were to provide the spearhead for a highly trained and victorious German army to make the short crossing to land along the Romney Marsh coast.

'It is a bit dreary-looking,' Ginger conceded.

'And this is a helluva long road.'

'But we're coming to a village now. Of sorts.'

'Of sorts being the operative word, Ginger.'

Built on sand a foot above sea level, at first sight the village appeared to be sinking into a stagnant swamp to join the English Channel to which it had once belonged. They passed a couple of semi-detached cottages with thatched roofs and clematis round the doors, their once pretty gardens now filled with cabbages.

'Diggers for Victory, Ginger.'

A small discreet notice on the gate of the second one read 'Eggs for Sale'. A young woman smiled at them from the doorway. 'Crumpet!'

'Aye, aye, Ginger! I'm making a note in my navigator's log.'

Then fields again, and ahead, to the right, a grey stone church tower half-hidden by trees and, right beside them, the beginnings of its ancient churchyard wall.

'I hate churchyards,' Horner sighed.

Ginger quickened his pace. 'I don't go all that much on them myself.'

And then, as if determined that they should not pass it by unnoticed, an obelisk reared its ugly head. Standing near to the wall and a couple of feet taller than the mass of headstones, soaked and darkened in the mizzling rain, it glared out on the road, demanding attention like the Ancient Mariner himself.

Like the Wedding Guest, they halted, their eyes suddenly riveted first by a carving of the Stars and Stripes on top of the obelisk and, immediately below it, that of an aircraft — their familiar friend, the DH 4.

'So what story do you tell, old friend?' Horner asked, quite cheerfully for him.

He leaned forward to read.

But the story was far from cheerful.

'Erected,' said the obelisk, 'by the villagers of Marshfield in proud and loving memory of the men of the 96th Air Bombardment Division of the United States of America who served at RAF Marshfield in the autumn of 1918, and who distinguished themselves in the successful penetration of the Hindenburg Line, continuing their attack until all had perished, but achieving their objective.

'Ten days later, the Armistice that ended the war was signed on the eleventh hour of the eleventh day of the eleventh month, November 1918.'

And at the bottom was carved in gold letters, 'They shall rise on wings as eagles.'

'What a load of old cobblers,' Jack Horner said. 'They'll stay in the ground, same as the rest of us. Come on, Ginger! Quick march!'

They tramped in silence until they came to a line of cottages, a general store, a post office, and a small builder's yard. Then a long, low white-washed pub cowering sulkily under a heavy, sodden thatch.

A swinging sign displayed the American flag again.

'The Stars and Stripes,' Horner read aloud. 'Bloody awful name for an English pub!'

'I expect they used to drink there.' Ginger often stated the obvious. 'The 96th.'

'Can't say I fancy drinking there much.'

'Any pub's better than no pub, Jack!'

'Maybe. But we don't seem able to get away from Yankee bastards, do we?'

After the Stars and Stripes, the village petered out and they followed the road in silence to where the first indication that an airfield was ahead materialised in the shape of a barbed-wire fence and, on the horizon, the familiar black rectangle on stilts of the water tower.

'We're nearly there,' Ginger remarked. 'Oh, and look!'

His voice rose eagerly. The barbed wire had suddenly grown into metal uprights ten feet tall, bent outwards with sharp spikes at the end of each. There was a big gateway with a red and white pole across it, and a small guardroom beside that. A newly made road led to a group of corrugated iron Nissen huts crouching like petrified woodlice. And between two of them, a gaggle of those most delectable items, blue-clad Waafs.

'Marshfield's got Waafs!' Ginger exclaimed.

'Of course they've got Waafs! They've all got them these days.'

'Not all,' Ginger corrected. 'Anyway, I wasn't banking on it.'

'I was,' Horner said.

'Get away! You'd no idea. Anyway, it's a bonus!'

They continued with a lighter step.

'They're keeping them far enough away,' Horner grumbled as it transpired that at least half a mile separated the Waafery from the main camp.

'Suspicious lot, the higher-ups!' Ginger smiled good-temperedly. 'But we'll have bikes. And there'll always be buckshee transport.'

'Like today? Like now?' Horner asked drily.

'Soon as we know the ropes, we'll be in like burglars.'

'With that fence?'

'We'll go in all legal through the gates.'

A hundred yards farther on, the new high fence gave

way to the old barbed wire of the perimeter and, half a mile beyond that, the airfield proper, or at least the 1939 apology for it. A guardroom full of service police, guarding the entrance barred by a red and white pole, the Station Headquarters block with its flagpole directly outside, the RAF flag drooping disconsolately in the mist. Farther away, a couple of rusty old hangars and a concrete control tower. No runways, only a field of green grass, and ancient huts that had once housed the gallant 96th. Clearly a Great War airfield hastily resurrected to repel the Hun once again, a Hun now so close across the Channel you could almost hear him draw breath.

The All Clear was sounding by the time the SP on the gate had directed them to the Sergeants' Mess — four large shiplap huts set crosswise on concrete blocks.

'Ginger! Did you see what I saw?' Jack Horner pointed to the rotting timbers at the base of one of the buildings.

'What? A Waaf?'

'No! A rat! A great big brown one. Popped in that hole.'

'Nah,' Ginger said. 'That's what the concrete blocks are for. To keep them out.'

'Trouble with you, Ginger! You never see what you don't want to see.'

'Nor smell what you don't want to smell,' he added when they pushed open the door of the Mess hall and he rightly grumbled that it stank of rotting cabbages, which Ginger denied.

'I smell no cabbages. I smell bacon.' Ginger rubbed his plump pink hands together. 'Bring on the bacon and the dancing girls.'

There was bacon, fatty, stringy stuff, and two fat Waafs to serve it behind the hatch.

Ginger chatted them up, found out that a number of new boys for the squadron had already arrived, and got an extra rasher of bacon for both of them, together with a dark brown slice of fried bread which oozed gobs of fat when their forks were dug in.

As they were swallowing their last mouthfuls, the tannoy blared out,

'All new arrivals report forthwith to 13 Squadron office for crewing up!'

Horner and Ginger exchanged glances.

'This is it!' Horner said, getting to his feet. 'Our life or death moment!'

Ginger waved farewell to the two fat Waafs, and fell into step beside Horner. 'Don't worry. We're going to get a good Skipper, I know we are.'

But he touched the rotting wood of the door jamb.

Horner scowled. 'Sez who?'

'Sez me! Sez my bones! I got a feeling.' He rubbed his stomach as they marched across the grass to the squadron office block. 'A good feeling.'

The crew room was noisy and smoke-filled, crowded with baby-pink faces and excited chatter. It was not unlike the market in *Far From the Madding Crowd*, which Gabriel Oak attended looking for a job. Only here it wasn't shepherds that were up for sale, but aircrew and their lives.

Gazing around, Ginger's self-confident smile wavered.

And then both he and Horner felt an arm round their shoulders, heard an exaggerated Scots voice announce, 'Welcome to the kindergarten, laddies!' as the big brawny bulk of Flight Lieutenant Angus MacGregor inserted itself between them.

MacGregor, Rutherford and Slade had been the only three Skippers to have survived the gruelling Battle of France. MacGregor was a superb and daring pilot, kindly and convivial, but for some reason trusted more in the air than on the ground. He had the dark red hair and the light blue eyes of the Highlander, though he affected a strong and rather irritating Glaswegian accent. He made people feel uncomfortable. Partly it was the artificial accent, partly those light blue seer's eyes, both proclaiming he wasn't quite what he seemed.

Or worse, that he saw more than was good to see.

Which was the truth. A long time ago, in his childhood in fact, he had discovered that he had inherited some of that Highland gift or curse of *tarbhseatachd*, the second sight. He had taken an inordinate dislike to the bike his elder brother had been given for his birthday, had begged him not to ride it, two weeks before he was killed colliding with a lorry.

It was not all gloom. MacGregor had on several occasions lightheartedly used his gift by offering to tell their futures to the prettier girls at parties. It was a useful line to shoot. Pleasurable too, holding a young girl's hand and telling her what she wanted to hear.

But lately the curse had tightened its grip. He had begun to see what he didn't want to see. In France, he had seen curious dark haloes around the heads of aircrew who later went missing. He tried to tell himself it was imagination, but what he really feared was that he was losing his grip, getting shit-scared, that if he went on like this he would be a candidate for the dreaded LMF, Lack of Moral Fibre diagnosis, feared by all airmen.

He could confide in no one. So his accent became more exaggerated, his demeanour more devil-may-care.

'Got myself a wee bairn of a navigator to take Smith's place.'

Smith like Rutherford was tour-expired and now on rest. 'Doesnae need a razor yet. Still got his milk teeth, I shouldn't wonder.' He sighed. 'I suppose you two laddies are looking for Rutherford's replacement?'

'That's right,' they answered in unison, their eyes darting hither and yon in the smoky gloaming, trying to spot a likely experienced-looking pilot.

27

'There's only one pilot here.' MacGregor pointed. 'That bonny wee bairn in the corner.'

Ginger and Horner followed the direction of his finger. Wee bairn the bod certainly was, but even his mother couldn't have called him bonny. Untidy blond hair. Spots visible even at this range. A loose and vacuous smile showing uneven teeth. He was proudly clutching his round hat, over which the clot must have poured a pint of oil to make it look like a veteran's, and being chatted up by a thug of a WOP/AG, a girlish blush rising up his dirty schoolboy neck.

'I don't believe it!' Horner growled.

'Nor do I,' Ginger agreed.

'Name of Maddox. Peter Maddox,' Angus went on. 'Introduced himself by telling me he'd looped a Blenheim.'

'He can't be Rutherford's replacement,' Horner said.

'He can't be our pilot,' Ginger breathed.

But he was.

As if suddenly aware of the identity of the two new-comers, Maddox came over with his right hand extended.

'Are you Horner?' he asked in a hoarse squeak as if his voice hadn't broken properly.

Horner nodded wordlessly.

'And you must be Johnson?'

'Yes,' Ginger said.

'I'm Pilot Officer Maddox. Your new Skipper.'

There was an uncomfortable silence. To break it, Maddox went on, 'I'm from 11 OTU.'

'How many hours,' Horner rasped, 'solo on Blenheims?'

'Nine!' Maddox said, as if it was something to be proud of.

Horner closed his eyes.

'Done your fighter affiliation?' Ginger asked.

28

Maddox shook his head. 'The Hurricane boys were too busy with Jerry.'

'Night flying?' Horner asked, opening his eyes wide.

Maddox shook his head cheerfully again. 'Weather was clampers. Not to worry. Wing Commander Cavendish said we'd do it here.'

'Jeezus!' Horner said under his breath, and aloud, sharply, 'OTUs have to train aircrew to full operational standard *before*,' he emphasised that word heavily, 'posting them to squadrons.'

Then his eye was caught by a notice on the door at the far end of the room: 'Wing Commander Charles Cavendish, Officer Commanding 13 Squadron.'

Horner grabbed Ginger by the arm. 'Come on, Ginger!'

Teeth gritted, his big jaw jutting, Horner marched them both in, bypassing the mildly surprised adjutant sitting in the outer office, and knocked on the CO's door.

Wing Commander Cavendish looked up bleakly from his desk as they came in and saluted.

'Yes?'

'Horner and Johnson, sir.'

'So what can I do for you?'

Amazing how antipathy, irritation, hostility and condescension could be conveyed in an aristocratic drawl, in so few words and in such an apparently polite enquiry.

And it wasn't just the drawl. Horner saw the irritated frown that drew together the black brows, felt his own gaze held by the the glitter of anger in the hooded eyes, perceived the flaring of the thin nostrils, the faint curl of the lips beneath the small black moustache, and knew they would get nothing from this poncy tailor's bloody dummy with his Gieves jacket and the polished 'A's of the Auxiliary Air Force in his lapels, signalling loud and clear that Daddy had paid for his flying lessons.

From his side of the desk, Wing Commander Cavendish, Eton and Oxford, now charged with the task of reforming and revitalising a decimated squadron, saw two potentially bolshie flight sergeants and prompted sharply, 'Well?'

'It's about the pilot we've been crewed up with, sir.'

'Pilot Officer Maddox?'

'Yes, sir.'

'Good type. Keen as mustard.'

'Sir, Johnson and I did twenty-six ops in the Battle of France. Only four more to do to finish our tour.'

It was not the most tactful statement to his commanding officer who, through circumstances beyond his control, had not yet been on any operations.

'I know that.' Cavendish put both his hands behind his head and leaned back easily in his chair. 'Jolly good show!'

'We've only four trips to do.'

'So you're a very experienced pair.' He proffered the velvet glove of a frugal smile. 'That's why I deliberately gave you to Maddox. You can build up his confidence. I'm relying on you two to see him through.'

'Who's going to see us through?' trembled on Horner's lips, but what was the use? What did this inexperienced toffee-nosed scion of the landed gentry know about operations and who did what in any crew? Instead, aloud, he expostulated, 'He's just a schoolboy!'

'So are they all.'

'But he's so . . . well . . . you've only got to look at him to see . . .'

Cavendish interrupted Horner. 'Experienced pilots are as scarce as hen's teeth.'

'Couldn't you get some in, sir?'

Perhaps it was said in all innocence, but probably it was not. 'Getting some in' in RAF slang meant going on operations, and this bolshie flight sergeant had no doubt heard and was subtly reminding his commanding officer that he hadn't a single one to his credit, had in fact extricated himself by devious pulling of strings from a safe bum-polishing chair at Air Ministry.

Cavendish's eyes narrowed. 'The RAF has not got any more experienced pilots,' he enunciated slowly as if to an idiot.

'Because they squandered them all in the Battle of France.'

'Not at all!'

'Sir, I don't think you were there.'

Wing Commander Cavendish simply ignored that and continued with steely clarity. 'The reason has been the weather. The OTUs have had to cut down on training.'

'So they pass out untrained pilots to fly on operational squadrons.'

'Quite untrue!'

'Maddox is one of them! He hasn't done his fighter affiliation. Or his night flying.'

In a second, Horner thought, he's going to remind me that there's a war on, and then I really will fall about. Instead Cavendish simply glowered at him with undisguised loathing. Now I've really blown it, Horner thought, and on the very first day. My CO hates my guts. No use asking him for any favours.

'Command,' Cavendish spoke slowly, 'has suggested that those exercises could best be carried out on the squadron's training programme. Which is what 13 Squadron is doing now.' He stared keenly at Horner. 'Don't worry. The squadron will not go on operations until everyone is top line. If you look at tomorrow's Detail you will see you are flying in the afternoon.'

'With Maddox?'

'Of course with Maddox.'

'But, sir —'

With crushing deliberation, Cavendish picked up a pen and began to sign a letter on his desk. Without looking up, he said, 'I'm sure you will soon settle down with Peter.'

'Sir . . . the RAF can't do this to us! Johnson and I . . .'

Cavendish tossed the letter into his 'out' tray and addressed Ginger. 'Is that all, Johnson?'

Horner opened his mouth to interrupt, but Ginger took his breath away by simply nodding and answering humbly, 'Yes, sir.'

Back in the crew room Horner exploded. 'Thanks for your help, Ginger!'

'That's all right, Jack.'

Horner clenched his fists and drew a deep breath. Ginger was a dead eye behind a Browning, but, Jeezus, on the ground he could be as thick as four short planks.

'We're landed with him now!'

'So it would seem.'

Horner began, 'Don't you see what's going to happen . . .?'

Then he gave up. Accept what's coming to you was Ginger's philosophy. No imagination, that was his trouble.

In their room in the Sergeants' Mess that night, the two of them hardly exchanged a word. Horner's silence didn't seem to worry Ginger. He cleaned his buttons and cap badge and made down his bed and then began to fiddle with his radio. He got Lord Haw-Haw who was rabbiting on about the imminent invasion of Britain and all the barges assembled and raring to land on the south coast in spitting distance from Marshfield.

That traitor's oily voice gave Horner the excuse to draw up the blankets over his ears and pretend to be out for the count. But he was too worried to sleep. During a friendship of nearly three years, there hadn't been a cross word between him and Ginger. Today had been the closest. Not a good start.

Horner valued their friendship above most things. They had both been close to death many times in France, and

32

that binds you together. And more important and more binding, they trusted each other. But now, Ginger was wrong. They had got through in France because of Rutherford's skill. A crew survived or died by the skill of its pilot. So they had to object to an inexperienced boy like Maddox. But he and Ginger had to object together. Otherwise authority in the shape of Cavendish would divide and rule.

And the little clueless clot would kill them all.

2

The following afternoon, the little clueless clot was throwing his weight about at Flights to the shielded amusement tinged with sadness of Leading Aircraftwoman Phyllis Armitage, a bright-eyed, curly-haired eighteen-year-old, pleasingly an inch or two shorter than he was.

In her brief time in the WAAF she had seen too many of these eager boys come and go. Now, wearing his ridiculous round hat with its oily crown, he was doing S-Sugar's visual, trying to look as if he knew what it was all about, kicking her tyres, peering at her oleo legs, gazing up critically at her Mercury engines and running a finger down a line of her rivets.

'She's on top line, sir!'

'I should hope so, Armitage.' He made another circuit of S-Sugar, and then clearly running out of items to observe or touch, he came and stood beside her. 'Know anything much about aircraft, do you, Armitage?'

She had been specially selected because of her knowledge of engines, and because of the shortage of fitters immediately taken on.

'A bit, sir.'

'Like it?'

'Love it. I wouldn't want to do anything else. They're wonderful things. Like birds!'

At that point, they were joined by the two other members of the crew, and instantly she recognised tension and trouble.

'This is Armitage,' Maddox introduced her in a lordly manner to the tall dark navigator with a big nose and jaw, and what seemed a permanent frown on his forehead. But he had kindly eyes underneath those dark brows, and when he smiled his whole face lit up.

'This is Flight Sergeant Horner. And this,' Pilot Officer Maddox waved his hand to a stocky rosy-faced bod with bristly ginger hair and a cheeky-chappie grin, 'is Flight Sergeant Johnson.'

'I'm Jack. He's Ginger.'

The boys shook hands with her. They both had firm hand-clasps. Her mother, or rather as she had now to remember to think of her, her grandmother, had always said you could trust a man with a good handshake.

'Armitage and I,' Maddox told the other two, 'have just finished our visual check, haven't we, Armitage?'

'Yes, sir.'

'No lipsticks, compacts or spanners in the works, I hope.' Ginger essayed a teasing smile.

LACW Armitage's grey eyes sparked angrily.

'Hey you! Just because I'm a girl doesn't mean I'm not a good fitter, think on!'

'Of course it doesn't! Don't take any notice of him.' Jack Horner looked at her kindly. 'That's Ginger's idea of a joke.'

'Well, I'm not laughing!' She stuck out her little rounded oil-streaked chin. 'My Chiefie'd have my guts for garters if there was a spanner in S-Sugar's works. And I'd give him them before he asked if there was.'

She spoke with a slight Yorkshire accent.

'I believe you!' Jack Horner gave his oddly beguiling smile. If anyone had told him he'd be reassured because a little bright-eyed sparrow of a girl was the fitter for his aircraft, he'd have fallen about laughing.

'Well, Ginge and I'll do our checks now.' He turned to

35

her as they began to climb into the Blenheim. 'What's your name?'

'I've told you her name,' Maddox said pompously, 'Armitage.'

'First name?'

'Phyllis.'

Horner and she both laughed simultaneously.

'That's an awful name! Doesn't suit you.' Horner shook his head. 'What do your Mum and Dad call you at home?'

Her smile faded. She shrugged.

'I'll call you Pip. That suits you.'

'Call me what you like,' she answered, her face still clouded.

She watched them mount the ladder on the port wing and disappear through the hatch, thinking there was a pair who could take care of themselves.

She turned to the gormless pilot still standing beside her and wondered what she was going to do about him.

Doing what she could about people and things had been her lot in life. She had been brought up by her Mam, now suddenly revealed to be her Gran, in a sooty terraced two-up-and-two-down in the middle of Leeds. It was close to the LNER station and the whole place shook when a train went by. They had done their best to keep it clean and make ends meet.

Her Gran was a strict Primitive Methodist, so having a good time was never even dreamed about. The nearest to fun was on the very infrequent times when Auntie Kathleen visited. She was quite young and pretty and wore tight skirts and laughed a lot. She'd married a feckless Irishman and was living in Eire. She once gave Pip a picture of herself, but her Mam, as she thought of her then, wouldn't allow her to put it up.

The only picture allowed up in the sooty little house, other than 'The Light of the World' and one of Jesus on the Cross, was a big one over the mantelpiece of an

36

angelic-faced little girl with blue eyes and fair ringlets. She was helping an enormous collie over a stile that led from one field into another exactly the same on the other side. The picture bore the unnecessary caption 'Helping Lame Dogs over Stiles'.

That, her Gran said, should be her motto in life.

'So where did you learn about aircraft, Armitage?' P/O Maddox folded his arms across his chest and squinted condescendingly down those two extra inches at her.

'Oh, they give us a course, sir. Have to pass it an' all. But I knew a bit about mechanics before I joined up. I worked on cars.'

'Your father's?'

'No, sir. My father didn't have a car.' Come to that, she didn't have a father. She had been clever at school and got a scholarship to Leeds High. But her Gran couldn't afford the school uniform.

'I worked at the local garage. Mr Smithers taught me how to service cars when his mechanic joined up.'

Although she had been taken on as office clerk, she had continued to service the cars even after Mr Smithers got a lad in, because the lad was as gormless as P/O Maddox, and she had ended up doing most of the work. That stood her in good stead when the RAF, like the other two Services, was appealing for women and she decided to join up.

Her Gran didn't object at first. But after Pip had been to the RAF recruiting office in Briggate, the main street in Leeds, and the officer there told her she would need her birth certificate — that had really thrown the cat among the pigeons.

Then it was revealed her Mam was her Gran and her real mother was the tight-skirted Auntie Kathleen, but the feckless Irishman wasn't her father, and all she could find out about her father was that he was dead or as good as.

Since she'd joined up, she had become used to men being dead or as good as. Full of life and fun one moment. Dead the next. Youngsters, not nearly as old as her father when he copped his clog.

One of the MT drivers in the hut returning yesterday from a duty run to Maidstone had seen a Spit go in the drink, two Me 109s shot down in flames. Another had crashed but she'd seen a parachute open.

It was to the Parachute Section, their visual checks satisfactorily completed, that Jack Horner and Ginger were now repairing.

'So who was giving the glad eye to LACW Armitage?' Ginger asked.

'I don't know, Ginger! You tell me.'

'As if you didn't know! I'll tell you something else. I think she gave you the glad eye back.'

'She's not that sort.'

'Wanna bet?'

'No.'

'You're right not to, Jack. They're all that sort. You just don't try hard enough, Jack. You need to be a bit more jokey.'

'Not with her.'

'You seem to know a lot about her in a very short time.'

'Give it a rest, Ginger. I'm not in the mood. I'm still thinking about Maddox.'

That wiped the smile off Ginger's face for a moment. But then they pushed open the door of the Parachute Section, and what did they find?

The Parachute Section was always dear to the heart of any aircrew. In the final instance, the parachute was the piece of silk that separated the living from the dead, and the packers who so conscientiously examined and packed them were by association guardian angels. Better still, for the most part guardian angels with pretty faces. It was apocryphal that so well were the parachutes inspected

38

and packed that they never failed you. The aircraft might, your comrades might, you might fail yourself, but your parachute, never!

And that damp Monday afternoon, there were three good-looking young Waafs behind the counter handing out the parachutes, one of whom would have lit up any day with a head of bright gold hair like the best Christmas tinsel and a large sexy mouth the colour of a new pillar box.

Ginger homed straight in on her.

'It's out of a bottle,' Jack warned ungallantly from the side of his mouth.

'I don't bloody care!' Ginger replied, making a silent apology to the Lord and the Methodist elders. 'She's a smasher.' And leaning forward over the counter, 'What's your name, Gorgeous?'

'Gorgeous'll do. But really it's Pam.'

'I'm Ginger.'

'You surprise me!' She laughed. 'Ginger what? Ginger Biscuit?'

'Johnson.'

She assumed a prim and proper expression and began busying herself with the forms for signing over the parachutes.

Jack Horner was dealt with by a dark-haired girl who whispered 'Good luck', and by the time they left the Parachute Section Ginger was cock-a-hoop at having made a date with Pam.

His euphoria ended shortly afterwards when they returned to the Blenheim and the inescapable problem of Maddox.

No matter how you looked at him, he was a clumsy bugger, and the cockpit of a Blenheim, with its haphazard control lay-out, was not the place for a pilot like Maddox. He stumbled going up the ladder into the aircraft. He got into the seat clumsily, and the attentive LACW Armitage had to help strap him into his Sutton harness like a baby in his pushchair.

The round faces of the airspeed indicator, the altimeter, the artificial horizon and the 360 degrees gyro — the most vital for flying survival — looked blankly down from the pilot's instrument panel. On the right, the twin revolution counters stood straight as soldiers, one on top of the other above the boost gauges. Under the panel to the left was the compass. Above the artificial horizon were the twin oil pressure and temperature gauges. On the left was the clock, the only instrument alive, its second hand relentlessly rotating. The red-topped throttles were on the right beside the mixture controls and the red and green undercarriage position indicators. Shuffling around in the cramped cockpit space, Horner and Johnson were apologising to the girl and swearing at each other as they pushed their way to their stations.

Horner reached the navigation table in the nose, checked the anglepoise lamp, plugged into the intercom the leads to the earphones in his helmet, checked the Identification Friend or Foe was on and the main batteries.

Ginger had struggled his way to the radio. Now he checked the transmitter/receiver before turning on the TR9 R/T.

'Marigold,' (Marshfield's call-sign), 'this is Bunter' (13 Squadron's call-sign) 'S-Sugar. Are you receiving me?'

'Strength five,' came the immediate laconic reply.

Up front, the Waaf had left. The ladder had been taken away, the hatch closed. Maddox was pressing the starter button for number one engine.

The port propeller wheezed protestingly around before the engine burst into life with a loud guffaw.

'Starting number two,' Maddox shouted through his open side window to the ground crew manning the starter acs (accumulators).

Then, with both propellers turning, after scurrying through the Before Take Off check, he waved the chocks away, opened the throttles and went squelching over the wet grass to the far end of the field.

'Bunter Control,' he called on the R/T. 'Marigold S-Sugar ready to roll.'

'Sugar cleared to take off.'

Maddox opened up both engines fully on the brakes. When he released them the Blenheim shot off like a bullet. But the take-off wasn't too bad. Apart from the fact that he got the tail wiggling like a tart's bottom, they left the ground still straight and mercifully in one piece.

But suddenly for some reason, only inches from the ground and still at full power, he put on full left aileron. The Blenheim did a steep turn to port round the control tower.

And then he had the gall to turn to Horner, a big uneven grin splitting his face, and say, 'Thought I'd let 'em know we'd arrived!'

'Look out!' Horner shrieked, resisting a temptation to hit him with the aircraft axe. 'Water tower's dead ahead!'

Maddox pulled hard over and managed to avoid it, but Horner swore he looked straight into the eyes of the outraged Flying Control Officer.

Once they had got their breath back, they cruised around the countryside, familiarising themselves with Hythe, Dymchurch, Ashford, Dover, and the outskirts of London. The southern suburbs were still smouldering after six of Kesselring's Gruppen had dropped their tons of bombs the night before. The bombers had got Woolwich Arsenal and Shellmex House. Battersea, Brixton, Camberwell, Clapham and Chelsea had all been knocked about, the damage clearly visible even with the intermittent covering of rain clouds.

'Keep a sharp look-out, Johnson,' Maddox called importantly, 'for the Hun!'

41

And then as they turned south and beyond the Channel they could see the low grey coastline of Occupied France. 'Jerry might have a go at us.'

Mercifully, he didn't. Only distantly did they see sign of enemy activity — a Spitfire getting the worst of it in combat with a Ju 88 over the Channel to the east. The last they saw, the Spit was heading for the sea.

After that, Maddox called, 'Course for base, Horner.'

Johnson winked at Horner. Most crews used 'Skipper', 'Navigator', 'Gunner', or Christian names. But Maddox was clearly going to act as if they were all at boarding school, whence he had so lately emerged.

He bounced on landing. Twice. LACW Armitage was waiting at Flights, little feet planted firmly apart, arms folded, a frown of concentration knitting her brows.

Then she put the ladder in place and climbed up to the open cockpit hatch. 'Everything OK, sir?'

'Top line, Armitage.'

He struggled like a Houdini apprentice to get out of his straps. 'Absolutely bung-ho!'

Ginger and Horner looked up to heaven.

Returning to the crew room, they stood beside Maddox as he signed the authorisation book — DCO (Duty Carried Out).

He signed it with his left hand.

Horner was struck dumb. And that really got through to Johnson as well. Once outside, Ginger exploded, 'He's a cack-hander!'

'Certainly is.'

'You know what that means?'

'Trouble.'

'That's why he's so clumsy.'

'Not just clumsy. Not just a cack-hander.' Horner was almost choking. 'A schoolboy show-off trying to fool us he's an ace!'

42

* * *

The big picture window in Wing Commander Cavendish's office at Flights gave a panoramic view of the whole of the grass airfield fringed by the huddle of Marshfield village two miles to the east. Since the first arrivals of the newly generated 13 Squadron a fortnight ago, that screen had been filled with hair-raising scenes of aircraft bouncing, swinging, ground-looping and overshooting as the Blenheims objected to their half-trained masters in their cockpits.

A noise like thunder shook the whole Flights hut.

Squadron Leader Slade and Group Captain Hurst looked up from the table in the CO's office round which they were all sitting, and watched a Blenheim bounce higher than a house three more times before coming back on the ground with an ear-splitting bang.

The Wing Commander had seen it all too often even to look up. 'Is it still all in one piece?'

'Yes, sir,' said Slade.

'You've all seen and heard the uphill task we've been assigned,' Cavendish went on. 'And you're only too aware that there are thousands of enemy barges twenty miles away, all being loaded up for the invasion. Group has given us three weeks to complete our training and become operational.'

'Ridiculous!' said MacGregor.

The Wing Commander put down his pen. 'What's that supposed to mean?'

'It cannae be done, sir.'

'And that's where you're wrong, MacGregor. It can be done, and it will be done!'

'Sir, they're as green as the grass! What hours they were originally trained on have been on unsophisticated aircraft — fixed undercarriage, flapless kites. Far too few

43

hours on Oxfords. And a pitiful introduction to the Blenheim. It's dangerous!'

'Not nearly as dangerous as the enemy waiting at the gates.'

'Sir, we've all seen their antics. They'll kill themselves if they don't get more training.'

'But they are going to get more training, MacGregor.' Cavendish's thin lips tightened. 'And you're going to give it them. Slade will be our new Squadron Leader A Flight, And you, MacGregor, as of now are our new Training Captain.'

There was a short pause while they digested that in silence.

'So can we get back to the business in hand?' Cavendish asked pointedly. 'The new boys have to carry out the exercises they did not complete at OTU, namely air to ground firing, fighter affiliation, night flying, and a long cross-country.'

'What about the weather?' Group Captain Hurst put in.

He had been at Marshfield ever since it was re-opened as a landing ground a month ago, and it had rained almost every day. An ex-RFC pilot of DH 4s in the last war, he had become responsible for this godforsaken place in the most dangerous corner of Britain. Not once had he even gone up in a Blenheim, let alone flown one. And having seen the gyrations of 13 Squadron around the Station, he had no desire to do so.

'We can't worry about little things like that with the enemy already at our throats.' Cavendish picked up a pen. 'We start the cross-countries tomorrow. Butterworth looks a reliable sort of bod, wouldn't you say, Angus?'

'None of them look reliable sorts of bods,' MacGregor replied, true to form.

'He's the only one to get an "Above Average" at FTS,' Slade put in. 'But —'

44

Hugh Slade had been attempting to do what he could on training before MacGregor arrived. Now he was only too glad to unload training onto MacGregor. The biggest problem which Cavendish had carefully not mentioned was that there were no dual controls on the Blenheim which meant the pilots' actual flying couldn't be checked out. All the instructor could do was to watch take-offs and landings which usually made him wince.

'No buts.' The Wing Commander simply continued with his list. 'Lennox seems to me a clued-up type. Have you any ideas, Angus?'

'I haven't had the chance of a word with them, sir. But from what I've seen —'

'Right then! Butterworth goes on the detail. Take-off ten hundred hours tomorrow. Let's choose the order for the other chaps.'

MacGregor reluctantly agreed that Butterworth should go off tomorrow, and Lennox the day after. Maddox could go on doing circuits and bumps and local flying before going last on the cross-country.

'Why, MacGregor?' Cavendish raised his eyebrows. 'Seems a keen little chap to me.'

'Too keen. Overconfidence masking underconfidence. The fellow needs to be watched.'

'They all need to be watched,' Slade was saying, 'but in our present situation —'

Suddenly through the open window came the sounds of a clanging bell and the screaming of a siren.

'The blood wagon,' Cavendish said.

Without a word, all four men made for the door. 'And the fire engine.'

The Group Captain led the way to his Hillman, jumped in, shoved the accelerator down to the floor.

The car hurtled across the grass to a Blenheim forlornly standing on its nose in the far hedge.

45

By the time the Hillman slid to a stop beside the ambulance, all three of the crew were out of the aircraft.

'It's all right, sir,' the Flight Sergeant pilot called out. 'We're all in one piece.'

'Which is more than L-London is!' Cavendish scowled. 'What happened?'

Slade answered for him. 'You came in too high and too fast, didn't you, Sullivan?'

Tractors came up with tow ropes. The Squadron Leader Maintenance and his Flight Sergeant arrived, The blood wagon departed with the three crew to be checked at Sick Quarters.

On their way back to his office to continue the training conference, Slade said, 'That's the third prang in a fortnight.'

'But at least we haven't had one casualty,' Cavendish countered.

'Yet,' said MacGregor.

* * *

Fifteen minutes later, he left the squadron commander's office in a state of mental perturbation. He had been sold a pup. By the good old RAF formula of giving troublemakers promotion or a position of responsibility, Cavendish thought he had disarmed him. Well, not altogether. It would take more than that spoilt, over-bred, overly rich Sassenach to disarm a MacGregor. MacGregors were the sons of kings. 'S rioghal mo Dhream — 'royal is my race' — was the MacGregor motto. MacGregors were fighters. And not just against the enemy, but against petty authority as well.

But MacGregor had to admit to himself that his right arm had been weakened and his claymore blunted by his new position as Training Captain. Something, in fact, that he had felt himself quite capable of being, but not, for

46

Chrissake, under these conditions. Not trying to square this awesome circle of too many pilots squandered in France, so many youngsters too hastily taken on and far too hastily semi-trained, resulting in yet more squandering not only of the lives of pilots, but also of their crews. Before the war ever began, ten per cent of the new Blenheims had been lost to accidents because new pilots were unable to handle their great leap in performance and complexity. Meanwhile Group and Command pressed the squadron to get into action at this most desperate state of the war. And perhaps worst of all, at this moment when, distantly but persistently, he himself was beginning to have doubts about his own nerve.

Yet who else could do it better? Who else could do it at all?

Before he addressed himself to the problem, he did what he always did when in doubt, he went for a long solitary walk. His father had been an estate manager in Sutherland, so MacGregor was used to seeking out the wisdom of the empty unsullied Highlands, alone except maybe for a dog at his heels.

Romney Marsh on a misty early autumn evening didn't compare, but it had its own almost eerie quiet. It did, that is, until he was returning from his walk via Flights, when Jack Horner came out of the hangar and hailed him.

'Bush telegraph has it you're i/c training.'

'God in heaven, some telegraph! Och, I only heard myself a half hour ago.'

'Is it true?'

'There was nae anyone else, laddie.'

Horner accepted that in unflattering silence. Then he added commiseratingly, 'A bloody awful job.'

'I know that well, laddie.'

Then Horner came swiftly, as was his wont, to the point. 'Maddox is useless. You'll need to fail him for a start.'

MacGregor frowned forbiddingly. 'That'll be up to me, laddie,' he said stiffly. 'Me and Cavendish.'

Then he stalked off, thinking, it doesnae take long to become a management man.

Maybe that was why, when he returned to the squadron offices, he really went to town. Still frowning, still not easy with himself, he nodded to the adjutant and went straight into the Flight office. Clearly Cavendish and Slade hadn't been able to give much time to the nuts and bolts of training. There was still a stack of log-books on the table, belonging to the latest arrivals, waiting for Cavendish's scrutiny. Also on the table, a rough programme, some queries on dates for fighter affiliation.

MacGregor drew up a chair and began on the stack of log-books, all new and blue and so sparsely filled, like the exercise books of new scholars at an infant school.

Conscientiously he made little notes as he worked, trying to assess who was good at what, and who weak. But they were all much of a depressing muchness. Only the log-books of two of the pilots stood out from the rest. Butterworth was the best by a short whisker, and Maddox — Jesus Christ, how had they ever let him out? — was the worst by a mile.

Twice as long as anyone else to go solo on Tiger Moths, then a lamentable period to master the Oxford. Three goes at converting to Blenheims. Twice his current instructor had passed him on to a colleague for another opinion, the comments column sizzling with controlled exasperation. But somehow he had got through, being passed out with the dismal assessment for pilot skill of 'Below Average'.

Christ, MacGregor thought, no wonder Horner and Johnson were shit scared. He'd have been the same himself. But what the hell could he do, caught between Cavendish breathing fire down his neck, and the poor material he had to work with?

48

At least, one decision was reasonably clear. Though he still said it was too soon, Butterworth was the only possible candidate for the first cross-country. Carefully he wrote out the Flying Detail for tomorrow and the next two days, and sent for a runner to come and collect it. He felt better for making that first decision.

Then he sat listening for a while to the BBC News. Blenheims from an unnamed airfield in southern England, which was probably Thorney Island, had attacked Hitler's invasion barges. That would no doubt make Cavendish and Group more eager than ever to get 13 operational and in with the action. Understandable. The proximity of those barges gave one an odd feeling. Just twenty miles of tonight's calm sea separating the British from an enemy who so far hadn't lost a battle. No wonder the powers-that-be were twitchy, maybe going to bed wondering if tonight was the night, or tomorrow the day for *Der Tag*, Operation Sea Lion, the Invasion of Britain.

However, those were their problems. His own were more immediate. He had no sympathy to spare for top brass.

It was gloaming when MacGregor got to his feet, pushed back his chair and stretched to his full lofty height. Grisewood, the adjutant, had left and gone up to the Mess for dinner. MacGregor closed the door of the squadron offices behind him and went out into the moist evening air.

A half moon had risen above intermittent cloud. As his eyes got used to the gloaming he could, from the slight hummock on which the offices stood, see the black rolls of barbed wire that edged the beach and, beyond, the white phosphorescent curl of the shallow waves.

Twenty miles away, he thought again. Maybe some Jerry bastard was also looking at the curl of the waves, almost eyeball to eyeball, maybe intoning Hitler's July directive

49

about his decision to carry out a landing operation 'to eliminate the English motherland . . . and if necessary, to occupy the country completely.'

MacGregor blew a good Scots raspberry over the water and was about to turn and get himself up to the Mess for dinner when he heard a sound behind him. It filled him with a quite disproportionate melancholy. And yet it was only the mournful sound of a dog howling at the young moon.

He heard that same sound again the next morning early when there was no moon and the sun was about to rise. His batwoman, a nervous girl with large horn-rimmed spectacles and a pleasant sing-song Welsh voice, had just called him with his morning tea.

'Did you hear that, Bronwen?' he asked her.

'No, sir! What, sir?'

'A bloody dog howling.'

'Oh, sir!' The airwoman's eyes blinked rapidly behind the horn rims. 'You're not flying today or anything are you, sir?'

'Not today, no. Why?'

'Oh, sir! It's unlucky. That's why.' She clapped her hands over her ears, lest she hear it too. 'A dog howling means a death.'

'Away with you, woman! Dinna be sae daft! It means nothing of the sort. The poor animal's hungry. Or its owner gone and left it.'

He waved her out of the room, laughing at her solemn face derisively. But he wished to God she hadn't said it.

And he wished that all the more ardently as the day went by.

3

And what a day for Marshfield and 13 Squadron! The beginning of Unlucky 13!

Early that morning, Group Captain Hurst received a telephone call from the police informing him that a red MG sports car belonging to F/Lt Phillips, the Station Medical Officer, had mysteriously collided with a tree, wrapped itself round it in fact, and that F/Lt Phillips was now in Canterbury Hospital awaiting surgery for various fractures.

F/Lt Phillips had been an amenable and co-operative medical officer with an unfortunate penchant for the bottle and fast cars. So his regrettable accident was less of a mystery to his commanding officer than it was to the police. He had been returning from a conference with the Group Medical Officer, and was clearly feeling no pain. A call to Canterbury Hospital revealed that he was unlikely to return to duty for the next few months, which left Marshfield without a medical officer just when the squadron was trying to get airborne and operational and casualties were unavoidable.

'Which leaves us,' Group Captain Hurst told the SAdO (Station Administrative Officer) 'up shit creek without a paddle. I've been on to Group. They gave me the usual bull about all our doctors being out in the Middle East, or been topped in France. But they've promised a replacement as soon as possible.'

'Give them forty-eight hours, sir. If no medic is forthcoming, then we halt the programme. That'll make them get their finger out.'

Getting fingers out was the order of the day as far as Cavendish was concerned. He brushed aside MacGregor's warning that he was still of the opinion none of the pilots was as yet ready for a cross-country, especially given the low cloud and the Hun activity.

'One cancels out the other,' Cavendish said with the certainty of an operational virgin. 'They can get into cloud in the unlikely event of a Hun straying onto their route.'

MacGregor gave Butterworth and crew a careful briefing. He had to drum into them every possible safety precaution he could think of.

'This is your route.' He traced the track drawn on the Mercator chart in front of them. 'This takes you well clear of balloons, prohibited areas and gun positions. You're inland, away from intruders. But you must watch out for the odd bandit.'

He paused and looked at the three faces now in deep concentration, with Butterworth industriously taking notes. 'First course 295 degrees magnetic to ten miles east of Bristol. Then turn south to the Quantocks.' He tapped his pencil on the map. 'Turn port to 110 degrees back to Marshfield.'

He suddenly became irritated by Butterworth's writing down everything he said. He pointed to Butterworth's head. 'There! I want it in there!'

Butterworth's face went a nervous juvenile pink as he dropped his pencil as though it was red hot.

'Fly at four thousand feet. That's well above all high ground. If the ceiling falls below that, return to base immediately. Report at every turning point. And if you have the slightest mechanical trouble, you're to land at the nearest airfield.'

The route would take them west as far as the Quantocks, then turning, skirting Portsmouth, a favourite target these days for the Hun.

Butterworth was an eager lad of nineteen with, thank God, an older navigator and gunner who had done a half-tour each in France. They listened attentively, noted the required heights, the presence of barrage balloons, obstructions and friendly but trigger-happy ack-ack which might mistake them for the enemy.

The cloud was broken and the sun shining when they took off, watched by Cavendish and MacGregor. Butterworth bumped a little over the spongy grass, held the aircraft down and then with a quick, controlled burst of power took off smoothly and competently.

Cavendish turned to MacGregor and remarked with a slight sneer as if to ask what the hell were you worrying about, 'Bloody good take-off.'

The same could not be said of the next Blenheim to become, but only by the grace of God, reluctantly airborne.

Maddox of course. Doing circuits and bumps, and missing death by inches.

The two officers watched narrow-eyed and with bated breath as S-Sugar seemed to fight the squelchy grassland every step of the way taxiing to the hedge, where it turned into wind. Brakes released, the Blenheim began zigzagging uncertainly before swinging to the left on take-off. For a moment, MacGregor thought they'd had it, and remembered Bronwen and the howling dog and shivered.

But no, thank God, clumsy, incompetent airmen must have their own guardian angel. They were airborne and away as Maddox corrected and hauled back heftily on the stick, and Horner and Johnson let out their breath in a concerted sigh.

'Did that deliberately,' Maddox said airily. 'Good practice.'

53

'You clipped the hedge,' Horner scowled. 'Did you do that deliberately?'

'We didn't clip the hedge.' Maddox flushed angrily.

'We did.'

'Don't argue, Horner. Get me a course for Maidstone.'

Horner did as he was told and didn't argue. But when they had landed, after a couple of bounces needless to say, and had taxied to Dispersal, he made a point of inspecting S-Sugar's undercarriage. And what did he find tucked up in the joints of her oleo legs, but a sizeable branch of thorn.

He thrust it gleefully into Maddox's face in the crew room, but Maddox simply refused to believe him. 'You've been over to the hedge and picked off a piece! You're doing this deliberately! You're sending me up!' He lowered his voice, 'I warn you, Horner, you are being insubordinate.'

Horner hadn't much better luck with young Pip.

'What's this?' she asked suspiciously when he presented the thorn branch to her. 'A crown of thorns?'

'Could be. My crown of thorns.'

'Get away,' she laughed. 'You're no Jesus Christ.'

'I'm a martyr.'

'No you're not.'

'I am. I'm a martyr to Maddox's flying. You saw it, didn't you?'

Her eyes clouded.

'It wasn't brilliant.'

'Jeez, that's the understatement of the year! It was bloody dangerous.'

'He has to learn.'

'But will he learn in time? I ask myself.'

'Anyway, what is this all about?' She waved the branch. 'It isn't a bouquet of red roses.'

'It's what Maddox clipped off the hedge on take-off.'

'Oh!'

54

'You might well say "Oh".'

'I thought he was a bit low,' she conceded. 'But he'll improve, He just needs confidence.'

'How about my confidence?'

'You've got bags of it.'

'No I haven't.' Horner smiled slyly, tiring of trying to convince her about Maddox and perceiving a possible advantage. 'If I had bags of confidence, I'd ask you to come out this evening.'

'Really.'

'What would you say to that?'

'I'd say you'd be dead unlucky.'

He looked crestfallen.

She took pity on him. 'Because tonight is Domestic Evening. For Waafs to make do and mend. Confined to camp.'

He brightened. 'So supposing I had the confidence to ask . . . maybe another evening?'

'Maybe,' she said.

At six o'clock she was just finishing her usual meticulous check of S-Sugar when Chiefie called to her from the doorway of the Flight offices. 'I'd like a word, hinny, soon as you've finished.'

He was standing by his table in the shabby little office, drinking a mug of tea. He handed her one already poured. Without preamble he said, 'Looks like A-Able's bought it.'

Her eyes widened. She felt a sick hollowness in her stomach. 'Butterworth?'

'Aye.' He drained his mug noisily and wiped his mouth with the back of his hand.

'Might have landed somewhere else?'

'Might. Might not.'

'Did he make any contact?'

'Not so far as I know.'

'Did he report any trouble?'

'Nope. Just flew off into the sunset. Or into the ground.'

'They haven't found any wreckage?'

'Not yet.'

'And he was one of the good ones!' she exclaimed bitterly.

'You can say that again! Makings of a good pilot. Nice little bugger.'

And that, she thought, scrubbing her oil-stained hands and sluicing her face in the tiny so-called rest room at Flights, was the epitaph of Butterworth and his crew.

She got a lift as far as the Station guardroom in a Stores van. The RAF corporal driver had heard about Butterworth being missing. Bad news travels fast on an RAF station. 'He'll just be the first of the many,' he said, parodying Winston Churchill's recent speech in the House of Commons paying tribute to the Few. 'It isn't so much the aircraft we're short of as the poor sods to fly 'em. Once Jerry's got rid of the RAF he'll just step over the pond. My Equipment Officer has put in a big indent for coffins, wooden, airmen for the use of.'

At the guardroom she thanked him grittily for an enjoyable ride and slammed the door. He wished her good night and, this being Domestic Evening, 'Good darning!'

After that she was glad of the half-mile walk alone in the cool darkness. The wind had risen, sweeping the sky. The waxing moon rode clear of the drifting swathes of rain cloud. There was the sound of gunfire far away, but no fires, no air raid warning. Just peaceful country sounds. A cow lowing, an owl hooting. And country smells, the swampy scent of the marsh mingling with crushed grass and some sage-like herb, the smell of wet leaves and dung. She tried not to think about Butterworth and his crew or how for Butterworth you could much more easily and likely substitute Maddox.

By the time she reached Hut 7 on the Waaf site, after

56

swallowing a few mouthfuls of battered cheese sandwich, a gruesome indigestible but filling concoction, in the Waaf Mess, all the girls had heard about A-Able. One of them, Doreen, had made a date with Butterworth's navigator, but it was for tomorrow so now it would never happen. As she sat on her iron bed, polishing her buttons, the tears dripped onto her buttonstick.

Pip busied herself with her own bed, stacking the three biscuits that comprised the mattress, making a sandwich of hairy brown blankets and coarse sheets, then rolling the sandwich as required in another banket like a liquorice allsort. After that she cleaned her cap badge, the buttons on her tunic and on her greatcoat, and polished her shoes.

All kit had to be laid out for inspection. Pip quite enjoyed that bit. She had never had so many clothes in her whole life, and she took care of them religiously. She even wore the blue and white striped winceyette pyjamas which everyone else despised. She was good with a needle. She darned a hole in her grey lisle stockings, sewed a button on her shirt, gave her bed space a brisk polish and then, unable to shut her ears to the muffled weeping, went over and put her arms round Doreen.

'She'll get over it.' Pam came breezing in half an hour later, with her lipstick all smudged. 'Ginger Johnson walked me down from the Parachute Section,' she whispered excitedly

'Was there any news?'

'No.' She shook her head. 'Butterworth and crew have handed in their 'chutes.' She looked heavenwards. 'Up there.'

At nine o'clock a deep and terrible voice boomed, 'A . . . a . . . tenshun!' as the door of the hut was flung open. In stamped Flight Sergeant Judson, the Waaf Admin NCO who, rumour had it, was an ex-Governor of Sing-Sing. She was smoothing the way for the Queen Bee,

Flight Officer Fortescue, who now entered to inspect the hut and the airwomen's kit. She was a deceivingly jolly-looking little tyrant, with round shiny cheeks, round currant eyes, a round body, and brown hair scraped up into a round bun on top of her round head.

But those currant eyes were as sharp as razors. Usually she could spot yards away an undarned hole or a missing item of kit, or a lock of hair on a collar. But tonight she had other things on her mind.

Without comment she walked down the two rows of girls standing to attention by their beds, then told F/Sgt Judson to stand them at ease. Then, drawing a deep, wheezy breath, she announced, 'I have an important directive to read. From no less than their Lordships of the War Cabinet.'

She paused, hoping for a sycophantic indrawn breath. When none came she continued. 'The subject of that directive, Operation Sea Lion, so called. The Nazi (like Churchill she pronounced the word "Nazzzi") threat of invasion.'

She then read out a list of do's and don'ts. Report any lights, any suspicious strangers, any parachutes seen dangling in trees or descending either singly or in numbers. Refuse lifts to strangers, refuse drinks from strangers, refuse to give directions or any sort of infor-mation to strangers. MT drivers of course knew it was a chargeable offence not to immobilise their vehicles every time they left them, and this precaution could not be overemphasised. Careless talk was now more than ever to be avoided. Should the landing take place, Winston Churchill had already given his pledge that, she read aloud in ringing tones, 'We will fight on the beaches, we will fight on the landing fields, we will fight in the streets. We will never surrender.'

At the door, she turned. 'And be particularly careful of your clothing. Never leave any item in the ablutions block or anywhere else. Enemy infiltrators have been known in the unhappy countries the Nazzzies have invaded to don female clothes.'

'Kinky bastards,' Pam whispered, trying to make Pip laugh.

'So never part with any item of apparel.'

When she had departed in an orgy of stamping and barked orders from Judson, Pam said, 'Ginger must be an infiltrator. They had a hairy trip with P/O Maddox. So he asked me tonight if he could have a pair of my knickers for luck.'

Which at least made everyone laugh.

'Lucky for who?' Pip asked.

'For all of them. Him and his navigator don't trust Peter Maddox. So Ginger wants my knickers as a mascot. You know what superstitious bods aircrew are.'

Doreen told them lugubriously that her might-have-been boyfriend had asked her for her cap badge but she hadn't dared to give it before kit inspection. Now she wished she had. And everyone began thinking about Butterworth and his crew again.

They brightened briefly when they got the stove alight. Bunty who worked in Stores had filled her pockets with coke from the fuel compound. This was eventually ignited with smears of margarine liberated by Alice who cooked in the Sergeants' Mess, therefore with access to all sorts of goodies. She had also brought along a package of tea, some sugar and a tin of Nestle's milk.

But as they all sat round the now tomato-red stove, sipping their hot, strong, sticky brew, the mood was sombre, not for the invasion, for who could really believe in that? The feeling throughout Britain was that certainly they were alone, but frankly they were better off without the Frogs and other unreliable foreign bastards.

It had all been said succinctly by King George himself:

'Personally I feel happier now that we have no allies to be polite to and to pamper.'

Throughout Britain Dunkirk had taken on the glory of a victory not a defeat. Dowding and his chicks were knocking hell out of the German eagle, and as a famous historian wrote of the British, 'They were instinctively stubborn and strategically ignorant.'

And ignorance, invasionwise, was bliss. On the other hand, Butterworth and his crew were immediate and known.

'I knew it was going to happen.' Bronwen cupped her tin mug in her hands. 'I knew it this very morning. And do you know for why?'

'No,' Pip said crossly. 'But you're going to tell us.'

Bronwen pursed her lips in the way she did when she was offended and said nothing.

'You were reading the teacups again,' Pam suggested pacifically.

'No. Didn't have to. If I had, I'd have known it twice over.' Bronwen drew a deep breath. 'I got it from one of my gentlemen in the Mess. F/Lt MacGregor.'

'So how could he know?' Pip demanded.

'He heard a dog howl.'

'So?'

'So that always means a death.'

'Rubbish,' Pip said.

'It isn't rubbish. Dogs know. Dogs smell death.'

'Lamp-posts, more like.'

'No, she's right,' Alice joined in. 'Our ration lorry driver, who's a regular boozer at the Stars and Stripes, he told me the airfield used to be haunted by a howling dog. It used to be here in the First World War.'

'That's a load of crap!' Pam and the others, except Bronwen, told her, shivering a little nevertheless.

'It isn't crap,' Bronwen said. 'You won't be told! Just

like F/Lt MacGregor wouldn't be told. But I bet he's laughing now on the other side of his face!'

* * *

Angus MacGregor was not laughing on either side of his face. He waited in Flying Control until 22.00 hours and then walked over to the Intelligence Section on the off-chance of finding Mark Pringle, the Intelligence Officer, still at his desk. Mark was a lonely man. An ex-university scientist. Rumour was that his wife had left him for another man, and he was still reeling from the blow. He was a cultured, polite, distant mysogonist. And he was still there.

'Come in, Angus. Sit yourself down. No,' he answered without MacGregor asking, 'no news of A-Able.'

'Group's been notified they're missing?'

'Yes.'

He poured Angus a slug of rum from the demijohn used for crew debriefing refreshments and handed it to him silently.

'I shouldnae have let him go,' MacGregor said, cupping the drink in his hands and staring into it.

'Come, come. We none of us should let any of them go.'

'We're rushing them through too fast.'

'Who is to say? And what is the alternative? Anyway, it was up to Cavendish. He's the one that cracks the whip.'

'Och aye, Cavendish!' Angus MacGregor sighed deeply. 'He's no doubt batting the bods' ears in the Mess about morale and the press-on spirit.'

'To give him his due,' Mark Pringle said, 'he does battle it out with Group as well. On the squadron's behalf.'

MacGregor blew a raspberry. 'Like over what?'

'Over getting in better-trained pilots.'

'And have we had a single one? No, sir!'

'More aircraft.'

'Another resounding duck.'

'He's threatened to suspend flying training until we get our replacement MO.'

'He'd never do that!'

'If the necessity arose, he might well.'

But it didn't.

At least on that score, Group in its wisdom moved quickly to fulfil Marshfield's need. A signal was delivered to the SAdO the following morning that Marshfield's replacement medical officer was proceeding forthwith on a temporary posting. Flying Officer Stamford would be with them that afternoon.

'I am glad we were firm,' Group Captain Hurst remarked to Wing Commander Cavendish when he telephoned him with the good news. 'It proves we can sometimes stick our heels in with Group and make them sit up and take notice.'

Cavendish winced at the Group Captain's mixed metaphors and agreed that on occasion firmness paid off with Group.

'Don't like the sound of him overmuch, though. Only a flying officer. Must be a real sprog.'

'They're scraping the medical barrel,' Group Captain Hurst agreed. 'But some of these youngsters are a good deal more clued up than the older types. Got all the new ideas.'

'Perhaps,' Wing Commander Cavendish agreed reluctantly. 'And perhaps more malleable. Anyway, when are you expecting him?'

'This pip emma,' Hurst said, showing his WW1 origins.

'Send him down to my office, will you, when you've had a word?'

'I shall be delighted to.'

And indeed he was, when the time came.

Group Captain Hurst neither greatly respected nor

greatly cared for his Squadron Wing Commander. He found him arrogant, high-handed and inexperienced. An unhappy combination, and a thorn in his own flesh. He himself might be regarded by the young as something of a dinosaur, a WW1 pilot who knew nothing of modern warfare, but at least he'd operated over enemy lines, in a DH 4, had seen the gossamer-thin wings of aircraft fold, had watched bodies of his comrades falling without parachutes, had twice returned with a dead gunner in the rear cockpit. He also knew the legend of the only squadron which had occupied Marshfield before 13 — the American Air Force 96th Bombardment Group. In between the wars he had been the manager of a small electronics firm. He was reasonably good with people, which the Wing Commander was not, but he always felt the Wing Commander was trying to usurp his position, making himself the real commander of Marshfield.

So when the transport from the station duly arrived and disgorged Flying Officer Lesley Stamford, his first thought was, This'll be a turn-up for the book. But serve Cavendish right.

At twenty-five, Flying Officer Stamford was a smart, good-looking woman with large blue eyes, straight black brows and a smile that the Group Captain found quite winning. He couldn't see her hair because, apart from a tiny roll, it was all tucked decorously under her very new-looking cap.

She saluted punctiliously, and sat down at his invitation for a brief chat. He could see, as he peered over his desk, that she had neat feet and ankles.

The Group Captain discovered that her father was a naval surgeon, that she had been in the RAF for only six months, was at the WAAF depot at Innsworth when this immediate posting had come through. She was delighted to be for the first time on an operational station and the poor girl was clearly very wet behind the ears.

After their chat, he sent her on her way to meet Group Captain Cavendish and waited, with his hands over his ears metaphorically speaking, for the inevitable explosion.

* * *

It was immediate.

As Lesley Stamford pushed open Wing Commander Cavendish's door he squinted down his thin nose while first incomprehension, then a massive cloud of disbelief, crossed his young/old face.

She saw a tall slim man in his mid-twenties possessed in his expensively cut uniform of a certain elegant foppishness, whom she instinctively disliked. She couldn't decide which she disliked more — that taut uncompromising face with its high cheekbones and tight-lipped mouth under that small black suitably Hitler-like moustache, or the fact that he could well have been a model for one of those Kensitas cartoons of the quintessential upper-class Englishman.

He watched her salute. He didn't invite her to sit down. 'Yes?' he asked sharply.

'Group Captain Hurst said you wanted to see me, sir.'

'To see you?' He was a man hiding in disbelief, fighting his destiny. 'Why on earth should I want to see you?'

'I'm Lesley Stamford, sir.'

Wrung out of him, shattering the composure of that well-bred face, 'I don't believe it! I just don't believe it! Even Group can't do this!'

Most women would have been intimidated. But her father had taught her to get used to intimidating men. So instead she asked quietly, 'Do what, sir?'

'Send you! Send you! You're a woman!'

'I did know that, sir,' she replied, still in that studiedly neutral, damnably disconcerting tone. 'So did Group.'

64

'How can they send a woman to a bomber station?'

'They already have, sir. Masses of them. Maybe you haven't noticed.'

'Don't talk to me like that! The women here are Waafs.'

'So? They're still women. They're doing useful jobs. Some of them doing dangerous jobs. Medicine isn't dangerous.'

'To your patients it is!'

'I resent that, sir!'

'Resent away, Flying Officer! And why are you a Flying Officer. Why not a Waaf Section Officer?'

'Because women medical officers take RAF ranks.'

'Really? Just to confuse us? To sell us a pig in a poke! And no,' he held up a well-shaped hand, 'you don't have to resent that too. I apologise. I withdraw that remark and the other. All the same, I can't be having you.'

And he stretched out his hand, lifted the receiver of the telephone to Group, and began yelling that he wasn't accepting the medical officer just posted in to Marshfield.

He was pale with anger. After a moment, he covered the mouthpiece of the receiver with his hand, and told her airily, 'Nothing personal, you understand, Flying Officer.'

'I understand perfectly, sir. I am a doctor, sir.'

He wasn't sure how to take that remark, but decided not to pursue clarification. Instead, 'Why do you call yourself Lesley?' he demanded, and before she answered, snapped into the telephone, 'Well, get him! Get him, man! I want to speak to the Group Medical Officer. I'll wait.'

'Because that's what I was christened, sir!'

'You could call yourself something else.'

'I don't wish to!'

'Well, sit down, woman, sit down! Don't stand there looking like —' he seemed to look at her for the first time.

'Well, looking like that. I am not personally objecting to you. I am objecting to your gender.'

'They are inseparable, sir,' she replied coolly.

But by that time he was connected to some medical officer at Group and was blasting away on all cylinders. 'I'm not putting up with her! Did you know she was a woman? Well, didn't you realise that would cause trouble? I don't agree! In fact, I couldn't disagree more! I do not want a woman. She won't be as competent as a male ...'

He waved a hand, and called to her over his shoulder, 'All right I withdraw that remark!'

Then he went on into the telephone mouthpiece. 'She'll be bad for morale. The crews won't accept her. I don't give a damn about your staffing problems. I know all about your losses in France. And yes, I know all about your Middle East demands. But you can't let all your competent medicos go there. We can't be left with the women! And I'm not having this one! Especially not this one! She's too wet behind the ears! She's too young ...'

He suddenly turned and threw at her, 'How old are you?'

'Ninety-five.'

'She's pert and insubordinate ... and ...' He drew a deep breath and looked over his shoulder at her again. Then he produced what he thought was the ace of trumps, 'She ... too ... pretty.'

Flying Officer Stamford had never been regarded as pretty. A more susceptible woman might have ben flattered. But she wasn't. The Wing Commander's attitude was too like that of her father who had, so her mother said, greeted the birth of a daughter with angry dismay. Only the birth of her brother two years later had mollified him. But her brother too had a mind of his own. He had refused medicine as a career, disliked the thought of the Navy, and had volunteered for aircrew. He had been killed a year ago.

Flying Officer Stamford sat with her eyes decorously lowered while the Wing Commander ranted on. In the end, faced with the ultimatum that it was her or no MO for the next month, he struck a bargain with Group. He would put up with her for a month on detachment. After that, Group promised a male RAF medical officer, and as soon as possible after that a male Squadron doctor as well.

'I think we can cope with you for one month,' he said.

'Would it not be for the Group Captain to decide that, sir?'

'Listen to me, Flying Officer, I don't like argumentative women.'

'And I don't like rude men.'

'It doesn't matter what you like,' he began, and then as if the remark had just penetrated, he exclaimed indignantly, 'Me? Rude? Good grief! What will you say next?'

'Bad tempered, sir? Overbearing, sir?'

'That's enough, Flying Officer!' He shoved his chair back and stood up. 'I'll take you to SHQ.'

'I've already been.'

'And no one objected?'

'To my being a woman?'

'Yes.'

'Why should they? The Group Captain was very welcoming.'

'Oh, the Group Captain!' he exclaimed scornfully. 'He doesn't have to run the squadron. A squadron that's had all hell knocked out of it. Dead men's shoes filled by schoolboys. No real discipline. No *esprit de corps*. Well, if you've done SHQ, I'll introduce you to the Mess. Make sure you get a decent room.'

'With a small barred window?' she asked him and he smiled cautiously as if that hurt his face muscles.

As they walked briskly past Flights towards the Officers' Mess, he expounded on how to run a successful squadron. The key words, as she might have guessed, were discipline and morale. Morale was where a serious and dedicated medical officer could make a valuable contribution. He was about to enlighten her on exactly how, when ducking out from under the wing of a parked Blenheim emerged two flight sergeants, two, Cavendish recognised, of the several bolshie ones.

They saluted Cavendish, and eyed his companion with wolfish interest.

As they got past, from a safe distance but just within earshot, Ginger Johnson let out a low wolf whistle.

'There you are!' Cavendish turned to the girl indignantly. 'Did you hear that? Whistling at you! And you an RAF officer! A holder of the King's commission! That proves my point! They're not going to see you as a medical officer. They're going to see you as a floozie.'

For the moment he was right.

Ginger and Horner stared after them bemused, momentarily forgetting that they were about to go on their first cross-country with Maddox. 'Not bad, not bad!' Ginger said, pawing the ground with his right leg in the well-known sign of masculine interest. 'Good underpinning too. Mind, not a patch on Pam. What d'you reckon? New Waaf officer?'

'No, you clot! Didn't you see the snakes on her lapel? She's the MO.'

'Jesus! I don't believe it! Unlucky Marshfield's got lucky at last! Cavendish won't like it, though.'

'No! He didn't look as if he'd won the Christmas raffle, did he? Bet he's spitting blood.'

The subject of the new MO engaged their conversation till they reached the crew room where they spread the good news about a new MO who was female and easy on the eye. Then they collected their helmets, received from Angus MacGregor a run-down on route hazards between Marshfield and Peterborough, the farthest point of their cross-country, and their minds returned to the sober business of how they were going to cope with young Maddox.

The crew room was less noisy than usual. After Butterworth's disappearance all the aircrew were pretty edgy for today's Detail. Mascots were much in evidence. One navigator was tying his girlfriend's stocking scarfwise round his neck, a gunner had a miniature teddy bear dangling beside his aircrew whistle, a young pilot officer had nipped out to do his superstitious libation of peeing on the tail of his aircraft.

Suddenly P/O Bates began anxiously slapping his pockets. 'Christ!' he exclaimed. 'I've left my lighter in the billet. Can't fly without that.'

He bolted off to retrieve his mascot, while Horner remarked dourly, 'What a load of crap! This mascot business.'

'Oh, I dunno.'

'Well I do. Stands to reason! What difference could a mascot make, you clot?'

'Might.'

'Might not.'

'Well, none of us can prove it, can we?'

'Yes we can! Butterworth had his mascot, didn't he? That bent penny, remember? Wouldn't fly anywhere without it. Fat lot of good that did him.'

'Well, I reckon it's worth a try. In the situation we're in anything's worth a try. I'm organising myself a mascot.'

'Organising? A mascot? What on earth is it, Ginger?'

'That's a secret. A gift from Pam. I'll show you when I get them!'

'Them? Them? Oh, Jeez! I can guess. You're a bastard, Ginger! A sex-mad bastard! I hope she slapped your face.'

'Well,' Ginger replied as they opened the door and went outside, 'she didn't. So there! She was keen to do anything to help us aircrew. Some girls are very keen on aircrew.'

He repeated that last sentence loudly as they came up to S-Sugar and they caught a glimpse of Pip at the top of the steps up to the wing. Her hair was tousled, her hands were covered in oil and she looked flustered.

'Where's Pilot Officer Maddox?' she called to them.

'Dunno! Why?' Jack turned, hearing steps. 'Oh, here he comes.'

'I'm not late,' he said, puffing up from behind them. 'I was just having a last word with MacGregor. I want us to give this cross-country everything we've got!'

'I hope not everything,' Horner murmured under his breath. 'Maybe we could hang on to certain things,' he lowered his voice and winked at Ginger, 'like life.'

'MacGregor seems to think . . .' Maddox was beginning importantly, when Pip called down, 'Bad news, I'm afraid, sir.' She came clattering down the steps. She held in one hand the 700, the aircraft maintenance form. 'There's a mag drop on Number One.'

Maddox, whose supercilious smile had collapsed at the words 'Bad news', now got his smile together again.

'A mag drop,' he repeated. Johnson and Horner exchanged glances as if to say, he doesn't know what a mag is, never mind a mag drop.

'How much?' Horner asked.

'Hundred and fifty.'

Horner raised his brows.

'That's all right,' Maddox assured Pip airily.

'No, sir, it's not all right.' She thrust out her chin. 'It needs work. The plugs need to be looked at. Maybe the magneto. I can't take the responsibility.'

Maddox was outraged. 'I shall be taking the responsibility,' he said, drawing himself up to his full meagre height.

'No, you won't, sir,' she told him quite politely, 'because I'm not going to sign the 700.'

That really threw the cat among the pigeons. Maddox

70

flushed with anger and embarrassment to the roots of his yellow hair. As Ginger remarked afterwards, not a pretty sight.

'I am the skipper of the aircraft . . .' he began pompously, but she said, 'It isn't just you, sir. I'm also thinking of your crew.'

Which offered him a tactful way out of the argument. He looked from Horner to Johnson, nodded as if he was giving in gracefully purely for them and marched off in search of MacGregor.

'Thanks,' Horner smiled at Pip.

'For what?'

'For not signing the 700.'

'You don't reckon I did that for you, do you?'

'Well, let's say it benefited Ginger and me.'

'Well I didn't do it for you, lad. I did it for me. For my work and what I think of it. I don't sign out a kite unless it's bang on. Even if Maddox had been the King of England I wouldn't have signed. So don't flatter yourself!'

Horner sighed heavily. 'There it goes again! Now I've lost it.' He began looking round the tarmac exaggeratedly searching for something.

'What's up?' she asked. 'What've you lost?'

'My confidence.' He put his hand to his head. 'I was just going to suggest a walk seeing you won't let us fly. If you're off this afternoon, that is.'

'I'm not. I'm on duty.' She paused. 'But how about coming to Flights and giving me a hand?'

4

Giving her a hand was the beginning, not just of a beautiful friendship, but of an odd courtship.

Why should it be more in the idiom of the times, Horner thought, to court your girl in the back row of the cinema or in the back seat of a jalopy if you were lucky enough to own one? Sitting astride the engine nacelles you learned a lot about one another, and everything he learned about Pip he liked, except her soft attitude to Maddox. That he didn't like and couldn't explain.

'Girls prefer officers,' Ginger told him, man to man, as he tried to sleek his scrubby red hair with palms full of Brylcreem before his date with Pam (a double date had been suggested but Pip had excused herself saying she had a headache). 'I don't say Pip does. But that's the gen. Given the choice, officers win hands down.'

Satisfied with his hair, Ginger slipped on his well-brushed jacket. 'And another thing. They prefer pilots to crew. So you've got two counts down to start off with. But chance your arm again! Ask her to the Sergeants' Mess dance, eh?'

Horner had every intention of so doing when the time became ripe, and it became ripe the next day, after their air-to-air gunnery training. Maddox had got so close to the drogue the Henley was towing that he almost cut the rope with the port engine's prop. Hair-raising.

That time, Ginger remained unmoved by the near-disaster because they had got so close he couldn't miss with his guns, and got over a hundred hits on the target.

He went off to celebrate with Parachute Pam and Horner volunteered again to help work on the engines alongside Pip.

'Congratulations!' she said warmly as he rolled up his sleeves.

'What for? Surviving?'

'No, Jack!' her smile faded. 'You know what I mean. For getting the highest score. Your crew.'

'Ginger, you mean. Ginger did it. Mind, we almost got the Henley as well. But that's another story. And that would have been Maddox's.'

'Why don't you like him, Jack?'

'It's his flying I don't like, love. And come to that, why do you like him?'

'He's OK really. I reckon he's lonely.'

She knew for sure that he was, because Pam, who had an ex-boyfriend in the orderly room, had discovered from Maddox's file that his parents were dead, and his guardians were Lydgate and Green, Solicitors, and that he had spent the holidays in the headmaster's house at some toffee-nosed school.

'Besides,' she went on, 'I reckon he'll get you through.'

'Through the veil? To the next world?'

'No, don't be daft! Through ops.'

'Why?'

'Because he's lucky. Someone up there.' She raised her eyes shyly.

'Getaway! Mind you, maybe someone up there doesn't want him to join the angelic squadron. That's a thought.'

'But he is lucky, isn't he? He gets away with things. My mother's boyfriend . . .' Strange, but that was the first time she had acknowledged the feckless Irishman aloud. ' . . . says it's better to be lucky than rich.'

Horner glanced across at her soberly. Then he lowered his eyes to tighten a bolt, and said with clumsy gallantry, 'Well, he must be lucky. To be her boyfriend. Your mum's.'

73

'I don't reckon he is.' She shrugged. 'No, forget I said that. It's not fair.'

'Do you get on well with your mum?'

'I used to think I did,' she said, and then her face seemed to close up. For an hour they worked in a silence broken only by the sound of metal on metal and Horner's tuneless whistling.

'That's about it,' she said, and stretched her grease-stained arms above her head.

Horner tossed his spanner into the toolbag and asked, 'Care to come for a stroll?'

She began wiping the oil off her fingers with a rag, before glancing at him sideways. 'What d'you mean by a stroll?'

'A walk.'

'OK,' she said, 'but not too far.'

Then she slid down the wing and did the long jump to the ground.

And as they strolled along the dyke that edged the first of the Napoleonic canals, Horner judged it the right moment to try to invite her to the Sergeants' Mess dance.

'When?' She was watching a skein of geese honking above them in the slowly darkening sky, her face glowing in the last horizontal rays of a crimson setting sun.

'Next Saturday.'

'I might,' she said. 'Or I might not. But thanks all the same.'

'That's a funny answer.'

'I don't like those sorts of do's much. I'd rather be out here.'

'Well, I'd like you to come,' he said. That seemed to do the trick. She stood on tiptoe and kissed his cheek.

Encouraged by that kiss, albeit a chaste one, Horner caught the Liberty bus the next morning into Hythe.

There were only two chemists in the town. In the first, a flashy blonde was at the counter. So he went to the

Boots store on the corner. But there was a woman serving there, too.

So he went to Ye Olde Tea Shoppe for a cuppa while he thought about what to do.

Eventually he went back to the first chemist, hoping the blonde would have gone on her coffee break. No such luck — there she was still purveying toothpaste and cough mixture. But at Boots an elderly man was now on the counter. Horner told him what he wanted.

Disapprovingly he produced the packet of French letters and sanitised it by covering it decently in a plain paper bag before handing it over.

That Saturday Horner dressed with especial care. Clean shirt, clean pants, clean socks, buttons and shoes brushed bright.

'Hu-hu,' Ginger remarked, interrupting his own preparations to ask, 'She said yes, did she?'

'She said she might.' Horner popped The Packet surreptitiously into his trouser pocket.

'Might what?' Ginger asked, and laughed.

The station band was blaring out as they arrived. Ominously the tune was 'Wish me luck as you wave me goodbye'. Vera Lynn's favourite tune.

They shoved their way to the Mess bar. The place reeked of sweat and scent and cigarette smoke. The floor was awash with beer. Straight away Ginger collected Pam from a gaggle of Waafs sitting in chairs against the wall, trying to talk animatedly to one another.

At first Horner thought Pip hadn't come. He looked around anxiously. Then he spotted her on the floor dancing with her Geordie Maintenance Flight Sergeant.

The officers made their entrance, clearly thinking they were slumming — the CO, the SAdO, a couple of flight lieutenants and half a dozen sprog pilot officers, one of whom was Maddox.

It was a source of some irritation that the officers never

invited the sergeants to their Mess do's, but expected to come to the Sergeants' without invitation. The WAAF CO, a round cottage loaf of a woman, who had been appointed because she was some air marshal's sister, arrived with one of her admin subordinates and the spotty-faced junior Intelligence officer. The female MO followed reluctantly behind. They all tucked in like gannets to the sausage rolls and ham sandwiches, and drank deep of the meagre rations of spirits, encouraged by the sycophantic warrant officer chairman of the Sergeants' Mess Committee.

The noise was terrific. If the Germans had bombed the station, no one would have heard them. There was a constant chorus of deep and shrill voices, the clatter of feet, the sound of breaking glass and ribald cheers and the band playing on.

Finally Pip managed to extricate herself from the embraces of her Flight Sergeant and came over to sit beside Horner.

'Enjoying yourself, Pip?'

'Yes. I think so.' She patted his hand. 'I am now.'

'What are you drinking?'

'I'd like a lemonade really,' she said shyly. 'I'm thirsty. I don't really drink much.'

He bought her a gin and lime, and watched her sip it with apparent innocent enjoyment.

Suddenly she glanced across the room and said, 'Look how he sits!'

'Who?'

'Peter.' She pointed to where the clueless clot was sitting on his own.

'So?'

'Don't you see? His right leg twisted round his left like the snake round the MO's badge.'

'So,' Horner repeated. 'Why shouldn't he? After all, he is a snake.'

'No, he's not. You know he's not. He's ever so lonely.'

'So am I.'

She pulled a derisive face.

'He hasn't any family.'

'Neither have I. Not to speak of.'

'Do you talk to him much?'

'Not if I can help it.'

'Why not?'

'I dunno. Just don't want to.'

'Has he any friends?'

'How should I know? He's in the Officers' Mess.'

Horner was about to ask her to dance when a ladies' excuse me was announced and abruptly she got up, walked across the floor and asked Maddox to dance.

An astonished smile spread across his face. He jumped eagerly to his feet, and then hesitantly put an arm round her.

It was a quickstep — 'Don't go out with college boys/ When you're on the spree/Take good care of yourself/ You belong to me.'

It was pitiful to watch. He couldn't dance. Had no rhythm. No balance. Being a cack-hander he didn't know his left from his right. Clung to her shoulders like a drowning man. If he'd been a boxer, he'd have been disqualified for illegal holding.

When a breathless, somewhat discomfited Pip returned, Horner asked, 'How are your toes?'

'No worse than before.'

But she looked a little uncomfortable, worried even.

'I nearly got the ref to separate you,' Horner joked.

'I'm not laughing,' she said crossly. She felt deeply embarrassed. Maddox had held her so tight that she had felt something in his trousers the size of a hefty torch, which even her limited knowledge told her wasn't a torch and wasn't usually there, and was something vaguely threatening.

'You didn't enjoy it, did you?' Horner grinned.

She didn't answer.

The next dance was a waltz. 'I'll show you!' Horner said, for the boys at Halton had been frequenters of the local Mecca Locarno Dance Hall and had learned a step or two.

She was as light as a feather, following his showy steps easily and gracefully, smiling. Now it was a gentlemen's excuse me, and MacGregor tapped Horner on the shoulder and took her away.

Horner watched them, frowning. He got himself another Bass, and putting his hand in his pocket, felt the packet of French letters.

Time was getting on, so after MacGregor returned her, he downed the rest of his drink, and told her she looked hot and suggested, 'How about a breath of fresh air?'

She gave him a funny sideways look, but didn't say no.

Outside there were already a number of couples seeking the privacy of corners and crannies and air raid shelters.

There wasn't much cover left. He propped her against the wall behind the ablutions and put his arms round her. She kissed very sweetly, but very innocently. A school-girl kiss. None of that tip of the tongue French kiss lark Ginger talked about. Horner was afraid to initiate it.

But he did let his hand rest on her thigh and then creep under her skirt. He felt the thick stockinette of black-outs, the heavy duty knickers the girls were issued with, not the unlawful silk and lace some of the naughtier girls wore. He rested his reconnoitring fingers momentarily on the top of her lisle stocking preparatory to crawling upwards through the tough barbed wire of her knicker leg elastic and over the top.

There came the statutory slap on the hand. But he let it rest in the position he had won in No-Man's Land before deciding to move forward once more into enemy lines.

He had calculated they were only eighty yards from the room he shared with Ginger in the Sergeants' Mess. He was just about to suggest it was cold out here, when suddenly there was a dazzling finger of yellow light that pierced the night like a miniature enemy searchlight.

There was an immediate and indignant howl of 'Blackout!' from the snoggers. It was totally ignored. The accusing searchlight flickered round them.

In the back beam was illuminated the WAAF Queen Bee, standing on top of the Mess steps now flanked by the burly bodyguard of her Waaf Flight Sergeant as she swept the darkness with her powerful torch.

'The dance is now over!' announced a stentorian voice. 'All Waafs back to quarters!'

So that was that. The rumour circulating later was that the Orderly Officer had caught a Waaf and a sergeant *in flagrante delicto* in the broom cupboard, and so Ma'am had decided on an immediate clean-up. When Horner returned disconsolately to his room he found Ginger lying on his bed beside Pam with her skirt right up to her waist.

It was an unfair world.

'You'll get caught,' he told them hopefully. 'Then you'll really be for it! Cavendish'll have your guts for garters.'

But they weren't. And Cavendish had other things on his mind.

5

'How's the training programme going, Charles?' Every other day, Air Vice Marshal Stalybrass would ring up from Group to make that tender enquiry.

'Not too bad, sir,' Cavendish would answer cheerfully. 'Problems, of course. But we're getting there.'

'Get there a bit faster, eh, Charles?' Stalybrass tried to make it sound like a joke but failed.

'We'd go faster if we'd newer and better aircraft, sir.'

'Blenheim's a bloody good kite, Cavendish. Don't blame your tools.'

But it wasn't just the tools. It was the airfield. It was the weather. It was the inadequately trained new boys. Two Pilot Officer Prunes – the RAF's personification of a flying clot – landed with their undercarriages up. Another came in so fast he ended in the hedge. Another came in so slowly he undershot the airfield by half a mile. There had been three ground collisions and one episode where an air gunner had shot his own tail off. Every time he saw Maddox come in to land, Cavendish's heart went into his mouth. But for some extraordinary reason, none of his antics resulted in any damage to the aircraft.

The AOC's monotonous question had now turned testily to 'When is 13 Squadron going to be operational, Cavendish?'

'Just as soon as we can possibly make it, sir.'

Then when at last they were making some headway, sea mist smothered the airfield. Every breath you took was salty. Then rain bucketed down followed by thunderstorms accompanied by hail and lightning. There were snow showers and freezing rain and night frosts. Out of the leaking huts crawled half-drowned rats, four-legged as well as two-legged. The airfield roads became rivers of water. The Sergeants' Mess was flooded. SHQ was temporarily abandoned. With no hard standings, Blenheims sank in the mud right up to the middle of their oleo legs.

Gigantically, heroically, splendidly, Marshfield began to live up to its name.

All flying had to be scrubbed. In a desperate attempt to keep the crews occupied, Cavendish laid on lectures on navigation and gunnery, organised physical exercises and route marches – all of which went down like the proverbial lead balloon. With only two Liberty buses a week to Hythe, there was nothing to do but drink and grumble.

The new boys began to lose their girlish laughter, with the exception of Maddox who threw himself into every exercise with the enthusiasm of a laughing hyena. His performance in the Mess games, such as high cockalorum and planting sooty footprints on the ceiling and riding motor bikes round the corridors, was as dangerous as his flying. But he always picked himself up after crashing to the ground, hotly protesting he was not hurt.

With so little to occupy their minds, the crews began chewing over Butterworth's disappearance. Rumours of high losses on other Blenheim squadrons flooded both Messes. Two young captains decided they had had enough before doing even one operation and were posted to the Glasshouse at Sheffield for Lack of Moral Fibre. Where before, hardly anyone had visited Station Sick Quarters, now there was quite a queue in the mornings with coughs and colds.

People began talking openly about Unlucky 13. It was discovered that the Air Council had decreed that there must be either twelve or fourteen feathers in the new airgunners' brevet, so even the RAF top brass admitted thirteen was an unlucky number.

In the sanctity of their room, Ginger, ever the optimist, declared to Horner that they need have no fears, they wouldn't have to complete those four ops before the end of their tour: 13 Squadron, like Marshfield, would collapse.

Nevertheless, imminent collapse or not, the training programme staggered on, frequently in bad weather. Maddox and crew completed their cross-country with no incident more dramatic than ground-looping on landing.

But after that the spectre of night flying raised its ugly head. Incredibly, the RAF had done almost no night flying between the wars. As a result, really experienced night fliers were few. Even Rutherford had been wary of it on the one occasion when they had gone up over France in a Battle. Instructors at OTUs were never keen to go up with their pilots and it was at night that most fatal crashes occurred.

Pointing out to Ginger their names on the Flying Detail in the middle of November, Horner said, '*Der Tag* for us tomorrow, Ginger boy! Prepare to meet your Maker!'

'It'll be clampers,' Ginger prophesied cheerfully. 'Cavendish'll have to scrub.'

Certainly the day started with black cloud getting lower and lower. But the night flying Detail carried on regardless.

Sitting in the crew room, looking at the muzzy line of paraffin glims, waiting their turn, Maddox turned the pages of an aviation magazine. Horner and Johnson sat in gloomy silence, while one by one the other three crews were passed out.

It became later and later. A thin drizzle started and the night flying programme fell way behind.

It was three in the morning when Cavendish put his head round the door and called, 'Maddox!'

Out the three of them followed to Blenheim S-Sugar, its idling propeller blade cutting into oily orange slices the light thrown from the guttering paraffin flares. Twelve of them formed the flarepath in a line to the pitch-black horizon stippled with rain.

Maddox followed Cavendish inside the aircraft for the single circuit that the Wing Commander would do with him alone.

The engines roared up to take-off power. Horner and Johnson watched S-Sugar shuddering over the uneven grass and tottering up into the sky. They watched the red and green navigation lights crawl round the sky, turning on the approach. Then hold off.

The main wheels touched the ground. Up bounded the Blenheim with a sudden burst of engine before banging on the ground again and this time staying there.

'He'll fail him,' Ginger said. 'Bound to.'

But he didn't.

Cavendish clambered out and beckoned Horner and Johnson to come in. Maddox said nothing as they settled into their positions.

Still overcast, still raining.

Maddox opened up. The engines roared at full power. S-Sugar zigzagged into the night.

Once airborne, Maddox lost the flarepath.

'Where is it?' he demanded shrilly. 'Horner . . . Johnson . . . what's happened to the flarepath?'

First he went left. Then he went right.

Ginger came up from the turret. 'The cack-hander's got himself all confused. Doesn't know his left from his right.'

'Or anything else,' Horner grunted grimly. 'You said we might not have to do our four. And boyo, looks like you're right!'

S-Sugar was whirling round in pitch blackness – first clockwise, then anti-clockwise.

'Horner . . . Johnson . . .' the voice had become quite plaintive. 'The flarepath! Which way?'

Horner said, 'Search me!'

'You're the navigator!'

'After all your weaving, we could be anywhere.'

'Johnson!' Maddox's voice over the intercom became even higher, even more desperate. 'Where's the flarepath?'

'Maybe there's an air raid, sir,' Ginger said helpfully, 'so they had to douse the lights.'

'They wouldn't do that to us!'

'They could.'

'Bound to be down there somewhere.' The Blenheim went into a tight turn, too tight for their speed. Johnson could feel the G in his stomach. The next moment the aircraft was shuddering into a stall.

'Speed! For Christ's sake, look out!' Horner shouted, getting hold of the stick and shoving it forward. 'Or we'll go into a spin!'

'I'm doing a three sixty!' Maddox shouted back. 'Call when you can see the lights.'

But no lights appeared. Now they were in cloud. Hail was hammering down on the Perspex of the windscreen.

'Johnson!'

'Sir?'

'Where are those lights?' Maddox said accusingly. 'You've lost the lights!'

'Me, sir?'

'You must be able to see them now! Where are they?'

'I can't see anything.'

'Then get on the set! Get me a QDM!'

Minutes passed.

'Johnson!'

Ginger stopped sending, and got back on the intercom. 'Sir?'

'Where's my QDM?'

84

'Static!' Ginger retorted.

'Surely you can get it! Surely you can hear?'

The noise from the hail on the metal sides of the Blenheim was bad enough without any static on the set. The aircraft was bouncing around in a black hole worse than Calcutta. Up and down went the wing-tips like red and green juggling balls.

Up front, Maddox went on struggling with his blind flying, weaving nonsense patterns in the night.

'God only knows where we are now!' Horner shouted up at him.

And then suddenly, a miracle! The rain stopped. The cloud lifted. As if whipped out of oblivion by the removal of the magician's cloak, dead in front appeared the letters MF flashing in red — the Marshfield beacon. And two miles beyond the pale yellow line of goose-necked flares.

That wasn't the end of it, though. True to form, Maddox turned left instead of right, lost the flarepath again. Then pushed the nose right down as if to sniff it out of the darkness.

Full flap down, losing height at five thousand feet a minute, through the windscreen ahead Horner caught sight of the dark shapes of huts, then a slit of light as a door briefly opened.

Seconds later, S-Sugar hurtled inches above the roof of the Waafery.

Maddox made a tight turn, mercifully the right way, straightened up and at almost full power crossed the threshold.

And then made the most perfect landing.

It was the best landing Horner had ever known any pilot make in a Blenheim. Ginger didn't know they were down. Maddox didn't either.

'Have you noticed,' Ginger said as they trudged back to the Sergeants' Mess, 'Maddox gets into the most

85

impossible scrapes . . . and then out of the blue, up comes something to save him?'

'The devil!' Horner said. 'He's got the luck of the devil.'

'Don't mind whose luck it is,' said Ginger, 'so long as it's good luck.'

All the Waafs tucked in their beds had heard their engines inches above their heads. Pip actually saw them — it was she who had momentarily opened the door.

Her reaction angered Horner. She didn't seem to realise how close to death they had been. Indeed many of the Waafs thought it very exciting, and when Ginger foolishly told Parachute Pam about the brilliant landing, Maddox became almost a hero in their eyes.

Pip said, 'He can't be as bad as you make him out to be. Did you give him a pat on the back?'

'Did I hell!'

She paused. Then she said, 'Couldn't you be more friendly?'

'Friendly? Friendly? I can't stand the little bugger!'

Horner noticed that she went out of her way to be just that. And the little bugger reciprocated. He kept appearing when Horner was working with Pip on the Daily Inspections, trying to help and getting in the way, but she seemed to encourage him.

'Why don't you tell him to piss off?' he asked her. 'He's just a bloody nuisance.'

'He's trying to learn.'

Horner was beginning to think Ginger was right and that Waafs preferred officers. What happened when they were duty crew seemed to confirm it.

Maddox's crew had to do a fuel consumption test on F-Freddie.

Off they went for four hours, cruising all over central England in (for once) blue skies and winter sunshine.

Pip was waiting to wave them in.

'Nice landing,' she said to Horner.

'Another fluke!'

'He's getting better. He'll see you through.'

'Into the next world.'

She clenched her fists. 'Don't say that!'

'I've just said it.'

'Listen, Jack,' she said as if repeating a mantra. 'He's got guts. He's got what it takes. And he'd do anything for his crew.'

'How come you know him so well?'

But she walked away and didn't answer. Off she went to help the bowser men with the dip-sticks checking the tanks.

Surprise, surprise!

Almost dry tanks! F-Freddie had been guzzling it down.

Chiefie scratched his head, searching for a reason. Then he said, 'Double engine change. Nothing else we can do.'

He stalked away in a temper.

Then Horner had an idea. 'He'll have flown all the way in rich mixture,' he told Pip.

Straight away she went over and asked Maddox direct. 'Did you go into weak mixture?'

He blinked. Looked puzzled. Then he hit his forehead with the palm of his hand.

'Crikey!' His face crumpled as though he was about to break down and cry. 'Pip, I forgot!'

Horner almost danced with joy. They'd got him! Really got him! Sheer carelessness. Appalling airmanship. Endangering his crew's lives with no enemy in sight. Cavendish would have to act now. He'd have his guts for garters.

All Pip said was, 'There you are! He's honest.'

It was what she did then that griped Horner.

Off she went and told Chiefie there was slack on the mixture controls. These were changed — and another crew did another fuel test.

Normal. Chiefie was as pleased as punch.

Horner hung around to reproach her. 'I suppose you were trying to save his confidence,' he said bitterly.

'That's right.'

'Well, bang goes all of mine.'

Then he began to walk away. 'He's not the first pilot to do that!' she called after him. 'It was just a mistake!'

Horner didn't turn. Slowly he returned to the Sergeants' Mess. It's Maddox she likes, he thought. Women are like that. Want to mother their little baby boy.

He opened the swing doors of the Mess and there in the hall saw a crowd had assembled round the noticeboard.

A silent crowd. A very still crowd. With nobody saying anything. Then he looked up at the board and saw why.

Pinned up there was Monday's Detail. The words 'Thirteen Squadron is now fully operational' hit him in the eye.

It was all signed by Wing Commander Cavendish.

6

Since boyhood Wing Commander Cavendish had been impressed by the story of that brave and dogged man Andrew Walker who, single-handed and working in the dark, had underpinned Winchester Cathedral when it threatened to sink into the peat bog on which it was built.

Now Charles Cavendish found himself in a similar situation. A telephone call that afternoon from Air Vice Marshal Stalybrass had informed him that Group's patience was at an end. Thirteen Squadron must become operational at once.

'Those youngsters should be rarin' to go!' Stalybrass boomed.

And yet far from rarin' to go, squadron morale was sinking into a slough of under-confidence and inadequacy. His underpinning was just two seasoned pilots. No wonder he felt alone and in the dark. No wonder that, like Walker, lacking any trusted confidant, he talked to himself.

That night he sat in his office, feet on the table, asking himself who the hell he could enlist to help him to pep up morale. The Group Captain in his opinion was a cipher, intent only on keeping his chair warm. Group was simply greedy for results, terrified of displeasing Command. And any Group that could land him with a medical officer now known throughout the squadron as Luscious Lesley, needed its corporate head examined. While the intelligence officer, who should have been a good up-and-at-'em officer, was only a marginal ally.

'Frankly,' Cavendish told himself, 'I suspect he has humanitarian leanings. He hasn't a press-on bone in his body.'

'How about MacGregor?'

'MacGregor is turning out worse than I supposed. There's something strange about MacGregor. Maybe overdue a rest.'

It had come to Cavendish's ears, actually through his batman who was having an affair with MacGregor's bat-woman, that MacGregor had heard a dog howling, and this bit of nonsense had given a real fillip to the super-stitions that haunt RAF stations in general and aircrew in particular. The superstition had been added to by the information culled from the village that Marshfield had been haunted by a dog ever since the Yanks were here in the Great War. Surely even sailors couldn't be worse than airmen.

So casting around in the darkness for possible material to shore up the squadron's sinking morale and get them into a press-on mood before their first operation, the only person he could think of was, to his shame, the padre. At his home in Lincolnshire, his father had in his gift the incumbency of St Mary's at Great Hartford. The cleric there was always a biddable, presentable chap, a good dinner guest and always open to his patron's suggestions.

'But not this Marshfield chap! He's not much cop,' he warned himself. 'A most unprepossessing person. Old Bicycle Clips, as the airmen call him. But at least, suppos-edly, he has the ear of God. And even if he hasn't, some amongst the chaps must believe that he has.'

It was a simple matter to persuade Group Captain Hurst that a church parade this coming Sunday would be timely.

'I'm very glad to hear you want one,' the Group Captain said enthusiastically. 'Usually you squadron types . . .'

'Scrounge off them? I know what you were going to say.'

'I'm right, aren't I, Charles? Usually you can't see the squadron for dust.'

'But not this time, sir. As you know we're into an important phase — the commencement of operations. Group has high expectations of us. We would like a church parade.'

'I didn't know you were a religious man, Charles.'

'Well, I'm not. Not unduly so. Just the right amount, I like to think. But I'm all for the God of Battle . . . how does it go? . . . Steel our soldiers hearts, isn't it? That sort of thing. The squadron like to think God's on their side. It puts heart into the men.'

He said much the same only at greater length when the padre telephoned him in response to the Group Captain's order.

'Sir, I'm delighted!' Bicycle Clips alias F/Lt Simon Wetherby's voice sizzled with the enthusiastic saliva that always seemed to flood his speech. 'That you actually want a church parade shows I'm getting through.'

He did not specify where or how he was getting through, but Wing Commander Cavendish replied, 'You're absolutely right, padre. I'm glad we're on the same wavelength. Now, if I might outline the points I think it would be a good thing to emphasise . . .?'

Simon Wetherby drew a sheet of paper towards himself, picked up a pencil and listened with it poised.

His delight at the Wing Commander's request was unfeigned. He had so far found Marshfield a tough nut to crack. Not that he hadn't found most of his duties, since he was ordained, tough nuts of different size and strength. He was a solitary soul. Ardent and well-meaning, loving even, but tending to be unloved. He was only too well aware that he lacked the physical and social graces which endeared people to one. His mirror told him he was an odd-looking chap — too tall with sloping shoulders and flat feet. He hadn't exactly had a call from God to join the ministry but he had a nameless desire to seek out some meaning in life. His Oxford tutor had expressed doubt about his choice, but he had gone ahead, had found theological college tolerable, and in his first parish as a curate had honed his social skills a little, and even had a mild flirtation with the churchwarden's nubile daughter. At the same time he had got on very well indeed with all the youngsters in the choir, a facility for which he had been grossly misunderstood.

It was Munich which had made him join up in a flurry of patriotic shame. Not by nature belligerent, Chamberlain's betrayal of the Czechs had made him briefly so. He had not exactly regretted his decision. He looked better in the skilfully tailored RAF uniform than out of it. His first posting to HQ Maintenance at Andover had been nauseatingly easy — well-fed older men wining and dining in a glorious country house.

Marshfield was the opposite, full of youngsters, most of whom wore the letters CofE on their green and red identification dog tags, so that they could have the appropriate burial, but who shunned the station chapel and who had christened him Bicycle Clips — he couldn't even drive a car, and that to them expressed his ineptitude.

'I'd like a good rousing sermon, of course, padre. Don't be ashamed of patriotism. That's why we're here. That's our duty! To fight the good fight. Isn't there a hymn that goes something like that?'

'Yes, sir. It starts with that line. "Fight the good fight/ With all thy might".'

'Excellent. Excellent! Just the right sentiments. That must be one of the hymns. There's another one I have in mind.' He hummed over the telephone wire. 'About soldiers arising.'

'I know it.'

'You're writing these down, I hope?'

'Indeed I am, sir.'

92

'And the one about trampling out the vineyards?'

'Well, I think we've probably got enough, sir. And it's a bit Yankee.'

'Perhaps. But no bad thing for that. Did you know the Yanks were here in the last war?'

'No, I didn't.'

'Well, they were. Very gallant, the Station Commander told me. Died to a man.'

'Oh, dear!'

'And that brings me to another matter, padre. A rumour's going around about a dog howling!'

'Oh, dear. Poor thing!'

'It's not a poor thing, padre. Certain weak-minded people are the poor things. Saying it heralds casualties.'

'Oh, dear!' the padre repeated, to the intense irritation of his hearer. He was about to compound his error by telling the Wing Commander that a dog belonging to one of the old ladies whose funeral service he had conducted had howled all night before she died, but he stopped himself in time. 'Oh, dear,' he said again. 'But what do you want me to do, sir?'

'Stamp on it, man!'

And then he hung up.

Next day the padre pored over the order of the church parade service. He consulted his one assistant, a gawky ACH called Trimble who was responsible for cleaning the chapel, polishing the cross and the altar rail, and on such occasions as church parade, donning a surplice and lighting the candles and playing the piano. Together they selected the hymns from the limited range that Trimble could play, and the lessons. Then the padre wrestled alone with the address.

Sunday was a mixture of cloud and a watery, wintry sun.

'Cavendish has a nerve ordering us to turn out for church parade!' Horner grumbled. 'But I wish he'd get a move on!'

93

There wasn't going to be enough room in the small station chapel, so half of the personnel would have to stand outside while the service was broadcast to them through loudspeakers.

As they assembled in ranks of three outside on the main station parade ground, Horner and Johnson were craning their necks to see if they could spot Pip and Pam in the squad of smartly turned out Waafs.

'A-tenshun!' called the big thick-necked brute of a Station Warrant Officer, and then gave the order, 'Fall out Jews and Catholics!'

Half the station mendaciously fell out.

'What are you? Jew or Cathoic?' Horner demanded accusingly of the equipment sergeant, who was smiling broadly as he sneaked past them, making his exit.

'Jew.'

'Then how come you were eating all those pork chops yesterday, you lying bastard?'

'Mind your own business, Jack-o.'

'I've a good mind to fall out myself . . .' Horner began.

'No. Don't,' Ginger said. 'Cavendish knows you're not a Jew or a Catholic. He'd spot you if you fell out. He reckons we're troublemakers as it is.'

'It's religious persecution! Letting them off and not us! And look at that! Now they're marching the girls in first. What a cheek!' Then his face softened, and actually broke into a smile as he spotted Pip marching briskly. 'She's a good little mover,' he said tenderly.

'Pam wanted us to go to church,' Ginger said.

'Why? To get you used to walking up the aisle?'

'No . . . to say one or two. To get us through ops.'

'Better than mascots, eh?'

'I'm willing to try anything, believe you me!'

After more hoarsely shouted orders from the SWO, a squad of RAF officers was marching past towards the chapel.

'Christ,' Horner sighed, 'I'm willing to try anything as well. But we need more than one or two prayers. Look at Maddox! He can't march any better than he can fly. Talk about two left feet!'

And to increase Horner's irritation the chapel was full by the time they got there. So Horner and Maddox, and the rest of the sergeants who hadn't claimed to be Jews or Catholics, stood at ease, their hymn sheets blowing in a rising east wind.

And then, just as Trimble hit the first notes of the National Anthem with which all church parades began, the air raid warning sounded.

'Carry on!' Cavendish told the padre when he glanced at him uncertainly.

So to the bass accompaniment of the Bofors guns of Station Defence and the distant roar of aircraft engines, they finished the National Anthem and began on their first hymn, 'The King of Love my Shepherd is'.

How had that crept in? Not to Cavendish's taste at all.

But to Pam's. 'If Ginger gets through this lot and I get him to marry me, I'll have this for my main wedding hymn,' she whispered dreamily to Pip.

Outside her intended bridegroom and Horner grumbled about the cold, now blustery wind and watched high up in the east a Spitfire and two Messerschmidts in combat, weaving in and out of the sunlight, soaring, diving amongst little dandelion puffs of white smoke.

'Shape of things to come,' Ginger said. 'The Spit'll knock them for six!' Then he closed his eyes as there was a distant rattle of cannon followed by the scream of an aircraft in a fatal never-to-be-recovered-from dive.

'Gotcha!' Ginger exclaimed without opening his eyes. 'Ker-ump! Told you! One of theirs.'

'Since when did the Hun fly Spits?' Horner asked him, not for the first time, and Ginger opened his eyes and there were just the two Messerschmidts in the sky and

95

lower down the tip of a column of black oily smoke. That shut him up. Shut the pair of them up. This time tomorrow or maybe the day after, they were both thinking . . . will we be here or will we be a column of oily smoke and someone trying to gather up what's left of us?

For the moment, there was no more sign of the Hun. The All Clear sounded before the service was over.

And what a pathetic apology for a service it had been in Cavendish's estimate. He was sorry he had ever called it. The sermon was an inept mixture of duty and, of all things, the brotherhood of man, a passing reference to Churchill's 'an evil thing that we are fighting' but not a mention of the real villainies of the Hun or fighting the good fight — nothing whatever to get the chaps in the right frame of mind for their first operational Detail tomorrow.

7

'Tomorrow never comes,' Ginger had said cheerfully that afternoon when, after discussing the alarming fact that operations were imminent, Horner had cheered them by saying that at least they couldn't be on the first operational Detail because they hadn't done their fighter affiliation yet.

They were both wrong. Tomorrow came and they were on the Detail.

They had just pushed through the swing door of the Sergeants' Mess when there, pinned on the noticeboard, they saw tomorrow's Detail with a list of crews on standby for 13 Squadron's first operation.

Fifth down was P/O Maddox and crew.

Horner stared dumbly at the noticeboard as if pole-axed.

Finally Ginger burrowed his way through the crowd, read the notice and burrowed back, his hair standing on end.

'We've got to do something, Ginger, and we've got to do it quickly.'

'But what, Jack? What?'

'We've got to see Cavendish. First thing tomorrow. We've got to thump on the table. Tell him we're not fully trained and we're not bloody well going till we are!'

'Hang on a minute, Jack!'

'Otherwise, Ginger, we're gonners.' Horner drew his finger across his throat.

Ginger shuddered.

'We've got to go in together, and tell the bugger the RAF can't send half-trained crews against the enemy.'

'But they can, can't they? They can do anything they like with us.'

'No, they can't. Sure, we'll fly. Sure, we'll fight. We've shown that, haven't we? We've shown that in France, haven't we? But this lark works two ways. The RAF's got to give us proper aircraft and training.'

'Cavendish will say they have.'

'How can he? They've given us ex-commercial airline kites tarted up with pea-shooters. And we haven't had our fighter affiliation. And Maddox is no bloody good.'

'Cavendish will say he is.'

'Jesus! Will you stop being Cavendish's mouthpiece? What d'you say we should do?'

'We'll just have to trust to . . .'

'To what?'

Ginger paused.

'If you say God, Ginger, I'll throw up.'

'Luck, I was going to say. Trust to our luck. And Maddox's.'

But trusting to luck or not, Ginger unwillingly allowed Horner to drag him into Cavendish's office at nine o'clock the next morning.

Angus MacGregor watched them go in. He didn't need a crystal ball or even his Highland intuition to know exactly what they were going in about or how they would fare.

He himself was champing at the bit, raring to go on this first operation which showed his nerve was as steady as ever. But Cavendish had insisted that he remained on the ground, only one seasoned pilot — Slade — being sent.

But that wasn't the only thing that had fazed him. He had wakened early while it was still dark, and he had heard the bloody dog howling.

On and off this time, it went on for about half an hour, and this time Bronwen, his batwoman, heard it.

'Oh, sir!' she exclaimed. 'I don't like it! Not one little bit. What d'you think it means?'

'It means you've slopped my tea all over the saucer.'

'Oh, sorry, sir! My hand was shaking. What d'you think the howling dog means?'

'It means there's some hungry animal out there. Probably the owner's abandoned it.'

'D'you really think that's all it is, sir?'

'Och aye, that's what I think.'

'Then I'll put out some scraps.'

'You do that, lassie.'

'But,' she had added, turning as she left his room, 'I'm ever so glad you're not flying, sir.'

Now he saw the two flight sergeants who would prefer not to be flying emerge from their bout with Cavendish, not with their tails between their legs exactly but nearing that quarter.

'So how was the Wingco this morning?' MacGregor asked them cheerfully.

'As reasonable as ever,' Horner replied shortly.

'Oh, my! As bad as that?'

'Worse! We told him we hadn't done our fighter affiliation. But did it make any difference?'

'Well, it wouldn't, laddies, would it? You're away to do your fighter affiliation in half an hour. There'll be a Hurricane from Manston in the circuit shortly to put you through your paces. I could have told you that before you went in.'

And should he also, he wondered, have told them he'd heard that damned dog howl again? But that thought was so stupid and irrational that he felt antagonistic to himself for even thinking it. And yet he did continue to ask himself if he should have told the others, just as he'd wondered for months if he should have told those chaps in France about the dark haloes round their heads.

'Maddox,' Horner said quietly and without malice, 'is a ham-handed clot. He'll kill the lot of us. He shouldn't have been passed out as a pilot.'

'Och, the laddie has his good points,' MacGregor murmured.

'Name me one.'

MacGregor was hard put to it. 'He's lucky. Most important that. Remember Napoleon. Chose his generals for their luck.'

'And look where that bloody well landed him! So what's all this about doing our fighter affiliation now?'

'That iss so, laddies. I've organised it. Rendezvous is over the airfield at ten.'

'And the best of North British luck to you, MacGregor!'

The lucky lad, Maddox was waiting beside S-Sugar. The aircraft was spanking clean. Pip was standing with them looking as proud as a diminutive mother sparrow with two cuckoos — one enormous, spick and span, engines humming, the other with two left feet and still covered in egg.

'Good luck!' she bade them, checking young Maddox's straps, and then suddenly squeezing Jack's hand as she eased herself past.

This time, Maddox didn't swing out on take-off. And pleased as punch with himself, he immediately addressed the two flight sergeants. 'Keep you eyes skinned for the enemy.'

'The Hurricane, d'you mean?' Horner asked.

'The Hurricane is the enemy. We've got to fight this as for real. He's going to wish he hadn't strayed into our airspace!'

Maddox himself was looking around all the time with his mouth as wide open as his eyes. Then, up at five

100

thousand feet, a Hurricane swooped out of a cumulus cloud on top of them. The game was on.

Maddox was in his element. A kid with a new and lethal toy. He didn't exactly loop the Blenheim as he said he had done, but he did everything else — he put the aircraft up on the port wing, then vertically on the starboard, raced up to the clouds at full throttle, dived to the ground almost vertically. He seemed to snatch the fighter role away from the Hurricane.

After an hour of this jousting, their playmate waggled his wings and made for home.

With a triumphant smile, Maddox called for a course back to Marshfield. He looked from Johnson to Horner as if awaiting their congratulations.

Suddenly, his expression changed. The pleased smile was wiped off his face. He turned green, leaned over the throttlebox and was sick.

Violently, noisily, horribly sick! All over the cockpit, all over himself, all over Horner.

Somehow he managed to land, clumsily, but not all that much worse than usual. Pip had heard something was amiss from the R/T in Flights. All concerned, she clambered up and helped him out of the aircraft, still heaving, choking and spluttering.

Horner wiped the sick off his jacket and felt a sudden leap of hope.

'Poor chap's airsick,' he told her with false concern. 'Must suffer from chronic airsickness. Shouldn't ever have been allowed to fly, should he, Ginger?' He winked.

Ginger winked back.

But all Pip said was, 'I'll take him to Sick Quarters.'

Then she put her arms round him, getting covered with yellow vomit at the same time.

She stopped the armourer's van, bundled Maddox inside and was away.

'There he goes,' Horner told Ginger as they watched.

101

'This is it! Someone up there's looking after us. We've been saved! Luscious Lesley won't send him off this afternoon. Not in that condition. She'll ground him. Can't do anything else.'

Cheerfully the two flight sergeants got buckets of soapy water and disinfectant and some rags from the hangar and started to clean up the cockpit of S-Sugar. Then they legged it up to Sick Quarters.

Pip was just coming out as they arrived.

'What did she say?'

Pip shrugged. 'The MO? He's still in there with her. He's scared she'll make him scrub for today.'

'Scrub for today? Scrub for good, more like!' Horner said under his breath.

'He seemed to think it was the smell made him sick.'

'Smell? What smell?'

'You know, S-Sugar having had a refit. I smelled it a bit myself.'

'You would say that,' Horner muttered.

'Not unless I did smell it.'

'Well . . . maybe we could fill her in a bit,' Horner murmured, striding down the corridor and opening the MO's door after the most perfunctory of knocks.

'We're P/O Maddox's crew,' Horner announced. 'We wondered if we could help? Explain what happened.'

'If you'd wait outside, I'll ring if I need you,' she told him sharply, and out he went.

She returned to Maddox.

Although his skin was pale and clammy and his pulse still racing, he was desperate to be given the all clear. He seemed genuinely to want to fly, loved it, he said.

He screwed up his eyes when she pressed his abdomen. 'Am I hurting you?'

'No, no! Not at all!'

She decided it was embarrassment more than pain that made him close his eyes. Nevertheless, a raised tempera-

102

ture, violent sickness and some abdominal tension. His breath too smelled strange, but she couldn't identify the smell.

'Have you eaten anything unusual? Been out for a meal? Down to the pub?'

'No, really, doc. It wasn't anything I ate. It was that awful smell.'

'But it hasn't made the other two ill. They're hale and hearty. So to be on the safe side, I'm going to admit you to Sick Quarters. At least for tonight.'

'You can't do that, doc! I'm on ops this afternoon.'

'I'm sorry. You *were* on ops this afternoon. As of now you're not!'

'Please, doc! Have another think.' He put a grubby hand on her arm. 'It's not just me. It's my crew! They're terrific chaps. Frightfully keen. They'll be furious!'

'They'll live with it.' Flying Officer Stamford rang her bell. 'Let's get them in now and tell them.'

She might well have added 'the good news'.

Rarely had she seen such spontaneous relief so quickly suppressed.

'Scrub?' the navigator managed to ask in a theatrically horrified voice.

'Scrub the op?' the gunner echoed in a similarly mendacious tone.

Poor young Maddox hadn't noticed the relief. All he saw was their faces made lugubriously long.

'I'm so sorry, men.'

Flying Officer Stamford eyed the trio curiously, wondering how on earth Peter Maddox could be so gullible, as she lifted the telephone to inform the Squadron office of her decision.

'I keep telling the doc it was just that awful smell.'

'What awful smell?' the other two asked in unison.

'I told you! Like hot castor oil.'

103

'Nah!' They laughed derisively, Horner adding, 'No castor oil on board to smell. It's never used these days.'

'Haven't smelt hot castor since working on the old DH 4s,' the ginger-haired gunner laughed. 'And they were obsolete years ago.'

But oddly enough, she suddenly remembered that smell of hot castor oil from an early model aircraft her brother had built. And strangely, that was what Peter Maddox's breath had smelled of.

But after that, she didn't give it another thought, because a few minutes later there was a quick knock on her door and in came Wing Commander Cavendish, hell-bent on reducing her to rubble.

First he tersely dismissed the two flight sergeants as if it were all their fault, and then he asked her what in God's name she was playing at.

'I'm playing at nothing, sir. I assume you're referring to P/O Maddox and his sickness?'

'Sickness my bloody foot! He needs to take a shower, change his uniform and get down to Flights.' He turned and glowered at Maddox as if he had a mind to order him to do exactly that.

'I am admitting him to Sick Quarters,' Flying Officer Stamford said as steadily as she could. 'And there he will stay.'

Alarmed by the raised voices, the chief medical orderly, Sergeant Tillotson, put his head round the door.

'Come in, Sergeant.' Flying Officer Stamford smiled slightly. 'I was just about to ring for you. We have an in-patient. Would you take P/O Maddox along to the ward, please. He's being admitted.'

Maddox gave his squadron commander an agonised apologetic glance as he shambled out like a whipped dog dragged off from his master.

As the door closed behind them, Cavendish was about to continue furiously when she held up her hand. 'I didn't want to embarrass you in front of one of your squadron, but let me make something clear from the outset. I will not have my medical opinion questioned by a layman. And certainly never in front of junior officers. Do you understand, sir?'

For a moment, Wing Commander Cavendish looked at her with total disbelief. Then he recovered and countered sharply, 'And do you understand the trouble involved in sending a replacement crew at this late stage?'

'I do. But it's irrelevant. In my medical opinion, Maddox shouldn't go. The rest is expediency.'

'Good grief, woman! You don't know what the hell you're talking about! Haven't I explained to you about morale?'

'The word is scarcely off your lips, sir.'

Suddenly she began to enjoy herself. All her young life she had had to put up with the overbearing, woman-despising attitude of her father. All her life she had wanted to unburden herself of her antagonism to him and all he stood for, had fantasised about exactly what she would say to him given the opportunity and the courage.

Well, now she had the opportunity and the courage. She was well rehearsed. She knew exactly what to say.

The Wing Commander listened. Then he said quite calmly, 'Now you've got all that off your chest, listen to me. Squadron morale is Number One priority.'

'Station health is mine.'

'They go together. But morale is Number One.'

'That could be argued.'

'Not with me. I don't argue. I say what is and what has to be done.' Then, holding up his hand at her indignant exclamation, he continued. 'If it gets around that any little bellyache or cut finger can get you off ops, we'll have half the squadron reporting sick.'

'That doesn't say much for your morale,' and while he was reeling furiously from that, she administered the *coup de grace.* 'For all I know, Maddox may have something infectious, some gastro-enteritis bug. Neglect that, sir, and we may have to ground the whole squadron.'

* * *

'I'm duty crew, so the logical one to go if wee Maddox is sick,' MacGregor told the still angry Wing Commander fifteen minutes later.

'The logical one not to go,' Cavendish replied irritably. 'I've got too few seasoned pilots as it is. And anyway, it wouldn't be fair on the new chaps. They're raring to go.'

MacGregor raised a cynical eyebrow, but said nothing. For the first time in his flying career he felt relief at not being allowed to go on an op.

'But, sir —' he felt impelled nevertheless to protest.

'But nothing, Angus! Shut up and get cracking!'

Again he felt relief. Why? Suddenly he remembered his batwoman's worried face and then her smile and her remark, 'I'm glad you're not flying today.'

Ye Gods, what was it coming to when a howling dog and a superstitious young girl could rob a MacGregor of his famous nerve?

Cavendish and he briefly debated who should go in Maddox's place, and in the end F/Sergeant Nash got the short straw.

Now again, why should he think of it as that? When he was selected for his first op, sure he was terrified, but he was also greatly honoured and, as Cavendish had said, raring to go.

MacGregor had a quick word with Nash and his crew and if they weren't raring, they gave a good imitation of it.

'Poor Peter,' Nash said, pale-faced but smiling. 'If you see him, give him our commiserations. Tell him there's always another one!'

From Flying Control, MacGregor watched them take

106

off into a light blue sky streaked with thin grey cumulo-stratus. Slade first. Beautiful take-off as usual. Then one after the other — P/O Fox, P/O Knight, Sergeant Jessel and, finally, F/Sergeant Nash.

MacGregor said their names aloud for some reason, like an incantation. He watched them form up, neatly and competently, the cold sun, the colour of egg-white, winking on their windscreens.

His own spirits began to rise. The operation was a comparatively easy one — an attack on the barges lying waiting for the invasion in the Scheldt estuary. Slade would take good care of them. They'd be home again within a few hours with that vital first op tucked under their belts. And squadron morale would begin to rise thereafter.

If it hadn't been for that damned dog and that slight worry about his own nerve, he'd have been fine.

So after he'd seen their departures chalked up in the appropriate boxes on the big blackboard, he left Flying Control and allowed himself the indulgence of a brisk walk which took him in the direction from which the howling seemed to have come.

In his own mind he was sure it was a live dog and, poor sod, that it might well be in some sort of trouble. He knew a fair amount about dogs, had always had one at his heels, and from that howl he reckoned it was a retriever of some sort. Oddly enough, as he thought about it, he had a clear vision of what it looked like. A brown retriever, he felt sure of that, though how one could be sure of an animal's colour from a howl, God alone knew.

He whistled to himself as he walked along, circling Flights in a southerly direction and avoiding the wet grass by continuing along the perimeter track till he came to the barbed wire that separated the Station from the turnip and potato fields of the nearest farm. Here the straggling

107

village began and there was a cluster of cottages, a haybarn and cattle shelter.

Reaching it, MacGregor stepped over the barbed wire and began to whistle for the dog — the low insistent whistle that a dog could hear for miles. Then he found himself calling its name. The name, like the colour, sprang into his mind without him thinking about it.

'Sam,' he called. 'Sam!'

A man working in the potato field paused a moment, glanced towards him and continued.

No one and nothing else stirred. He could hear a rooster somewhere, and the cry of gulls — but no dog barked, and no dog appeared.

And yet, as he turned away, he had the sudden certainty that a dog followed at his heels. Twice he turned.

But there was nothing there.

* * *

MacGregor was in Flying Control again twenty minutes before the Blenheims' estimated time of arrival back at base.

The minutes ticked by as they all stared at those empty boxes on the blackboard in the column headed 'Actual Time of Arrival'.

'Should be in the circuit any minute now,' The Flying Control Officer said, and glancing questioningly at the airmen on the W/T consoles, then the two Waafs on the R/T, 'Anything?'

The airmen shook their heads.

'Nothing, sir,' said the Corporal Waaf.

'Try them again.'

'Bunter Zebra . . . this is Marigold Control. Are you receiving me?'

The loudspeaker was switched on, but all that came over, magnified and eerie, was the static. A static that

108

howled and chattered as if about to start up a human call.

After twenty minutes MacGregor could stand it no longer. He walked out onto the balcony. He lit a cigarette. Twice he thought he heard the throb of distant engines in the east, but they came no nearer, turned into the desynchronised beat of German aircraft, several of them by the sound, making for London.

He went back inside.

Wing Commander Cavendish and Group Captain Hurst had now arrived, huddled inside their greatcoats. They waved away the mugs of coffee the W/T operator offered them, stood with their arms folded, their eyes flicking from the blackboard to the clock creaking away the minutes on the wall.

Overdue. By five minutes, by ten, by fifteen.

'Try calling them up again.' The Flying Control Officer told the R/T Waaf.

'Hello, Bunter . . . Zebra . . . Bunter Dog . . . Bunter Orange . . .'

Still nothing.

The Waaf on the telephone had been ringing around other RAF stations in the hope that the aircraft had diverted.

None of them had been contacted. No messages had been heard on Darkie, the emergency message receiver.

An hour later, a tight-lipped Cavendish rang Group and reported all five Blenheims missing.

8

The loss of the five crews had a devastating effect on squadron morale. The usual remedy after a bad loss was for an RAF squadron to have a party in the bar and drink and sing bawdy songs through the night.

Not this time. The crews were too young and green, and they hardly knew the words of the songs anyway. With Slade gone, MacGregor did his best. But the alcohol merely made the youngsters morose, and one by one they sidled off to bed.

MacGregor and Cavendish would have welcomed another operation as a means of getting them in the saddle again. But instead, Group gave them three days' stand-off to recuperate, which was a bad mistake.

Then a week of fog and rain kept them on the ground. Finally, the next op, which MacGregor was to lead, was announced.

And in the morning he woke to hear the howling of the dog.

But worse followed. Sitting down in the dining-room for breakfast beside Lennox, an ex-policeman, who was slightly older and more sensible than the others, Lennox told him he'd just heard that P/O Bates was reporting sick.

The rot was setting in. MacGregor hoped to high heaven that Luscious Lesley would have the gumption to send Bates packing, otherwise the squadron would fall apart.

Flying Officer Stamford was halfway through her morning's sick parade when P/O Bates reported. A suspicion, similar to MacGregor's, briefly crossed her mind, but not for long. Bates was one of the youngsters whom she knew quite well. She was on good terms with most of the squadron. They were so like her young brother that she felt a real affection for them, had been on the occasional pub crawl with them, and she was always urged to come and sit at the aircrew table when going in to the Mess for lunch or dinner, a fact which caused Cavendish to make his long face longer still.

She had somewhat cut him down to manageable size, too. The week after she arrived she had carefully read through the Wing Commander's personal file, and after that she understood him better.

As she had guessed, he had been born with the proverbial silver spoon. Home was Gayton Hall, his father the Lord Lieutenant of Lincolnshire. Eton and Oxford continued what Gayton Hall had begun. Then the Auxiliary Air Force. Naturally he got Exceptional assessments for flying skills and rapid promotion. The daring young man on the flying trapeze was all set for the highest echelons of RAF power. But as the squadron was moved to France, the daring young man was proved all too human after all. He was hospitalised for glandular fever. No wonder he detested sickness, and detested anyone who pretended sickness even more. Left behind in Blighty while his chums went on to death or glory in the Battle of Britain, he was given, when he recovered, a stooge job at Bomber Command Headquarters until some string-pulling, well-heeled fairy godmother waved her wand and gave him 13 Squadron at Marshfield.

'Come in, Bill! Sit down,' she said to Bates as he came into the surgery. 'Did the pud get you after all?'

She had sat beside him yesterday at lunch and they had all groaned about the leaden weight of the lemon sponge pudding. Bates was a red-faced rugger-playing smiley Liverpudlian. He had dropped a lump of the pudding on his plate and sworn it had cracked it.

'No, doc, no. Take more than that. It's my throat.' He smiled apologetically. 'Feels like I've swallowed a couple of razor blades.'

'Any other symptoms?'

'A bit dizzy.'

'Headache?'

'A bit. Like as if the lid of my head flaps up as I walk.' He smiled again. 'I wonder if you could give me something. I want to be on the top line for the op.'

Flying Officer Stamford pulled the angle-poise light closer, lifted a spatula and looked down his throat. His tonsils and uvula were reddened, but not excessively so.

'Do you tend to suffer from tonsilitis, Bill?'

'No. I'm fit as a flea. Never suffer from anything, really.'

She probed around. He had a badly decayed wisdom tooth with the gum inflamed all round it, and she wondered if that might be the source of the trouble. She felt his glands and they were only slightly swollen.

She was aware of his eyes on her face. She had the impression that now he wished he hadn't come. He looked impatiently at his watch.

She shoved a thermometer in his mouth and thought carefully. To ground or not to ground, that was the question. He wasn't really ill enough. And she'd heard a rumour that this operation was going to be an easy one, a real trip around the bay. She tried to examine her own integrity. If she did ground him, wasn't some part of her wanting to cock a snook at Cavendish? Showing him she wasn't his man?

She smiled vaguely at Bates as she waited for the thermometer to cook. She decided she would ground Bates if his temperature was at all raised.

It wasn't.

'I think you'll be OK,' she said and he brightened

visibly. 'I'll give you a couple of pills to take now and some gargle, and that should do the trick.'

'Thanks, doc,' he said jumping up. 'You're a wizard!' He planted a brotherly kiss on her cheek. 'Like I said, I want to be on the top line! Thanks.'

'And if it isn't better in two or three days, let me have another look at you.'

In two or three days. Christ, how stupid could she get!

A now smiling Bill Bates watched as she wrote in the Disposal column of the sick parade daily record, M and D standing for Medicine and Duty, and gave him a chit to collect the gargle and the pills from the dispensary.

'Thanks,' he said again at the door. 'The others would have killed me if I'd had to scrub.'

The others would have killed him — the words haunted her.

Who killed whom?

I killed them.

I said the sparrow with my bow and arrow.

I killed them all.

* * *

None of MacGregor's anxieties showed on his face as he sauntered down to Operations at noon with Ryan, his trusted air-gunner who had been through France with him, and Lyttle, his new navigator on his first op. Mac-Gregor exuded confidence, bursting with get-up-and-go spirit.

Coming in to the briefing room, he was relieved to see Bates and his crew sitting in the front row. Good for Luscious Lesley!

Plumping himself down next to Bates in front of the platform on which stood a big blackboard with a curtain across it, he joked with the six crews he would be leading.

113

Behind them the swing doors opened. The Station Warrant Officer barked, 'A-tenshun!'

Led by MacGregor, they all stood up.

In came the Group Captain and Wing Commander Cavendish who mounted the platform and stood beside the Intelligence Officer and the Met man.

The CO addressed them. 'Gentlemen, you may smoke.'

Hurst and Cavendish sat down beside the blackboard.

There were six seconds of agonised suspense as Pringle walked slowly towards it and drew back the curtain.

Pinned with brass drawing-pins on the map below was a white ribbon running north-east from Marshfield up the Channel till it crooked to the right at the beginning of the Scheldt Estuary.

The same target over which those five crews had disappeared.

There was a massed indrawn breath. Then total silence.

'Barges again, chaps,' MacGregor called out. 'Jerry's just about given up on those barges. It'll be a piece of cake!'

'Yes,' Pringle said. 'It is the barges again. Not so many this time. They've really had a mauling. And —' He pointed his billiard cue to three malevolent red blobs around Flushing. 'You'll be glad to know that those three batteries of 4-inch AA have been moved inland. Furthermore, this time there's going to be a simultaneous high-level mass attack on Le Havre, Boulogne, Calais and Dunkirk by three squadrons of Wellingtons. The strategy is to get Jerry to scatter his fighters to protect the remaining barges in the south. Then in comes 13 Squadron suddenly snaking in on the deck below the radar up the Scheldt and into the Walcheren Channel. You will drop your bombs in formation on the barges. Then continue up the Channel, turning left at the north end of Walcheren, back into the Channel and home. In and out again before Jerry realises he's been attacked!'

114

Now Flying Officer Flanagan, the Met Officer, took Pringle's place.

'More good news now, boys—'

Flying Officer Flanagan was renowned for his duff met reports, and an ironic cheer echoed round the room.

'Cloud cover! Honest! Stratus five hundred feet above you, but visibility three miles at sea level.' He paused. 'And Base is going to be CAVU. Lovely for landing.'

Next, the Signals Officer handed out the frequencies and the cartridges for the Colours of the Day — two greens.

Now Cavendish got to his feet. 'Did my damnedest to lead you all today. But the AOC wouldn't budge. As you know, Blenheim COs are still barred from operational flying. But I'll be up there with you in spirit. I know you're going to put up a tremendous show. And we'll have a hell of party when you're all back home!'

Group Captain Hurst finished the briefing with, 'Jerry has no idea of the present 13 Squadron has got for him. Good hunting . . . and the best of luck, chaps!'

As the crews streamed out to the waiting lorries, MacGregor said, 'Money for old rope! Go for it!'

On their way to the aircraft, he had a final word with Maddox, whom he had put next to him on the port side of the formation so that he could keep an eye on him.

'Don't get too enthusiastic, Peter. Hang on to my wing. Do what I do. Don't go out on your own. And for God's sake, don't get lost again!'

Caught up with the excitement of the op, the nervousness had left the young faces. 'Money for old rope!' they kept repeating. MacGregor's mind was calm now, too full to think of anything but the job in hand as he got out of the lorry and began walking to F-Freddie with his crew, feeling that something of the old 13 Squadron spirit had been injected into them all.

He signed the 700, got into the aircraft and began to

settle himself down on the cushion of his parachute that fitted into the metal container of the pilot's seat.

It was too far forward as usual after the Waaf fitter had done the DI.

'Women!' he grumbled as he adjusted it two slots back. 'All suffer from ducks' disease.'

He moved his body backwards and forwards, checking the seat's steadiness. A friend of his with short legs had had the seat propelled right back by the take-off. Couldn't reached the controls. Crashed. Urquhart was his name.

That first action of his pre-flight check completed, and the engines started, methodically and in the same name-linked way he went on to the next one, his hands gripping each lever and touching each switch.

Hydraulic selector down. Trim neutral — Fanshawe had the rudder tabs fully starboard and ended up ninety degrees to the right of where he started.

Mixture normal — Yates had it in weak and stalled back onto the runway. Revs fully fine — poor Chalmers earthbound in Coarse. Flaps twenty degrees — nobody but that Prune Parkes would have tried to take off with them fully down. Gills closed — Riley had them open at OTU and couldn't get over the hedge at the far end.

Then he swung the spectacles of the control column, ailerons fully left, then fully right. Red-haired Travers had tried to take off with the locks on and crashed. Then he pushed the stick full forward. If Noakes had tried them that dark night in France, he'd have found he couldn't move them.

With each action he did came the unfortunate face to fit in. A good memory and a good imagination were an asset there, not so good elsewhere.

Then he opened up the throttles to +9 boost before throttling back to test each magneto in turn — all well below 100 drop.

Up in the nose, Lyttle checked the bomb panel and reported it OK.

Now at the rear in the turret, Ryan had tested the W/T and was adjusting the belts of the .303s of the twin Brownings to guard against a stoppage.

'Guns OK, Skipper!'

MacGregor waved away the chocks. Then he inched both throttles forward.

Gently F-Freddie started to roll. Followed by the other six Blenheims, sedately he led the procession to the western end of the field and wheeled into wind.

Slowly he opened the engines to +9 boost, curbing the torque that swung the aircraft right. Gathering speed, the Blenheim raced over the grass.

At 80 mph he began easing back on the stick.

Gently, almost imperceptibly, the aircraft left the ground.

'Undercarriage up!' he said aloud to himself, slamming up the lever. Then he lifted the flaps.

A cacophony of sound enveloped Marshfield as the Blenheim engines roared up to full power. Up rose a startled grey cloud of peewits from the marsh, immediately followed by a screaming flock of seagulls as one by one the seven Blenheims pounded over the grass.

Out of the corner of his left eye, MacGregor saw a blue bunch of cheering Waafs as, like horses in a steeplechase, the seven Blenheims leapt over the hedge and roared up into the crystal-clear sky.

Seconds later, with weak mixture, plus one and a half boost and 2400 rpm selected, they were scudding over the barbed wire defences and the heavily mined beach, over the white fringe of foam to within inches of the brown waters of the Channel, on a course of 089 degrees.

Glancing to port, MacGregor saw the grinning face of Maddox tucked in so close he could see his baby-blue eyes and the smile on his pink lips.

He frowned, and gestured him to keep away. The last thing he wanted was to end up in a tangle with Maddox. Of all the sprog crews he had had to deal with, he'd had to take the most trouble with Maddox after seeing some of his circus act take-offs and landings. The man's navigator, Horner, had been a damned nuisance, pestering him to ground the boy. But MacGregor couldn't do anything about it, because in some extraordinary way, after getting himself and his aeroplane into a situation that even the most skilful pilot would be hard pressed to recover from, something always seemed to come from somewhere to save him.

The sea remained flat calm. From the turret, Ryan reported heavy firing to the south.

Glancing to starboard, MacGregor saw the blue sky crayonned over with grey puffs threaded through with silver and red.

He picked up his microphone. 'The Wellingtons doing their stuff!'

'Good old Wimpies!' Lyttle said. 'Keep it up, boys!'

Ten miles to starboard now, up over the horizon came the beaches of Dunkirk. Little movement there, but the formation was moving ever closer to land. Buildings could clearly be seen now, and even as they watched, the sky above them erupted in a thunderstorm of yellow explosions.

A stream of fire with a smoking tail was zooming vertically downwards.

'Wimpy going down!' reported Ryan from the turret. 'And another! Poor buggers!'

Over on the right, white waves were breaking on a corn-coloured beach. Up came the grey stone entrance to Ostend harbour. People running on the breakwater. Flashes of gunfire and, high above them, the Wellingtons now being pestered by fighters.

Zeebrugge flashed past. Still hugging the water, Mac-

Gregor swung slowly to the right. As one huge bird with left wing outstretched, the formation entered the Scheldt.

Everything was quiet. A fishing-boat drawn up against a wooden landing quay. Cars travelling along the road moving east. A field full of cabbages, wilting in frost.

Then suddenly, to port, MacGregor saw the narrow mouth of the Walcheren Channel filled with row upon row of brown barges.

Immediately the whole formation wheeled to the left, straightened up. With throttles hard against the stops, inches above the water, bomb doors open, at 230 miles an hour, the seven Blenheims hurtled towards them.

Now they had been spotted. Streams of glittering white cannon fire mixed with brown blobs of four-inch ack-ack were spouting around them. F-Freddie's cockpit filled with gun-smoke as Ryan began firing the twin Brownings in the turret.

Two hundred yards away now . . . one hundred . . . fifty.

MacGregor pressed the pilot release tit on the stick.

'Bombs gone!'

In the corner of his left eye, he glimpsed the 250lb eleven second-delay bombs lazily falling from the bomb bays of S, K and L. Seconds later, above the noise of the engines and the rattle of gunfire, he could hear them exploding on the wooden decks of the barges.

'Christ!' Ryan shouted. 'Bang on, Skipper! Fire, smoke, planks of wood . . . that'll teach 'em to crack nuts in church!'

Port wing vertical just above the dirty harbour water, MacGregor wheeled F-Freddie round for Lyttle to photograph the flaming red and yellow debris. The whole inlet now was a mass of fire punctuated with streams of flak. Half-suffocated by smoke, three times MacGregor circled the boiling cauldron.

'Thanks, Skipper,' Lyttle said as he returned to his desk with the B24 camera. 'Got some good ones.'

119

Ryan was still firing as MacGregor straightened up and began zigzagging north-west along the Walcheren Channel.

'See any of the others, Ryan?'

'Not a sign, sir.'

'They'll be halfway home by now,' said Lyttle as they hurtled out of the Channel and began turning a hundred and fifty degrees to go home.

'Watch out for fighters!' MacGregor called.

'Can't see any,' said Ryan.

But the visibility was dropping all the time. The blue sky had turned grey. Damp mist, no longer smoke, filled the Channel.

And coming out of it, MacGregor saw a huge ghostly shape hugging the coast and steering south-west.

A ship — ten thousand tons at least. A strange-shaped ship — neither tanker nor merchant vessel but midway between both. One thick funnel. A high, sharp bow. A blunt cruiser stern to which clung wraiths of mist like grey seaweed.

He swung the Blenheim to port for a better look.

Immediately the air exploded with yellow stars of flak. Seconds later, silver cannon fire streamed just above the Blenheim canopy. An Me 109 flashed immediately above MacGregor's head. Then another came right at him from the front. He had to wrench the Blenheim into a ninety-degree right bank to avoid collision.

'Christalmighty!' He slammed the throttles against the stops.

Immediately a dew of fine water drops smudged the windscreen. Within seconds, F-Freddie was swallowed into the belly of a cloud.

'Three cheers for the Irish!' With a relieved smile MacGregor climbed away from fighters and flak into denser and denser cloud. 'Saved by a duff Flanagan forecast.'

Lyttle came forward and laid a neat message slip on

the throttle box — 'Course for home, 254 degrees. ETA Marshfield 15.59'.

The next moment they were caught in a huge band of warm, moist air that had swept up from the Bay of Biscay to the cold waters of the English Channel. Blindfold in a grey prison at a safety height of 2,500 feet, MacGregor grimaced at Lyttle. 'This bloody stuff's going on for ever!'

Coming as low as he dared risk descending, he had a go at trying to get in to Shoreham, Tangmere and Thorney Island — each time seeing houses and trees just in time to pull back and roar up into the overcast.

Nowhere appeared open. Ryan reported the W/T jammed with static and call-signs of returning Wellingtons seeking homes.

On the point of running out of fuel, MacGregor suddenly saw a mist-streaked end of a runway perched on the edge of a cliff.

* * *

As soon as Flying Officer Stamford stepped out of Sick Quarters, she smelled the mist rolling in from the sea. Romney Marsh mist holds its own special eeriness. She felt its clammy cold touch on her face and neck as she walked briskly to the Airwomen's Mess to carry out her afternoon inspection. Even before the logistics of getting the seven aircraft safely on the ground had dawned on her, she had felt uneasy.

She was glad to get into the steamy heat of the WAAF kitchens. Apprised of her coming, everything was spruce and hygienic. The cooks had their hair covered, their nails spotless, there was nothing decaying in the larder. Even the vat of usually greasy water, where the airwomen dunked their irons, their individual knives, forks and spoons, was clear and piping hot. The only fault, as she put her head out of the rear door to look at the vegetable store, was a bowl of sodden meat and gravy.

'What's that doing, Sergeant?'

'Oh, sorry, ma'am. One of the cooks says there's a stray dog around. We put it out for him.'

'Well it doesn't look as if he wants it, does it? I should take it in. It'll attract rats.' She smiled to show she wasn't going to snag them for that, and sighed gratefully as the sergeant uncovered a tray of tea and scones for the final sweetener.

She was drinking her tea by the warmth of the ovens when an airwoman's head appeared at the hatch connecting the kitchens with the Mess hall.

The sergeant frowned at the airwoman. 'Are you off shift already?'

'Not off altogether. I gotta go back. There's a flap on at Control. His Nibs is doing his nut. Panic stations all round. Marshfield is clampers.'

In the preceding hour the mist had thickened and an early darkness fallen. Already one of the ACHs (aircrafthand) had gone round putting up the black-outs at the windows, so they couldn't see out and the weather had sneaked up on them unawares.

'Ten-tenths, his Nibs said.' The airwoman was relishing the drama. 'He told me to grab a wad and a hot drink and get my proper tea later. The kites are all up there somewhere. There's one clot trying to get in here, but the rest are putting down where they can.'

'Sooner them than me!' The sergeant looked towards the ceiling and shuddered.

Faintly, they could hear the sound of engines.

By the time Flying Officer Stamford got to the door, the engines were thundering overhead. She stepped through the black-out trap and into the suffocating fog.

She screwed up her eyes, trying to look up into the black overcast, but there was nothing to be seen. She could hardly see the corner of the Mess building. She couldn't get Bates out of her mind and for some stupid reason she prayed that it wasn't Bates up there.

*   *   *

In fact those engines belonged to S-Sugar, milling round in thick cloud for the last hour, trying to get into Marshfield.

Twice Horner had had a glimpse of the village. Twice Maddox had nearly hit the church tower on a crazy blind descent. Throughout his blind-flying aerobatics he had been shouting at Ginger to get him an alternate, and Ginger had been shouting back that every frequency, even the emergency one, was taken up with Wellingtons demanding the same thing.

'Position, then, Horner! Get me a a position!'

'Anywhere between Land's End and John o' Groats, sir.'

'Haven't you been plotting our course?'

'You've been flying every course on the compass, sir.'

S-Sugar continued to toss this way that way, up down and sideways.

Horner turned his head, looked back at Ginger and raised his eyebrows to heaven. 'Round and round the mulberry bush!'

'What's he going to do?'

Horner shrugged. 'Search me!'

In the cockpit now, total silence. Outside the propellers churned a thick mixture, grey as gruel.

And then, suddenly, Maddox leaned right forward and jammed his forehead against the windscreen.

Abruptly S-Sugar stopped weaving. Maddox settled on a course of 070 degrees.

And now of all things, he began pulling back the throttles.

123

The needle on the altimeter began to unwind.

'What's he up to, Jack?'

'God only knows, Ginger.'

The altimeter was registering 700 feet and the needle was still unwinding. Horner leaned aross and began desperately to push the throttles forward.

Maddox screamed at him, 'What did you do that for?'

'We'll hit a hill in a minute!'

'Nonsense!' Maddox pointed ahead out of the windscreen. 'That aircraft! Can't you see him, man? He's leading us in! He's taking us back to Marshfield.'

Maddox pulled the throttles back again even farther.

Horner peered into the gloom.

'What aircraft?'

'That big biplane!'

'I can't see him.'

'Two-seater. Gun in the rear cockpit.' Maddox began jumping up and down in his seat with excitement. 'There he is! To port! Going down fast now!'

From the back Ginger called nervously, 'What's happening?'

'Says a biplane's leading us in.'

'Can't see nothing.'

'You and me both, mate!'

Maddox suddenly reached out his arm and banged the undercarriage down.

'What the hell?' Horner roared. 'Are you trying to kill us, man?'

'Didn't you see him waggle his wings? We're on the approach.'

Ginger had come up to stand behind the navigator. 'What's got into him, Jack?'

'Mad! He's off his head! Get right to the back!' Horner pointed to the altimeter needle slipping past two hundred feet. 'We'll hit the ground in a minute.'

Johnson hurriedly departed aft. Horner slid his seat

right back, put a parachute in front of his face and braced himself.

Then suddenly out of the gloom ahead — a fuzzy light.

The sounds of the engines died away. Horner felt a slight jar — the flaps going down.

Another light. Then a muzzy glow to starboard — the Chance Light.

Another light.

He felt the nose lift — then heard the slightest whisper of tyres.

S-Sugar began slowing up. There was a shriek of brakes. Then all forward movement stopped.

Ginger rushed up from the back and began to open the emergency escape hatch. 'Quick, Jack! Let's get out before she burns!'

'Hang on, Ginger! We haven't crashed.'

'What's happened then, Jack?'

'We've arrived.'

'Where, Jack? For God's sake, where?'

'Not in heaven, Ginger. Not yet anyway. This is Marshfield — where we get off.'

* * *

When Flying Officer Stamford left Sick Quarters the fog was still dense. She had been relieved to hear from her sergeant that the aircraft in the circuit had been Maddox's and was safely landed. She didn't feel like eating a meal and headed straight for her room. She passed the bar where Maddox was celebrating his skill in landing with anyone who was willing to let him buy a drink. In her room, she took off her jacket and was about to run a bath when the Mess tannoy broadcast, 'Flying Officer Stamford, phone call. Upper corridor.'

The upper corridor was where the WAAF officers were accommodated in the Mess and the telephone box was halfway down between the Queen Bee's room and the bathrooms.

She slipped her uniform jacket back on, walked down and lifted the receiver.

Cavendish's taut voice twanged over the line. 'I want you down at Sick Quarters,' he ordered without preamble. 'Now.'

'Is someone ill?'

'No.'

'Has something happened?'

'Yes.' There was a pause while he cleared his throat. Then he announced starkly, 'One of our aircraft has crashed. They've found it. You will be required to receive the bodies.'

Then he hung up.

A doctor, she told herself, should be used to that sort of thing, especially an RAF doctor, especially one on an operational station. At the same time she felt the necessity to steady herself by holding onto the telephone cradle as if it were a lifeline. The corridor spun. Crackling laughter came through the Queen Bee's door as her radio belted out *ITMA*.

It was a nightmare. She would soon wake up.

Then she took hold of herself. She went back to her room, combed her hair, dabbed some rouge on her pallid cheeks, put on her cap and burberry, slung her respirator and marched herself down to Sick Quarters.

Cavendish's car was outside. Cavendish was inside. He awaited her arrival, his arms folded across his chest, his eyes narrowed, studying her face for signs of weakness.

Sergeant Tillotson was standing beside him. He smiled faintly at her. 'Several of the aircraft are still missing, doc,' he told her. 'But the army rescue laddies have found B-Baker.'

'Did anyone survive?' Her eyes travelled from Sergeant Tillotson's face to the cold, pale mask of Cavendish's.

126

'Hardly,' Cavendish answered. 'They went straight into the hill west of Marshfield church. We're lucky to have found them so quickly. They're bringing them here by military ambulance.'

'Which crew was it?' she asked, feeling that she already knew the answer.

'Bates,' Cavendish said. 'Good lad. Good pilot. Pity.' And then with a shrug, as if that was the end of his tribute, 'They should be here within the hour.'

It was the longest and the shortest hour of her life. They sat in the MO's consulting room which had two comfortable chairs. There was one Sick Quarters orderly on duty as well as the medical NCO, and she made them a cup of Camp coffee thick with Nestle's milk.

Cavendish paced angrily up and down in unbearable frustration. Flying Officer Stamford would have liked to do the same but her legs felt too wobbly. So she retreated to the safety of her swivel chair behind her desk and the appurtenances of authority and medical knowledge.

'The aircraft is a write-off,' Cavendish paused in his pacing to tell her. 'Cat 3. Stores will have to send a Queen Mary.'

She had the feeling that Bates and his crew no longer existed. They'd been, like the aircraft, written off. The crew was dead. Long live the crew. But for herself, Flying Officer Stamford doubted she would ever lose them.

She had slipped hours backward in time. Staring across her desk, she could see Bates, his apologetic smile as real as Sergeant Tillotson's anxious one, as he glanced from her to Cavendish. In the glass pot of disinfectant on her desk was the treacherous thermometer. The arbiter of life and death. Why the hell hadn't it registered a temperature? Why the hell had she made it so important? Why the hell had she let them go?

Eventually she heard the sound of a heavy vehicle snarling into the Sick Quarters compound.

This was it!

'I'll tell the driver to take them direct to the mortuary,' Sergeant Tillotson suggested and hurried to the door.

Cavendish turned to Flying Officer Stamford. 'You'll need to do a brief examination of each one. Or of what remains of each one.'

Courtly as always, he held the door open for her, allowed her to precede him down the corridor which led to the small block used as a mortuary.

The ambulance was drawn up outside, and the big side door of the mortuary was open in front of the black-out screen. Two army corporals were unloading three body bags.

'That's it, sir!' The corporals addressed Cavendish. 'We'll be on our way. Trouble all over tonight.'

He thanked them politely, helped her up the step and closed the door behind them, eyeing her keenly.

It was icy cold inside the mortuary, the lights glaring. Sergeant Tillotson was already masked and gloved and had the first — she couldn't designate it a body, shattered, bloodstained bits of a doll — on the table.

Numbly, she slipped on the gown and the gloves he held out for her.

It was Bates. The near faceless one was Bates. Half of his head had been stoved in by the impact, the smiley mouth torn apart. A section of his broken jaw hung loose, and in it she saw that decayed wisdom tooth. That's how she knew the body was his.

Nothing at medical school had prepared her for this. Her stomach rose. The room tilted, danced round her. She retched, covered her face with her hand and blundered out. She knew she couldn't examine him. Couldn't examine the others. Nor would she try.

Cavendish followed her swiftly into the corridor. He caught her arm. Then he put his hands on her shoulders. He didn't dig his fingers in or shake her or slap her face or offer any violence. And yet his whole attitude, his whole being was full of a personal violence towards her. He seemed to be deliberately overpowering her and everything she was.

'Get back in!' he hissed. 'Do what you have to do! If you don't you're not worth *that* much here!' he snapped his fingers. 'You're not worthy of the Squadron or the uniform you wear!'

And that was it. Back in she went.

And did what she had to do.

9

Three hundred miles to the west, MacGregor had suc-
ceeded in landing on the cliff-edge runway at Predannock
in Cornwall. Next afternoon, the moment the fog cleared,
he flew back to Marshfield.

As he opened the Blenheim's small side observation
window, the usual damp scent of marsh and mud greeted
him. But when he taxied round the perimeter there was
something else. Something in the faces of the ground
crew as they waved him into Dispersal that made him
sense that something else had happened.

MacGregor got out of the aircraft and asked straight
away, 'What's up?'

'B-Baker's crashed, sir.'

'Bates?'

'Killed, I'm afraid, sir.'

'And the crew?'

'Dead too.'

His satisfaction at the obvious success of the attack on
the barges had evaporated by the time he led his crew
into the Intelligence Officer's room.

'Tough luck about Bates,' he said to Pringle. 'What
about the other crews?'

Pringle looked up from the debriefing reports he was
making out. 'Rawcliffe landed with his wheels up on the
North Downs. Lennox and Harris came in from Gatwick
this morning. Ashley is still stuck at Northolt.'

'And Maddox?' MacGregor asked anxiously. 'What's
happened to Maddox?'

'Oh, Maddox landed back here yesterday afternoon.'

'Yesterday?'

'That's right.'

'But wasn't there thick fog?'

'There was.'

'Then how the hell . . .?'

Pringle put away the other completed debriefing reports and took out a fresh one. 'According to him, a big biplane led him here.'

'Fleet Air Arm kite?'

'828 Squadron left for Malta a fortnight ago. The nearest big biplanes are seven hundred miles away on the carriers in Scapa Flow.'

'Then what and whose was it?'

'Whose it was God knows. From Maddox's description, the nearest I can think of is that it was a DH 4.'

'From the last war?'

'Yes.'

'Didn't know we had any left.'

'There's a few in Iraq.'

'Then how the hell . . .?' MacGregor asked again.

'Your guess is as good as mine. So now shall we get on with your debriefing?'

MacGregor's crew gave an almost identical account of the attack to those which the other crews had given him. Just as Pringle finished it off and was about to put it with the others, MacGregor said, 'Oh, by the way, coming away from the attack off Walcheren Island, we saw a strange ship.'

Immediately Pringle was all ears. 'Tell me.'

'Wasn't either a tanker or a merchantman. Superstructure was between the centre and the stern. Odd bulky hull.'

'Did you take a photograph?' Pringle asked eagerly.

'A photograph?' MacGregor laughed. 'Didn't get a

chance. Four Me 109s bounced down on us. Lucky the fog was there to dive into.'

For a man who kept his feelings well hidden, Pringle looked uncharacteristically disappointed. 'Well, if you do happen to bump into her again, Angus, I'd be very obliged to get a good photo.'

'D'you reckon she's of some significance?'

'That size. With that protection. Could be.'

But, secretive as always, he wouldn't say any more.

'So how did Wing Commander Cavendish take last night?'

'Grimly.' Pringle pulled down the corners of his mouth. 'Heads will roll.'

*   *   *

Flying Officer Stamford was of the opinion that her head would be the first so to do. But surprisingly, Cavendish made no attempt to capitalise on her near-desertion.

He came to sit next to her the following evening at dinner. He actually smiled at her warmly. 'You've had your baptism of fire, Lesley,' he told her. 'It was a very distressing duty. But you did it admirably in the end.'

He was less amiable with MacGregor. 'You're supposed to be the Training Captain,' he told him. 'Both Bates and Rawcliffe made the most elementary of mistakes. Coming down through cloud not knowing where they were. Christ, man, that's the first thing that should be drummed into them!'

Meanwhile the rest of the squadron quietly licked its wounds.

Maddox had no wounds to lick. Maddox saw himself as cock of the walk, the only pilot who had successfully brought his aircraft home in appalling conditions.

For the next few days, while sea mist smothered the airfield, he was down at Flights strutting around S-Sugar, and engaging the flight mechanics in reluctant conversation. He had, in the face of irrefutable evidence that no other aircraft was in the circuit, relinquished his unlikely story about the good shepherd aircraft that had guided him down. Now it was pilot skill and that sixth sense which only the really gifted natural pilot possesses.

'I'm lucky,' he would say modestly, 'very lucky in having that intuition, that sixth sense.'

'And he is that,' Pip told Horner, after listening to Maddox for the umpteenth time. 'He's really lucky! He gets into a difficulty and,' she threw her hands wide, 'something always gets him out of it.'

'He gets himself into difficulties,' Horner grumbled. 'A good pilot would avoid the difficulties in the first place.'

But she would have none of that argument. She was the most starry-eyed of Maddox's admirers.

Parachute Pam ran her a close second, and even Ginger was coming round to the idea of Maddox not being all that bad, although the most he would say aloud was, 'He's learning.'

Ginger himself was learning, too. About women. Over the years, he and Horner had exchanged accounts of their sexual adventures whenever they had been out on a date. Up until coming to Marshfield, they had both been in the same virgin state, and there had been an unspoken rivalry as to which would kick the ball into the net first, though both were equally frightened of scoring an own goal that turned out to be a baby.

Now, since Marshfield and Parachute Pam, Ginger was setting himself up as something of a sex expert, a real high scorer. But Horner doubted that. Ginger was just as scared of women as he was, and Pam herself, although saucy and sexy-looking, had a religious streak and had said the prime rule of the game was a ring on the finger first.

Pip was different. Pip was a good girl and good fun

133

too, but in a more tender way. What Horner liked best was talking to her, either working on the aircraft or sitting in the NAAFI, or while they walked along the canals. He learned a lot from her. She pointed out the water rat poking its nose from a hole on the river bank, the grass snake wriggling between the reeds. She taught him how to listen to the birds, to identify the thrush, pigeon, robin and warbler.

'How come you know all this when you lived in the Smoke?'

'Leeds isn't the Smoke proper. And you can hear birds even there,' she laughed. 'I used to walk a lot in the park. I used to read books. We learned Nature at school. And when it was cold we used to get robins in our back yard, and thrushes, and pigeons. There was one robin would eat from your hand.'

'No self-respecting robin would eat from my hand,' he said.

'Happen not. Because you're too impatient.'

He was that all right. More impatient than she could ever know. For despite the fun of just being with her he felt something else. He felt an urge, not uncommon in aircrew, to have It before they handed in their dinner plates. To die a virgin like Bates seemed as some dereliction of duty imposed by nature, a denial of their manhood, indeed a denial of their ever having lived at all. In short, there was a strong compulsion to be laid alive before being laid dead.

Then too, there was the matter of not wasting the little packet, and just as bad, the thought of the Waafs from Stores, who collected and sorted the sad little bits and pieces of deceased airmen's effects, finding that packet.

On the second day of yet another period of clampers, when Horner had finished helping Pip and the armourer to belt the bullets for the Brownings, he suggested diffidently that they might take the Liberty bus to Hythe that evening and have a drink and a bite.

She hesitated for a moment. And then said yes.

The evening started well. He held her hand as the bus rattled and wheezed the six miles into Hythe. Casually, or as casually as he could make it, he remarked that she seemed to get on very well with Maddox.

'He gets on better with a number of bods these days,' she agreed.

'D'you like him?'

'Yes.'

'D'you fancy him?'

She clicked her tongue irritably. 'Why d'you ask that?'

'Because I want to know.'

'He's not my type.'

'What is your type?'

'Tall, dark and handsome.'

'That leaves me out, then.'

She didn't either agree or disagree.

Just before the bus reached Hythe, clumsily Horner suggested, 'I suppose girls prefer officers to common-or-garden flight sergeants?'

For a moment she turned her head and looked at him, her brows drawn together as if she was going to get angry. Then she said gently. 'I don't know any common-or-garden flight sergeants.'

And he was emboldened to ask, 'Who do you know, then?'

'Just one rather special one.'

He didn't say anything for the rest of the way, lest he spoil that moment. Arriving in a damp and desolate Hythe, he walked with a light and springy step until they came to one of those pink plaster 1920s hotels near enough the sea to smell it, but not so close that you were staring at rolls of barbed wire.

'How about this?'

Pip seemed impressed. 'It looks posh.'

135

In past years it probably had been, but now the pink carpets were scuffed, the wallpaper peeling away, a grumpy receptionist eyed them from a reception desk in need of a coat of varnish. She said she supposed they could have a meal. Meanwhile, yes, the cocktail bar was open.

Open and empty. A very elderly waiter with sore feet brought them their order — a gin and lime and a pint of Bass. They sat on a saggy sofa by a potted palm, stared at unnervingly by empty chairs.

Dinner in the dining-room was some sort of fish, clearly identifiable by its smell, accompanied by cabbage and mashed potatoes with lumps in them like glass. The sweet was a dried egg custard.

But Pip enjoyed it. She had never been in a hotel before, let alone eaten a meal in one. Until she came to Marshfield she had never tasted gin or wine, either.

After a weak and wishy coffee, they returned to the lounge, and Horner prowled around. With the ingenuity of a man with a Packet burning a hole in his pocket, he found double glass doors that led to the garden at the back. There was just enough light to see a tiny path with a summer-house at the top.

'Looks wizzo out there,' he reported back to her. 'And it's stopped raining. Fancy a breath of fresh air?'

'You're a right fresh air fiend,' she told him drily, but she followed him out into the night. There were little ornamental lamp-posts at intervals down the path, not lit of course, and loops of wire that must have held fairy lights slung between the bushes.

'I bet in the old days it was lovely,' she said.

'A real lovers' lane,' he suggested hopefully.

A thin moon had risen and a few stars. The summer-house was open, and there were damp cushions on the bench that ran round the inside.

They sat down together. He slipped his arm round her shoulders, and they cuddled up for warmth.

136

Then he bent down and kissed her. She had an eager but untutored mouth. He tried to insert his tongue between her tightly bunched lips, but her teeth were clamped. It was the first time he'd seriously tried a French kiss and he clearly needed more gen from Ginger. Pip didn't seem to like it, and all he got was a sore tip on his tongue.

He tried putting his hand up her skirt, but he didn't get as far as he had got at the Sergeants' Mess dance. She slapped his hand very smartly. But not so smartly that he didn't touch silk. He was amazed and encouraged. Girls didn't break Air Ministry Orders and wear silk instead of black-outs without mischief in mind.

Pip had in fact been prevailed upon by Pam who did quite a lucrative sideline in knickers. Torn or ripped parachutes which the Equipment Officer allowed them to write off U/S TFWT (unserviceable through fair wear and tear) could be cut and sewn into a vast number of dainty French knickers. Pip had paid her two shillings, a special cheap rate for friends, not because she had any intention of showing them to Horner or anyone else but because they made her feel feminine. She had also bought a new lipstick from one of the cooks — made out of lard and cochineal (another quite lucrative sideline) — and had managed to get hold of a tiny bottle of Evening in Paris perfume from the NAAFI. All in all she had felt good.

What didn't make her feel good was this fumbling up her skirt, and trying to touch her where she shouldn't be touched. At the same time, she remembered Pam's strictures on how young men needed to have It. Pam had confirmed her suspicion that the torch in Maddox's trousers meant he wanted It. And Pam had expounded on how they all basically wanted It. How it made them feel better, fly better, live longer. And any day now when the weather cleared, these lads would be off on ops again, dicing with death. She was between the devil and the deep blue sea.

So to make up for the slap, she took Horner's face in both her hands and kissed him lovingly on the lips. Emboldened, he tried stroking her breast, or what could be felt of it under her buttoned-up tunic.

Tunics must have been designed specifically to discourage that sort of thing. Thick serge with thick pockets and many brass buttons. The 1250s, (identity cards) were kept by the Waafs in their top right-hand pocket. Pip's late pass was in her left. So neither Horner nor Pip had much of a sensation out of the stroking and, after a while, Pip said she was cold and maybe they should go inside.

So back they went and sat on the big pink sofa. Jack ordered a whole bottle of wine. The wine made her talkative. She told him about working in the garage at Leeds, and the gormless lad.

'He was just like Maddox.'

'Oh, him! Why d'you have to bring up him?'

She shrugged. 'I don't know. It's just that the gormless lad caught on quite well after a bit. And Maddox is catching on, isn't he?'

'Perhaps. Perhaps not. I wouldn't call it exactly catching on.'

'Anyway,' she said coaxingly, 'tell me about Halton.' She gave him a shy, admiring smile. 'They trained you well.'

'It was OK.'

'What did you work on?'

'Old engines eventually. The DH 4 was my favourite. But first we had this awful exercise. They gave us each this lump of cast iron and we had to build a hexagon out of it. Just using a hammer and chisel. Then it had to be filed till it was smooth and dead accurate. If it was more than a thousandth of an inch out, we had to do it again. We had to hold it up to the light and if a crack of light showed through, that was it. Start again.'

'Did you pass muster?'

'Yep.' He nodded. 'And d'you know what then?'

'No.'

Something seemed suddenly to strike him. He gave her a shy smile. 'We had to make a female hexagon to fit exactly over it.'

'That must have been difficult.'

'Difficult to get the two to match just exactly right.' He suddenly reached over, took her hand and squeezed it. 'I hadn't thought about it till now. But . . .' he sighed, carefully picking his words. 'Sometimes,' he went on slowly, 'You get people that fit in just right. Like you and me.'

She smiled tenderly. He wasn't being poetic. He wasn't saying, 'My love is like a red, red rose/That's newly sprung in June', but she knew what he meant, and what he meant was just as good if not better. And it was romantic and funny and sad.

She squeezed his fingers. 'My love is like a perfectly fitting hexagon,' she told herself. She wanted to laugh and cry at the same time.

She didn't want the evening to end.

And then he spoiled it all. He asked, 'I suppose you didn't think to get an SOP?'

An SOP was a Sleeping Out Pass. Pam had warned her. Once a man asked that, it was the same as asking, 'Do you do It? Will you do It?'

Pip shook her head vehemently. 'No, of course not!'

Alarmed at her vehemence, he patted her arm reassuringly. 'That's all right! Do you want to go back to camp now, then?'

'No,' she shook her head again. 'I've got a late night pass. Till midnight.'

'If you wanted to, we could stay even longer than that.'

'How?'

'We could stay here and break into camp.'

'When? Where?'

139

'By the gun emplacements. It's dead easy. No one would see.'

'But when?'

'In the morning.'

'You mean staying the night here?'

'That's right.'

She glanced around, clearly tempted. 'I'd like to. But in single rooms. And I wouldn't,' she hesitated, not knowing how to put it into the right words. 'I wouldn't . . . I wouldn't . . . do It.'

He nodded. He had guessed already that the Packet would not be called upon to do its duty tonight. It was, as the RAF would put it, 'Surplus to Requirements'. He even dismissed the idea of trying to book two single rooms close together.

He poured himself another glass of wine, and after he had swallowed it, he rose and said rather stiffly, 'I'll see if they can accommodate us.'

The receptionist watched him approach. She had kept her eyes on the pair of them for the last hour, and she clearly anticipated some impropriety from them.

His request for two single rooms appeared to faze her. 'We don't have any.' Then she leaned forward and whispered confidentially, 'We do have a nice double room left. Sea view, so a bit extra.'

But he shook his head.

He returned, spreading his hands. 'No single rooms.'

He sat down and drained the last of the wine bottle.

'I'm sorry,' Pip said softly, leaning over to pat his knee. 'I'm really disappointed.'

'Not half so disappointed as I am!' he muttered, and then just as she was feeling a bit guilty, he laughed.

She loved him for that laugh. It was something that she knew she would hold in her memory for all the barren years that she already guessed were to come.

10

The bad weather held its grip on Marshfield. A seemingly immovable low pressure area sat over the Western approaches, blanketing the south coast in mizzly rain and mist.

Flying Officer Simon Wetherby, the Station padre, looked out of his office window and was glad of it. Thirteen Squadron had made such a miserable start to its operations that any respite in them was a mercy. Hamstrung too by their lack of aircraft, it was bound to be a while before he would have to watch those Blenheims taking off, reassure some young girl who had formed an attachment with one or other of the crews, refuse as politely as possible Wing Commander Cavendish's request that he wave off the bombers with a hand raised in blessing, and then wait like the rest of the Station to hear how many returned.

Worst of all, of course, was when they didn't return. Already only a few weeks into his sojourn on an operational station, he was finding it hard to reconcile patriotism and the prosecution of all-out war with even his rather watered-down brand of Christianity.

Mercifully he had not had to conduct the funeral service over Bates and his crew. At their relatives' requests, their coffins had been sent back to their homes for burial, with strict instructions to the local undertakers that they must, for security reasons, remain closed, filled as they were with sand and burned bones. But the padre had had to talk to the relatives on the telephone and those calls had tested his nerve and his conscience.

It was after them that he began to suspect he had made a mistake in joining up.

'Why did you?' His new-found friend, the Intelligence Officer Mark Pringle, asked him that same evening as they sat in the bar of the Stars and Stripes, the shabby thatched pub on the edge of the village. 'Why did you join up in the first place?'

Simon Wetherby had been drawn to Mark by his air of quiet competence, and their friendship had progressed through a shared loneliness. Neither of them was a hard-drinking, press-on type. They drank the occasional half pint of beer together in a corner of the Mess bar while the hard drinkers and the young boys chug-a-lugged endless tankards, or walked upside down on the ceiling with blackened feet.

Mark, as Intelligence Officer, knew the crews well and was highly respected, but Simon Wetherby, with his flat feet, shambling gait and owlish spectacles, was not. Nevertheless, under Mark's wing, he was tolerated.

'Why did I join up?' Simon Wetherby held his half-pint glass in both his hands and stared into it. 'Munich, I suppose. I felt guilty about Munich. We had a treaty, we should have honoured it. Chamberlain was wrong. It wasn't Peace with Honour. It was Peace with Dishonour. Besides,' he shot his friend a naïve, apologetic glance, 'I didn't like the parish I was in. And they didn't like me!'

Mark Pringle laughed, and then his rather ascetic face clouded over. 'I joined for less noble reasons.'

He sat back in his chair, a hard polished Windsor chair, and glanced around at the shabby brown Lincrusta walls, the dartboard set askew, the wooden bar in which was set a demijohn of pickled eggs, and behind which stood a mournful-looking bartender with a drooping walrus moustache. There was only one other drinker besides

142

themselves, a man with a great beer belly sitting on a bar stool talking in whispers to the bartender.

'I joined up,' Mark Pringle said, 'primarily because my wife left me.'

'I'm sorry.' The padre avoided looking at him. He himself had no experience of women and no way with them at all. He liked them all right, but like someone who couldn't eat rich foods, they didn't like him.

'She left me for someone else. One of my Cambridge colleagues, no less. Working on the same project.'

'Very hard to forgive.'

'Impossible. I don't even try. Nor did I try to live with it. I left Cambridge.'

'But you could have been reserved.'

'So could you. So could a number of the boys on the squadron.' He smiled. 'And it wasn't a very important project. I was in the foothills of nuclear physics. Not up there with the Powells and the Rutherfords. I reckon I'm more use here.'

'I'm not.'

'You're good for morale.' But he said it without conviction.

'Not according to the Wingco.'

'The Wingco's a hard man to please.'

'Too press-on regardless,' Simon Wetherby agreed.

'Yes, well, don't let's talk about him in a public bar.' Mark Pringle suddenly became careless talk conscious, not because either of the two locals in the bar was liable to be an enemy agent, but because, with encouragement from Simon, he might have said too much about a subject that vexed his conscience — insufficiently trained youngsters being sent to their deaths.

He drained his glass, reached over and picked up the padre's. 'Same again? My shout this.'

Wetherby nodded. As always the unaccustomed drink made him feel light-headed, made him forget his own feelings of inadequacy for the job, made him forget Cavendish's hostility. Owlishly he smiled across at the man with the beer belly, who raised his glass and said, 'Your good health, Rev.'

'And yours, good sir!'

'Bloody awful weather if you'll pardon my French, Rev.'

'It is indeed.'

So they had just got on speaking terms when the bar door opened and in came F/Lt MacGregor, a tall brawny Scot with, in the padre's opinion, a strangely divided personality.

'Why halloo!' MacGregor assumed a shocked expression along with his false Glasgow accent. 'So this is where you hide yourself, padre! And you, Mark!' He put his hand on Pringle's shoulder as he stood at the bar. 'Away with you, man!' He thumped his other hand down on the counter. 'Put that wallet back where it belongs, the drinks are on me.'

The man with the beer belly and the bartender brightened. But then MacGregor, at his best, had that effect.

'Bring your chairs closer up to the fire,' invited the man with the beer belly,

'Aye,' said MacGregor, 'into the body of the kirk.'

And immediately they were forming a cosy circle round the small wood fire.

'*Deoch slainte*!' MacGregor raised his glass. 'Your good health!'

'Good health and good luck to you!' said the man with the beer belly.

'So what d'you reckon to Marshfield?' the bartender asked, wiping the beer foam off his walrus moustache.

'Och, I'm glad you asked, squire. I like it fine. Next best place to bonny Scotland. Scotch mist, you've heard of that. Home from home.'

They all laughed.

The man with the beer belly said, 'The lads before you liked it.'

MacGregor opened his eyes wide and questioningly. 'And who might they be, squire?'

'The Yanks.'

'That's going back a wee bit isn't it, squire?'

'Last war. The Great War. A fine memorial to them in the churchyard. Well worth looking at, Rev.'

'And were you around then, squire?' MacGregor enquired.

'I were a lad. But around. I'll tell you something else. I built some of them hedges round the field.'

'They're still going strong.'

'I knew my trade.'

'Tell me,' Mark asked. 'what did the Yanks fly?'

'Why, DH 4s. Biplanes. Saw them fly in from that window. Smelled 'em, too! The castor oil, you know.'

'Castor oil?' MacGregor queried.

'To grease the pistons. D'you remember that, Wilf?' he turned to the bartender.

'Don't remember the castor oil. But I remember the Yanks.'

'Did you work here then?' Simon asked the bartender.

'Oh, aye. Sweeper and washer-up. I got the lease ten years back.'

'Wilf's risen in the world!' The man with the beer belly winked. 'From pot-boy to landlord.'

'The Yanks were OK,' Wilf went on. 'Open-handed. Democratic. The CO used to sit in that very chair you're sitting in now, Rev. The young lad, the last one to come and the last one to go, Robinson his name. He sat on that stool just under there, where we've got the dartboard now.'

'I remember him,' the man with the beer belly said. 'A funny little lad with fair hair. Captain Shea, the CO, took him under his wing, looked after him like a dad. The lad

145

was supposed to be eighteen, but we wondered, didn't we?'

'That's right. An' they always brought their dog. Lay in front of the fire. Never moved till they moved.'

'What sort of dog?' MacGregor asked, frowning.

'Retriever, I reckon. Wouldn't you say, Wilf? A retriever.'

'Aye.'

'Have any of them ever been back?' Mark asked.

'Back?' Wilf and the hedger laughed sardonically.

'No, mate. Never,' said the hedger. 'Couldn't. All killed. In some famous attack. Right at the end of the war. Made all the difference, that attack, they say. But they were all shot down. Not one of them was left. And the dog just disappeared.'

A silence followed, broken only by the sizzling of the logs. Wilf and the hedger drained their glasses and set them down noisily and hopefully.

'I know,' said the hedger determined to prolong the encounter. 'You got a photo somewhere of the Yanks, Wilf? Used to be up there over the bar where you've got them paper hop-bines. Where did you put it?'

'At the back somewhere.'

'Well, get it, Wilf! Get off your backside! The RAF gents'd like to see it.'

'If it's not too much trouble.' MacGregor got out his wallet. 'And let's have another round. No, I'm in the chair still! And who's for pickled eggs?'

The hedger was. 'He's a right slackarse is Wilf,' he said through mouthfuls of egg as the licensee disappeared behind to do his bidding and there came the sound of drawers being opened and papers riffled through. 'But he never throws anything out, so it's bound to turn up.'

A moment later Wilf returned carrying an old and fading photograph, torn at the corners where it had been pinned to the wall.

'There they are! All of them, God rest their souls, as

146

you might say, Rev! In front of a DH 4. Signed their names for us. Nice-looking bunch.'

He handed over the photograph. MacGregor, Simon and Mark pored over it.

They saw fourteen airmen, all but two looking disconcertingly young. They could just as easily have been 13 Squadron, only they wore the brown drab of the US Air Force.

MacGregor read the names aloud: 'Captain Shea, Kingsland, Rex, Gallagher, Mitchell, Bateman, Womack, Hollingsworth, Grodecki, Virgin, Mackay, Hartman, Martin and Robinson.'

In front of them was a retriever. He knew instinctively that it was brown.

'A Chesapeake retriever,' Angus MacGregor said softly.

'Now that's right. Fancy you knowing that! Now I remember!' the hedger exclaimed, 'That's what the Yanks said it was.'

'You'll be telling us next you know its name,' Wilf said, drawing deeply on his tankard.

'Sam,' MacGregor said. 'His name was Sam.'

Wilf laughed and wiped his moustache and said, 'You've been having us on. You knew all along. Someone told you.'

'I also know,' MacGregor said, 'there's a dog hangs round the airfield now. I've heard it myself.'

And that wiped the smile off their faces.

* * *

Two days later, the smile was wiped off Mark Pringle's face. Not unduly suspicious by nature, for if he had been, how could his wife have so successfully deceived him, he was becoming increasingly suspicious of Group and the role for which they had earmarked Marshfield and 13 Squadron. Now he held in his hand a signal from Group which had just been decoded. A copy of the decoded signal was to be forwarded to the Wing Commander Engineering and to the Squadron Leader Armament Officer.

If one didn't ask the question why, on the face of it this was good news, indeed an answer to Cavendish's prayers or rather his expostulations, and would cause the Wing Commander and the Group Captain considerable rejoicing.

The signal stated that the first two of the six replacement Blenheims would arrive at Marshfield in three days' time and that, weather permitting, a special training programme was to be embarked upon immediately, while at the same time the squadron would remain on the Battle Order.

Big stuff. But why? Mark Pringle wondered. Why?

The aircraft, it seemed, were to be new ones fresh from the Bristol factory. These had been fitted with extra fuel tanks to increase range, and with the newest Fraser-Nash turret as well as the usual .303 Brownings.

Why? Mark Pringle wondered again.

He had another, very important 'why' to add to those. One that surely must have engaged the minds of his superiors at Group and Command: why had all five Blenheims perished on that first operation? On what should have been a fairly routine stooge job attacking the invasion barges. Pringle couldn't get out of his mind the fact that 13, because it was their first baptism of fire, had been given the easier target, the handful of barges up towards the Scheldt. They had apparently all been wiped out, while the more experienced Wellington crews, attacking a more difficult target at a more difficult height, had returned to base relatively unscathed.

So this further question must be asked. Had those five aircraft stumbled unwittingly on something else?

If so, what?

Furthermore, had Group any suspicion that they might?

His keen intelligence officer's mind went squirrelling round that suspicion. It was bad enough to try to read the mind of a madman like Hitler without having also to try to read the inscrutable mind of one's own Group. And Europe now was just a vast, dark fortress with every port and estuary and creek marked with black swastikas.

There were, thankfully, scatterings of pro-Ally resistance groups throughout enemy-held territory, but these were as yet not well organised, and insufficient intelligence was getting through.

Tactful enquiries from his opposite number at Group elicited little except that 13 should thank its lucky stars they were being equipped with new aircraft. Not only the first two aircraft would be arriving forthwith, but the possibility of further replacements in double-quick time.

Had Group some special interest in Marshfield? Pringle got as far as asking. And, yes, came back the jovial reply. One only had to look at the map to understand the reason. Perched on Romney Marsh, eyeball to eyeball with that coast which the enemy now occupied from the Arctic Circle to sunny Spain, Marshfield's position was what interested Group.

'And 13 Squadron rejoices in a very press-on Wing Commander,' Pringle's opposite number told him.

'One,' Pringle replied, but only to himself, 'who has never been on a single operation.'

It didn't take a master's degree in physics to work out that excessive pressure from Group on an eager-to-succeed and inexperienced Wing Commander, himself leaning on an inexperienced and under-trained squadron, would sooner or later equate with the heavy loss of young life.

And then, the following morning, the WAAF Code and

Cipher queen, a stern-faced widow in her thirties, put a message on his desk just for his information and interest.

It was from one of the few Resistance contacts on the Dutch-German border. It reported extraordinary activity around a previously unimportant port along the Scheldt. Workers had been bussed in. A makeshift landing-strip had been laid down, extra fighters moved into the area, guns hidden in a small woodland.

Pringle flicked through the maps of the area. Then he opened the filing cabinet and brought out the briefing map for 13's first and fateful operation.

He ran his finger along the red line of their projected route, frowning. That route would have taken them to this now strangely active area. Their attention would have been focused on the barges, and on an operation that was unlikely to prove difficult. They would have been unprepared for a heavy and sudden fighter attack.

He brought the matter up at the afternoon's Operations meeting. 'Water under the bridge,' Cavendish told him. 'One of those things. You know better than I, Mark, you can't place much reliance on these so-called intelligence reports.'

'Sometimes it's all we have.'

'Even so. We must treat them with considerable scepticism.'

'We do. But if there are extra fighters and signs of unusual activity . . .'

'My dear fellow, there's bound to be a great deal of coming and going in that area, now *Der Tag* is on hold. One day the fighters are there, the next they're not. Maybe they're getting geared up for Hitler's new spring invasion. Maybe they're up to other mischief. Got their sights on somewhere else. Meanwhile we can't have any fanciful theories. Our job is to get the crews trained onto the top line. Prepared for anything. Rarin' to go. We can't second-guess what lies behind operations. Now we're

150

getting new aircraft, that's good news. Couldn't be better! Don't look a gift horse in the mouth, old chap.' He rubbed his hands. 'We're in business.'

'And on ops again as soon as the weather clears?'

'Exactly. It can't come a moment too soon. Thirteen wants to be where the action is. I wouldn't take *that* much notice,' he snapped his fingers, 'of that so-called intelligence. These well-meaning little chaps on the ground have no overall picture. They see an extra fighter, they see a few extra guns, and they're tap-tap-tapping away.'

'Sir?' Pringle appealed to the Station Commander. 'Do you think it might be important?'

'Just a straw in the wind, dear boy, I would say. A straw in the wind.'

But a straw shows the way the wind is blowing, Mark Pringle told himself, giving up the unequal struggle, as he walked to the Officers' Mess for a quiet beer and the relative calm of a chat with Simon Wetherby.

*   *   *

But Simon had his own cross to bear. His cross, too, bore Cavendish's imprint . . .

'He nearly blew me out of the chapel office,' he moaned into his half pint.

'What was it this time?'

'The same as before. Not pulling my weight for morale. Told you he thought that. Asked me if I didn't know there was a war to be won. Gave me a few texts which he thought I should weave into my next sermon, and told me he expected me to be waving at the end of the runway for the next op.'

'And you told him what?'

'That I would think about it. And he told me that our Group padre — I knew this of course — had no difficulty

151

whatever in reconciling blessing the bombers with his ideas of Christianity.'

'He wouldn't have,' Pringle said, and smiled. 'Anyway, it'll be a while yet, I hope.'

'He also told me to scotch any rumours about the dog. Interesting, I thought, in view of what we heard at the pub.'

'You don't believe the rumour?'

'No, of course not. It's just a silly superstition.'

Pringle nodded. It struck him as ironic that a man who not only believed in Christianity, but who felt able to dedicate his whole life to it, could despise superstition. For wasn't Christianity ninety-five per cent superstition? Its whole vast edifice built on a two thousand-year-old story of a dead man rolling away a stone, and getting lifted up bodily to heaven, on a handful of so-called miracles — water into wine, loaves and fishes multiplying, someone in a coma suddenly rousing? Incomprehensible!

'You see, if I thought it would actually help the boys, I would go and wave them off. But at the same time I keep thinking, how can God be in a bombing mission? How can He possibly want me to bless that?'

'If you think Hitler is evil, then I suppose you might just. Always supposing you believe in God in the first place.'

He scooped up the glasses and went up to the bar for refills, and when he returned Simon, to get away from his own troubled career, began asking him about his work at Cambridge.

So Cambridge was on Pringle's mind when he went to bed. His heavy sleep was filled with vivid, fragmentary dreams of Cambridge. Not about his wife or her paramour, strangely enough. But about work, about people he hadn't thought of for years, about their work on atoms and nuclear fission and, overlaying it all, Rutherford's announcement three years before the war began:

152

'Gentlemen, remember the genie is now out of the bottle.'

Why should he so suddenly and vividly remember that? Why should his overworked subconscious be telling him that?

He dismissed both the dreams and his questioning of his subconscious with several cups of strong coffee, and a plateful of gristly sausages and reconstituted dried egg, before walking briskly to the Section. Water still streamed down the window-panes and gurgled in the gulleys.

Amongst all the bumf on his desk which he gradually worked through was another Intelligence flimsy, this time via Group and already decoded. Its source, a small enclave in the Norwegian undergound. This was clearly a further info to one which Group in its wisdom had received some weeks ago but had not thought worth communicating to Marshfield. It said that the plant previously mentioned was now in operation, that its output was not just the deuterium oxide, but other components of The Project. And that a large armed merchantman was taking on supplies.

Deuterium oxide, that rang an ominous bell. And the armed merchantman? Could that be the strange vessel, neither tanker nor cargo, which MacGregor had glimpsed? It now had a name — the *Derflinger* — according to Group.

Pringle walked over to his maps. The enclave was at the head of an unimportant fjord. The village, originally a fishing and logging community, with behind it a small mine and a hydro-electric installation.

That was all. And yet putting those three pieces of the jigsaw together, his mind was already beginning to envisage a terrifying scenario.

If he had been a praying man he would have prayed earnestly that he was wrong.

153

Over in the Parachute Section, Pam was praying for the bad weather to hold. Ginger, she was telling the other girls, was about to come to the boil. A few more dates and who knew?

The news that replacement Blenheims would soon be arriving had been greeted philosophically by the packers. It meant 13 Squadron was on the up and up. The boys got browned off with kicking their heels, and even if ops did mean less time for dates, they looked forward to the big achievements promised by Wing Commander Cavendish. Some of the simpler even believed that 13 would become, as he had assured them, the crack squadron of the RAF.

'And then we'll see bags of action,' one girl said.

'Bags of casualties,' piped up someone else.

Then Ginger came in, and they all shut up.

All except Pam of course.

'Well, well, well!' she said. 'Look what the wind's blown in! Haven't they got you boys doing anything useful to keep you out of mischief?'

'We've just been to a lecture.'

'What was it this time? Flower arranging?'

'Air-to-ship gunnery and ship recognition. Some bloody ship called the *Derflinger* that Group's having a love affair with.'

He watched her admiringly as her deft fingers stowed the lines of a parachute, then the canopy, and then rammed the pins of the rip cord home. Silently he prayed he'd never have to use one of them, but that if he did, it would be one she'd packed.

'They're putting on an extra flick at the cinema tonight, Pam. Thought you might like to come.'

'What is it?'

'*Goodbye, Mr Chips.*'

154

'Goodbyes are all we ever get,' she began to say and then thought better of it. She wished she hadn't even thought it. It was too true. Ships that pass in the night. Here today and gone tomorrow. Hell!

'OK then,' she said instead.

'Jack wants to make it a foursome.'

'Suits me. So long as you bag the back seats first. And supposing Pip says yes.'

Pip agreed reluctantly. She would much rather have gone for a walk even in the wet, and she was reluctant to sit, slapping Jack's hand while Pam giggled and wriggled in response to Ginger's.

In the event, she didn't have to do that. Jack didn't even try anything of the sexy stuff, except to slip an arm comfortably round her shoulder, much needed because the camp cinema was just a concrete block of a building, hastily thrown up last year, and the damp and the cold seeped in. The floor was concrete too, but there were thinly upholstered tip-up seats and the back row was like a long bench, where couples could get astonishingly far advanced in their courtships.

Pam had secured four places, reserving the best, the most intimate ones against the far wall, for Ginger and herself.

The film was sweet and sentimental. The strange thing was that Jack seemed to be the one most absorbed by it.

Ginger, in Jack's presence, behaved at first with decorum, then, egged on by Pam, they began their heavy breathing and squirming.

The projector broke down only once, which was a record. A group of rowdies at the front yelled and stamped as the film went into a crazy overdrive, but the projectionist got it going again in minutes and the lights didn't go up, which saved Pam's blushes.

Then, just before the weepy end, big handwritten letters appeared on the screen: 'Enemy Aircraft in the

155

Vicinity, Take Cover, Take Cover', and that time up went all the lights.

Pam hastily pulled down her skirt and buttoned up her tunic, and there were lots of other girls doing the same

A tannoy announcement filled the auditorium: 'This is an Alert. All personnel not on essential duty proceed to the air raid shelters.'

'Number Three round the corner's the best,' Pam said, 'isn't it, Ginge? Floor's quite dry, doesn't smell hardly at all.'

'Who could ask more?' Jack smiled and began pushing towards the exit. Pip followed. And then as she looked down the rows of emptying seats, she saw Maddox two rows farther down, standing alone, not like a young RAF officer, but like a child abandoned.

She called to him. He turned his head, and then she saw the silly little blighter had been crying.

'We're going to Number Three shelter,' she called. 'Come on! Come with us! Look slippy.'

'What the hell did you do that for?' Horner hissed in her ear, as they all shoved into Number Three and Pam burrowed ahead of them and, practised air raid shelter enthusiast that she was, got them all seats in the darkness.

'What did you bring him along for?' Horner hissed again in Pip's ear.

It was difficult to talk because the Bofors guns all round the airfield were banging away and spent cartridges kept rattling down. There was the distant crump of bombs, but trust Jack, he didn't seem to give a damn about the outside effects, he just continued seething about Maddox sitting on the other side of her.

'I felt sorry for him,' she whispered back into Jack's ear.

'You're wasting your sorrow,' he whispered back.

Then suddenly she laughed out loud.

She couldn't tell Jack what she was laughing at. But the

156

clueless little clot, the cheeky little lad who wept at sad films, had got his hot little hand on her knee.

She let it rest there for a count of three, and then she lifted it firmly and put it back where it belonged. No words were exchanged.

And not many words did she exchange with Jack for the next few days. Cavendish kept them all busy with lectures and shooting practice and even a squadron gas drill.

The new aircraft arrived, and that tempted Jack Horner down to Flights to inspect the new toys. He was still a bit sulky about Maddox tagging along to the air raid shelter, but he was keen to look over the new aircraft. Like Pringle, he was intrigued by the two outer wing tanks, each holding an extra 94 gallons of fuel.

'What d'you make of them?' Pip asked, watching his face.

'They'll let our boy wonder have a bit more time in the air.'

'Seriously.'

He shrugged. 'We're going farther in.'

'To Germany?'

'Where else? Or spending more time looking.'

'For what?'

'Ah, there you have me, love! Looking for trouble, I suppose.'

He laughed.

She gave a pretty fair imitation of a laugh herself.

The appearance of Ginger interrupted that brief conversation. Ginger was keen to get into the new turret, to try the foot pedals and the twist grip handles, and have a look at the gun sight.

Walking back to the Waafery, Pip felt a sudden wind in her face, saw the sky was clearing, the overcast melting away.

The bad weather respite was over.

157

11

At twenty hundred the following day, the next Battle Order was pinned up.

F/Lt MacGregor did the pinning in the Officers' Mess, ate his dinner alone while the rest gathered round the notice-board, then went for a walk. Went for a walk with, of all things, a cold sausage in his pocket.

Could anything be more mad? He consoled himself with the thought that lots of things could be more mad. No, he wasn't losing his nerve, he wasn't afraid of tomorrow's op. He wasn't giving credence to those who said the airfield was haunted by a dog, because the last thing he wanted was to be lumbered with the ability to see *chumbachdach*, ghosties or spirits or things that went bump in the night. He convinced himself he was going for a walk in case there was some hungry animal out there.

It was perfectly possible that the Yank's Chesapeake had left progeny, and that progeny had had progeny. In wartime far too many people abandoned their animals because they couldn't get the food for them, or they left the area, and this howling dog might be one of them.

He walked briskly. The airfield on this late autumnal night was dark and mysterious, full of soft marshland smells. A high, clear sky arched overhead. Not the airman's favourite sort of sky with few trails of concealing cloud, but showing an awesome magnificence of stars.

No dog howled. He heard cats fighting behind the Airmen's Mess, farther westwards beyond Flights an owl hooted. He could hear the squeak of voles or mice in the drainage gulleys. A vixen screamed near the southern curve of the perimeter track by the farm. At that point he stood and whistled, but no dog came. He had no sensation of a dog following him as he returned to the Mess.

And back in there, tomorrow's pilots were looking reassuringly cheerful. As he passed the open door of the games room four of them were playing darts. Farther along, two were propping up the bar. The third, Maddox, was trying to horn in on their conversation and tell them again his special recipe for landing in the fog.

MacGregor crept past the bar and went to bed.

He had a sound and dreamless sleep.

Bronwen roused him with his cup of tea. As she was going out, mindful that he was going on ops she asked solicitously in her sing-song voice, 'You didn't hear the dog, did you, sir?'

'No, Bronwen. He's gone away. Found himself a home.'

'I'm ever so glad, sir.'

'So am I, Bronwen. For him, I mean.'

But, to his shame, it wasn't just for the bloody animal, it was for himself. It wasn't that he was afraid. But he felt a whole lot more confident of the success of the operation now the howling had stopped.

*   *   *

But it hadn't.

At 11.50 hours, ten minutes before briefing was due to begin, as he pushed at the door of Intelligence, just faintly and faraway he heard the howling. He stopped so suddenly in his tracks that Ryan, following behind, cannoned into him.

'Sorry, Skipper.' Ryan looked at him questioningly.

'My fault.' MacGregor slapped his top pocket. 'Thought I'd forgotten to post a letter, but I haven't.'

159

'Ah, some lucky girl.' Ryan sighed.

'Och, just one of many.'

They both laughed.

Pringle was already on the dais, talking to Cavendish. Even without exchanging more than a hand raised in distant greeting, MacGregor thought he sensed the Intelligence Officer's mood of sternly suppressed excitement.

So what was going to be so special about this op? he asked himself, taking his seat in the front row and folding his arms across his chest.

Pringle's face as usual was inscrutable. Nothing, he hoped, showed the alarm, tinged almost with a feeling of *deja vu*, which he had felt since receiving the target information three hours ago. Every word of that signal had sounded in his mind like the tolling of a bell. His suspicions of the last few weeks as good as confirmed, what he had hoped were his overimaginative fantasies declared reality. The connection was made, though as usual Group weren't admitting it. The nuclear deduction was inescapable. The Germans had been the first in the field. They must be working all out on a nuclear bomb and now, with the resources of all Europe in their power, they were probably well ahead.

Pringle looked round the youngsters trooping in. Half-trained, with only a few weeks' operational experience under their belts, these were the unlikely heroes to have to damage and delay that awesome scenario.

Only seven serviceable aircraft, including two of the new long-nosed Blenheim 4s, could be mustered. Mac-Gregor was leading Ashley, Simmonds, Lennox, Maddox and two new boys. At least some of them had been blooded with that one op, which was something, and they had tossed for the new aircraft Tommy and Queenie, a toss-up which Ashley and Simmonds had won.

At twelve hundred hours exactly, Pringle unveiled the first map on the beginning half of their trip.

It was the same map as the previous Scheldt op, same low-level tactics. Having done it before, all the crews reckoned they could do it again and swallowed the same intelligence briefing as before without comment.

It was when, with some trepidation, he unveiled the second map showing the last part of their journey, that the Ohs and the Ahs and the gasps went up. They were to fly at nought feet fifty miles across Holland to a small town practically on the German border called Steinheim.

'It's not as bad as all that.' Pringle forced a smile on his face to conceal his conscience about what was in his mind but which he was not allowed to tell them. In his most encouraging tone he went on, 'There's very few gun positions. The airfields are mostly away on the coast or in the Ruhr. The terrain is as flat as a pancake. No balloons. And if you hug the deck, fighters will be too scared to attack you.'

More cigarettes were lit. The muttering died down.

'The target is easy to recognise. Here's a photograph smuggled out by the Dutch underground.' He passed out copies for each crew to take with them. 'As you see, it's beside a lozenge-shaped lake that will reflect light and act as a beacon for you. Two tall, thin chimneys, a squat, round cylinder like a gas tank beside them. Three typical one-storey buildings with crenellated roofs. A rectangular eight-floor block ending in a paved courtyard. A new wide, straight road leading through a pine forest to the factory. No other buildings for miles.'

Nobody said anything. Nobody moved. None of them had expected to make such a deep penetration into enemy territiory.

'Now Group has been particularly careful to ensure you arrive at last light. You will just have time to recognise the target, drop your 250-pounders, turn round and scarper for home, leaving poor F/Lt MacGregor behind to pick up the pieces and take the photographs.'

161

They managed a slight titter at that.

'Now for the good news. As you would expect, there is one battery of four-inch AA protecting the factory. But it will be almost impossible for them to get the muzzles down and keep you in their sights, you'll be flying so low. Two multiple pom-pom cannons, yes. But the new Blenheim 4s will put them out of action with their forward-firing Brownings. And by the time they get their fighters airborne, you will be in pitch darkness on the way home.'

He paused for greater effect. 'Finally, Group has asked me to tell you that this factory is manufacturing a powerful new fighter, the Focke-Wulf 90, which is a menace to you and all other of our bombers. So I'm sure you'll want to put it out of action before they have a chance to take a pot at you.'

Even as Pringle said the words, he thought how tinnily untrue they sounded, so different from his own ideas about the target. Steinheim was on the main line from Flushing where new buildings were being built and where PRU photos had shown the strange-shaped ship berthed. Could it be that it carried a highly sensitive, half-processed explosive, difficult to handle, which should be delivered as close as possible to the factory where it was to be treated?

'Oh, and by the way, before I leave you,' he tried to say casually, 'that particular building at Flushing quay is going up remarkably fast. Group would be obliged if, when you pass, you'd take a dekko at what's going on, and if you get a glimpse of that strange half-tanker half-merchantman you've learnt about on your ship recognition classes, the one called the *Derflinger*, they would be even more obliged.'

He climbed down from the platform and Flanagan took his place.

A slow handclap greeted him, accompanied by the cry, 'Here comes the duff merchant.'

The Met man's ruddy Irish face puckered with embarrassment. 'Honest, boys, it wasn't my fault!'

'Blarney!' they shouted back at him.

''Twas Group. Honest. Their forecast. All I did was —'

Someone began singing, 'When Irish eyes are smiling.'

At least the laughter broke the tension. By the time he had delivered a forecast of 'Just the right weather, boys. No wind to take you off course. Clear across Holland. A layer of stratus just above the target to climb into if you're chased. And half a moon to light your way home', the atmosphere had changed.

The rest of the briefing — navigation, signals, emergency and escape procedures continued without comment. Pockets were emptied. Emergency rations, German money, a compass, a German phrase-book were issued.

Cavendish said his little piece about his sorrow that he wasn't allowed to go with them, and Group Captain Hurst promised that the bar would be open on their return and the first round was his.

MacGregor took over for a few last words. 'Keep close, but not too close! Keep your TR9 R/Ts on for order changes. I'll tell you if we have to split up. Then go your separate ways. After bombing, we'll return home singly. It'll be getting dark, so don't get too close to the ground, but fly at your lowest safety height.'

Out into the cold they went. One by one the lorries moved towards Dispersal.

Watching them, Pringle thought how brave they were. What dangers would be waiting for them? Off they went in the prime of their youth like lambs to the slaughter. Then he stayed watching them till they moved out of sight to the other end of the airfield.

Five minutes later, the seven Blenheims were taking off.

163

By the hedge at the far end, a bunch of Waafs were waving as the aircraft roared off, and there, towering above them like a flagpole, with them but somehow apart from them, he saw the thin figure of the padre, his head bowed.

The formation flattened out over the coast and turned onto a course of 06 degrees. The English Channel was like chopped green glass below them.

MacGregor had again positioned Maddox next to him on the port side. Outboard of him were Ashley and Simmonds in the new Blenheims. Everyone appeared to be flying quite expertly — not too close to one another, not too close to the water.

There was no sign of enemy activity. The coast of France was calm, still under the weak rays of the winter sun. No flak. No other aircraft. No ships.

Lyttle came up with a change of course of three degrees starboard. 'Seems nice and peaceful, sir.'

MacGregor nodded. 'Let's hope it keeps that way.'

'Just one snag, sir,' the navigator said apologetically as though it was his fault. 'We're slipping behind.'

'How much?'

'Six minutes already, sir.'

'Christ!'

MacGregor looked down at the sea and saw the tongues of white waves flopping over the sea from the north-east. The wind was dead against them.

'North-easterly wind, sir,' Lyttle continued. 'Forty knots. Getting stronger all the time.'

'What's our ground speed?'

'Down to 135.'

'Wasn't the met wind he gave us calm?'

'It was, sir.'

'Damn Met!' Suddenly the whole danger of their situation presented itself. He took another look at those white

164

caps. The grey-green had almost disappeared under what resembled a ruck of white horses.

'Getting worse!'

'That's right, sir.'

'What's our ETA if this wind persists?'

'Fifteen twenty-five, sir.'

'And sunset?'

'Fifteen thirty-three.'

MacGregor felt a certain relief. 'So we'll have a few minutes of last light?'

'That's right, sir.'

'Always provided,' MacGregor said slowly, 'the wind doesn't increase.'

'Might decrease, sir,' Lyttle suggested optimistically.

But it didn't. By the time the formation reached Flushing, still flying in a tranquil sky with no sign of enemy activity, they were a further five minutes late. Down on the quay there was no sign of the ship, although there was some activity going on. But by now MacGregor was very concerned about what he should do.

A strong feeling that he should abort and go home was in conflict with an equally strong feeling that such a course, having come so far, would be sheer chicken. Particularly as there was no evidence that they had been spotted and there was no sign of any opposition.

You never knew. The wind might die down. It might even turn into a helpful tail-wind.

Lyttle came up silently with a course chit of 070 degrees, and MacGregor edged the formation to starboard.

Down below he could see the huddles of houses still in sunshine and, plain as a pikestaff, easy to follow, the mainline railway to Steinheim only fifty miles away.

MacGregor began humming 'The Bonny Banks of Loch Lomond' and told Lyttle he was hungry and what about a sandwich.

The navigator came up and handed him a thick wad filled with hard yellow cheese, announcing at the same time that he had managed to get a couple of bearings and they were now a further three minutes behind.

A wave of panic swept over MacGregor, quickly suppressed under a light-hearted smile.

'Going to be dark when we reach the target, sir.'

'Better get a move on, then.'

He pushed the throttles forward to +2 boost. The engines roared unevenly. Bringing them into synchronisation, he saw the needle on the airspeed indicator move up.

But not enough. Not nearly enough. They would be gobbling petrol now and it was a long way back to base.

'Could we go faster, sir?'

Ruefully he shook his head, pointing to the two long-nosed Blenheims to port. 'Only for boys with overload tanks.' He gave an exaggerated yawn. 'Reckon 190 will be OK!'

But ahead now, up there over the horizon, had come an irregular wall of cloud grotesquely sculpted into an army of grey trolls brandishing jagged spears of lightning. The Blenheim began lurching and bumping, buffeted by the uneven wind, and with it, almost in unison, went the six other Blenheims in a chorus of ragged dance.

Under the overcast, it had become darker. Rain spotted the windscreen. Holding the photograph of the factory in front of him, MacGregor peered ahead.

Nothing he could recognise yet. No lake. No chimneys. He could see the railway below and that was a comfort.

MacGregor reached for the sandwich on the throttle pedestal, took a bite. But his mouth was too dry to swallow.

It couldn't be long now. They'd be over the target in a few minutes, surely. And still no sign that their presence had been spottted.

Suddenly a crimson fountain erupted from the ground.

166

Cannon fire threaded through the formation. Bursts of four-inch flak began exploding all round. And then they were through.

MacGregor breathed a long sigh of relief. 'Everyone still OK?'

And then, as he turned his head, on the port side, he caught a momentary glimpse of the two new long-nosed Blenheims and he froze in horror.

Their sprog pilots had jinxed too much in a desperate effort to evade the flak. Knocked off course, each had fatally turned towards the other. As though in agonised slow motion, MacGregor watched the long noses of T and Q close, touch, crumple.

The next second, both Blenheims had spun onto their backs, blazed, broken up, fallen in shattered fragments. Only Maddox remained on his left.

On the ground, a blaze of yellow flames, a column of black smoke rapidly disappearing behind them as the formation sped desperately on.

'Oh, my God . . . My God!' MacGregor snatched up his microphone. In a voice cracked with emotion, he called over the R/T, 'Break up! Break up! Formation to proceed to target independently!'

* * *

In S-Sugar, it was Horner from his navigation window who saw what had happened and shouted forward.

Scanning ahead from side to side, Maddox had simply noticed that he suddenly had no companions to port.

Alerted by his navigator that there had been a collision and hearing MacGregor's order to break up, immediately he pushed the throttle hard against the stops, went into a steep climb and then a turn, calling out to Horner and Johnson, 'Watch out for other aircraft!'

167

Far behind them, getting smaller, he could see the fiery inferno of the two new Blenheims. He made no comment.

'Poor buggers,' Horner said.

There was no sign of the other aircraft. And now from the ground, up came a stream of white cannon fire.

'Jerry now knows we've arrived,' Maddox called out. 'Johnson, keep a sharp look-out for fighters.'

'I always keep a sharp look-out for fighters,' came the laconic reply.

Maddox seemed intent on going round in circles at six hundred feet, presenting a perfect target for even small-arms fire. Up came a longer white fountain of cannon fire from the ground.

'D'you want to be shot down?' Horner shouted at him.

'I'm waiting for your course to target, navigator,' Maddox shouted back.

'Way you've been weaving, could be anything.'

'Any sign of that railway?'

'None. We've lost it.'

'That village, then?' Maddox pointed to ten houses clustered round a spired church.

'How the hell should I know?'

'You've got a map, haven't you?'

Too shaken from the collision to argue, Horner moved the lubberline on the compass to 065.

'Let's try that for luck.'

Maddox turned the Blenheim to port. Down they went to the ground on that course.

It was getting darker by the second. Flashes of lightning lit up the horizon ahead.

'Look out for the lake,' Maddox called out. 'Look out for those two chimneys!'

On and on they flew. Still no sign. Already they were thirty minutes behind ETA at the target.

Ahead, dark shapes on the ground and the lightning cracking open the grotesque troll figures in the sky.

Maddox put his face right against the windscreen.

'What are you doing that for?' Horner asked.

'I don't want to miss it. See anything, Johnson?'

'No.'

'Well, it's down there somewhere.'

'Reckon we've gone over it,' Horner said.

'We haven't! We haven't!' Maddox became quite frantic. 'I'd have seen it.'

Horner looked at his watch. 'Have to turn back soon.'

'Why?'

'I want to make base, if you don't!' Horner tapped the instrument panel sharply, 'FUEL!'

But Maddox was taking no notice. His head was pressed hard against the windscreen, his whole body suddenly tense.

He pointed ahead. 'Look!'

Horner came forward. 'What?'

'There! There it is!'

'I can't see anything.'

'I can! There! Dead ahead!'

The black boiling sky suddenly rolled sideways. Through a gap in the cumulus build-ups, Horner could now see the wisp of promised moon gleaming in the stormy sky and reflected on the water.

'The lake!' At the top of his voice Maddox shouted. 'To port! The lake!'

His shout was answered by a loud bang. Momentarily the aircraft was enveloped in an eerie phosphorescent halo.

'Lightning,' Maddox called. 'We've been struck by lightning.'

'Lightning my foot!' Horner yelled back at him. 'It's bloody flak!'

The night was filled with yellow bursts of shells. The fuselage echoed with the sounds of shrapnel. The beam of a searchlight came up and fingered the sky, searching.

169

'The factory,' Maddox pointed. 'The factory!'

Caught in the sideways glow from the searchlight, Horner suddenly saw the two tall chimneys side by side.

Maddox called, 'Bomb doors open!'

But already, down in the nose, Horner had opened them, checked the fuses, made the bombs live.

Still right down on the deck, the Blenheim was skating over crenellated factory roofs. Up loomed the big bulk of the cylinder. Maddox wrenched the aileron control full travel port.

Within inches of its curved metal side, S-Sugar slid round it, straightened up, zoomed into the gap between the two chimneys. Out of the bomb bay in a cluster fell the four 11 second-delay 250lb bombs.

Maddox banged both engines against the stops and pulled the aircraft into a steep climbing turn to port over the lake.

With a shattering white explosion, the night behind them dazzled into day.

Watching the smoke and the burning buildings, Ginger was too awed to speak.

Horner put a course chit for Marshfield on the throttle box. '280 degrees.'

Turning onto that course, Maddox asked, 'See any sign of the others, Johnson?'

'Not a sausage.'

Horner had gone back to his desk. 'They'll have got here before us.'

'Late for the party, sure,' Ginger retorted, 'but weren't we just the life and soul.'

'Where are their fires?' Horner asked.

'They'll have missed,' Ginger said with evident satisfaction.

'Jerry hasn't missed, though.'

'Whad'you mean, Jack?'

'Our starboard engine.'

'What's the matter with it.'

'Spitting blood.' Red sparks were trailing out into the night.

Ginger could hear the protesting creaks of the old aircraft being bucketed around.

'Just burning oil.'

'Listen!'

'I can't hear anything.'

An eerie whine was piercing the darkness — up to a crescendo, then down to a whisper. Up again, down again, up again, down again.

'My God!' Ginger groaned. 'Oh, my God!'

Both of them rushed up front and saw, in the greeny glow from the shaking instrument panel, Maddox struggling with the controls.

He pointed to the starboard rpm indicator. The needle was soaring to the top, then diving to the bottom, in time to the engine's banshee tune.

'Losing . . .' Maddox stuttered through his clenched teeth. 'Difficult . . . height . . . must have height!'

'Airspeed!' Horner howled back at him. 'Look at your airspeed!'

The needle on the dial was falling . . . 130 . . . 120 . . . 115.

Horner grabbed the control column and pushed it forward. 'We'll be stalling in a minute.'

'Stop it!' Maddox snapped back at him. 'We're all right. We're holding.'

He was unable to feather. The propeller was simply windmilling around, adding immensely to the drag.

. . . 105 . . . 100 . . . 95.

At ninety-five the needle on the airspeed indicator stopped falling. Somehow or other Maddox was holding that height at that speed. Somehow or other he was managing actually to climb. Slowly, painfully, inch by inch, the whole fuselage shaking and vibrating, in spite of the failed

171

engine, S-Sugar reached two thousand feet, then sank into black feathery cloud, the nose swinging violently 30 degrees either side.

'Your course!' Horner yelled at him. 'Hold 280!'

Standing beside him, the two crew watched the Blenheim's gyrations. Left, right, up, down.

'He can't cope!' Horner shouted at Ginger. 'His bloody instrument-flying! Look at it!'

'He's doing his best, Jack!'

'Best? He'll have us halfway down France in a minute!'

'At least we're still airborne.'

'But for how long?' Horner pointed to the drunken needle swimming around the alcohol in the compass. 'And look at his speed now! Eighty-five knots.'

He leaned forward again and grabbed the controls. 'Here! I can do it better!' The Blenheim lurched sideways, then the port wing lifted almost vertical in a steep turn. 'We'll be landing back in Germany next!'

A scuffle was developing before Ginger intervened.

'Stop it, Jack! You'll have us over!'

'Navigator,' Maddox's squeaky voice asked plaintively, 'where are we?'

Horner exploded. ' "Where are we?", he says! How the hell do I know where we are, *sir*?'

'Course!' Maddox shouted back at him. 'What's our new course?'

Milling round in dark cloud, still rocking from side to side, the propeller still sending out its terrifying high scream, S-Sugar waltzed wildly lower and lower.

'Better brace yourself, Ginger!' Horner called. 'We'll be hitting the Ardennes next!'

'Course, navigator! Course for home!'

Maddox took his right hand off the control column and, like a child demanding food, began thumping the throttle box. 'Johnson, get me a QDM!'

But Ginger was already at the back on the set, trying

172

to get onto the emergency wavelength through a cacophony of sound.

Twenty minutes later, S-Sugar stumbled out of the overcast, still sinking lower and lower at 95 knots. Ginger triumphantly shouted, 'Got 'em! Got 'em! Course 290! And they're standing by to guide us in!'

The wind was still strong behind them. A sliver of moon danced on the Channel waters. Led by successive courses to steer, S-Sugar crossed the English coast.

Ahead was the flashing MS of the Marshfield beacon and, just beyond, the string of double-row small pearls of the flarepath.

Swinging from side to side, with Maddox playing tunes of up-and-down power on the good port engine, the Blenheim lined up on the approach.

Maddox put his landing-lights on. Standing beside him, Horner called out the height and speed.

'Three hundred feet... 250... 90 knots... 85... Watch it! Hundred feet and ninety knots. You're too high! You're too high! Throttle back! Back! Back!...'

Sugar slid over the hedge.

'You're too fast! Cut the engine! Cut the power!... Christ!'

Sugar hit the ground on the port wheel, soared back into the sky, came down on the starboard wheel, bounced... bounced... swung starboard onto the grass... then with a screech of brakes and a reverberating sideways slide, S-Sugar came quivering to a stop.

*   *   *

Flanked by an ambulance, two fire engines and a tractor to tow the damaged aircraft to the hangar, Cavendish had been waiting in his car for nearly an hour, anxiously looking east for the first sight of S-Sugar. Now, as the Blenheim slowed to a stop, still in one piece, he accelerated over the grass and picked up the crew to take them to Intelligence.

The other crews had been debriefed, had reported all bombs on the target and were now in the Mess bars, celebrating. Certainly it was tough that Ashley and Simmonds had been lost, but that was considered a small price to pay for the utter destruction of such an important factory that was likely to be shown on MacGregor's photographs.

Once in Intelligence, the question that both Cavendish and Pringle wanted to know was why S-Sugar was so late.

There appeared to be no answer to this, until Cavedish asked Horner, 'What time did you bomb?'

'15.50.'

'But the others bombed at 15.30.'

There was a moment's silence. Then Maddox said, 'We guessed they'd arrived before us, sir.'

'By the fires?'

'There were no fires, sir.'

'No fires! No fires? They'd just set the whole factory alight!'

'We saw nothing, sir.'

'How could you possibly not have seen them? Those fires would burn all night.' Cavendish's voice rose. He turned on the other two. 'Surely you saw something, Johnson?'

'No, sir.'

'Horner?'

'No fires, sir. Just darkness.'

Cavendish thumped one fisted hand into the palm of the other. Slowly, bitingly, emphasising every word, he said, 'Flight Lieutenant MacGregor has given me a graphic account of the burning factory at 15.30. So have three other crews at exactly that time. Yet you say at 15.50 there was nothing! How the hell can that happen, Maddox?'

174

Maddox's mouth trembled. 'I don't know, sir.'

'I know, Maddox!'

'Sir?'

'You got separated. You were in a different place.'

'We were at the right place, sir! The factory was there, the —'

'But it wasn't the right factory!' Cavendish interrupted. 'You bombed the wrong factory.'

'No, sir,' Maddox was close to tears. 'It was the right factory in the right place!'

Cavendish covered his eyes with his hand as the horror of the situation dawned on him. Where the hell had the little clot bombed? Was it a Dutch factory? What in God's name were going to be the repercussions? Group would be furious.

'You couldn't have carried out the orders you were given for your briefing, Maddox. This is sheer dereliction of duty. I've a good mind to have you court-martialled for this.'

The congratulatory atmosphere in Intelligence disappeared. Now it was all doubt and recrimination. Horner and his navigation were cross-examined in the Navigation Section. Everything was in order until the crews split up after the collison.

'After that,' Horner said, 'Maddox flew all sorts of courses. I couldn't keep up. We were corkscrewing about in the sky. How could any navigator cope?'

Supported as it was by Ginger, his story was accepted.

'All the same,' Ginger added, 'the buildings were there. The lake was there — just as we were briefed by Intelligence.'

MacGregor's photographs, taken at last light and in smoke, were disappointing. But though the buildings were difficult to identify, there was no doubt about the degree to which they were on fire.

'Maddox has got to go. The sooner the better,' Cavendish told MacGregor. 'Back to OTU for further training.'

'He did a good job bringing S back on one engine,' MacGregor pointed out. 'I've never known a Blenheim able to maintain height on one engine.'

Cavendish simply brushed that aside. His view of MacGregor had not changed.

And in his own mind it was not only Maddox who would have to go.

12

Angus MacGregor sought the sanctuary of his room in the Mess after that heady mixture of near-euphoria, sorrow, anger, frustration and accusation that had filled the debriefings.

He had never seen even Cavendish first so triumphant and then so angry, a dangerous and explosive combination, nor seen a young sprog pilot in tears.

All in all, they had triumphed, hadn't they? Thirteen had completed a successful operation. MacGregor had seen it with his own eyes, the blazing roof, the tumbling walls, the weird pyrotechnics, the clouds of orange and black smoke.

And yet. And yet . . .

He had also seen Ashley and Simmonds slice into each other. He would remember that split-second for ever, remember yelling out a useless warning, remember himself and Ryan sitting for a moment totally frozen, while down those shattered fragments fell, twisting, spinning, bursting, disintegrating.

But the rest had survived, thank God, and all but the little clot had bombed the right target. Why so uneasy? he asked himself as he closed the door of his room behind him. Ashley and Simmonds had bought it. But they were not the first or the last. And this feeling wasn't only because of them.

Wasn't his uneasiness partly due to the fact that he'd heard that bloody dog again and it had presaged losses? It wasn't just a farmyard dog as he'd told Ryan, it was that same retriever. He knew that howl, and yes, he had to admit it, he was afraid.

He was also afraid that morale, so dear to Cavendish's heart, would really take a plunge, despite the mission's success, and that Cavendish would have to take that out on someone. He'd already indicated to Maddox that he despised both him and his airmanship and was out for his blood. Not that MacGregor had any particular brief for Maddox, but he had a brief for justice, and to bomb the wrong target under those conditions was not unusual. Cavendish, being an operational virgin, couldn't possibly understand that. MacGregor also felt sorry for Maddox's crew. They had looked ready to murder each other.

It all added up to a bad night. He hardly slept and when he did doze off, he kept waking himself, screaming out to Ashley and Simmonds.

Then it was morning and it was Bronwen waking him. 'Oh, sir! I wouldn't have wakened you, but you was having such a bad dream! You was sitting up. Calling the dog, sir!'

'Away with you, woman! I was doing no such thing. You're a wee story-teller, Bronwen.'

'Oh, sir. I swear!'

'You just wanted a natter, Bronwen.'

'No, sir. But I do want to say, I'm ever so glad to see you back. I was worried.'

'You're always worried, Bronwen. It's on account of being Welsh instead of Scots.'

'My friend Johnny was worried, too.'

'Johnny being the Wingco's batman no less.'

'That's right, sir. The Wingco thinks ever so highly of my Johnny. Says he'd make a good butler and maybe he might give him a job in civvy street. Johnny says the Wingco was in a terrible state last night, what with all that about Mr Maddox, and then someone mentioned the dog to him, and that really got up his nose!'

'And what a nose for any dog to get up!' MacGregor laughed. 'Now be a good girl, Bronwen, and get me some toast and a wee spot of marmalade. I'm knackered. I'm going to lie in till lunch-time.'

'I'll bring you your lunch, too, if you like, sir.'

'Och, no! But thanks. I'll be human again by lunch-time.'

And so he was, more or less. The dark feeling of unease had left him. He showered and dressed. Bronwen had cleaned his buttons till they were like gold, and polished his shoes. He walked briskly down the corridor and was about to skirt the bar when he saw Maddox, sitting alone in a corner hunched over an untouched half pint. He walked over, snapping his fingers for the barman to draw another two pints and to bring them over.

Like a number of other people, he had sometimes hoped uncharitably that Maddox would get egg on his face, but when it happened it wasn't a pretty sight.

'Why, halloo, Peter! Bit early for serious drinking.'

'Oh, sir.' Maddox immediately flushed with abject guilt. 'This is my first.'

'I'll believe it, laddie. Thousands wouldn't.'

Maddox attempted a feeble smile. He had been over to Flights in the hope of seeing Pip, but she wasn't on duty, and the RAF corporal who was exclaimed to him over the damage to Sugar's airframe. 'You collected a packet, sir!' He didn't add, 'and all for nothing'. But that comment had seemed to Maddox to hang in the air.

'So how are we this morning, Peter?'

'Awful sir. I feel awful.'

'You look a wee bit grey round the gills. Drink up!'

Maddox wet his lips with the beer and raised mournful eyes to MacGregor. 'I've let everyone down. But I can explain . . .'

'Ho'd your wheesht, man! Close the hangar doors! No shop in the Mess, remember!'

179

'But now no one wants anything to do with me.'

'That's codswallop, Peter. Everyone knows you're still learning. You'll know next time.'

'Will the Wingco court-martial me?'

'Course not.'

'But he has taken me off the Battle Order.'

'You'll be back on it in no time.'

'I was so sure I was spot-on.' Maddox dipped his face into his tankard, like a weeping girl into a handkerchief. He really was a case.

'Bombing's a very inaccurate science at the moment, Peter. The boffins need to work on it, and so do we crews. But you can't cry over spilt milk. Just let it give more power to your elbow. Put it behind you, except to say that it's a lesson learnt. That maybe you're too ready to think you're right.'

And that was the understatement of the year, Mac-Gregor thought. The laddie was either up like a self-confident balloon or down like a deflated one. But after a couple more pints, Maddox looked almost cheerful and certainly drunk.

'Now off you go, Peter! Lie down. Have a good sleep. Things will look a lot different in the morning.'

That was of course the usual remark you made to anyone whom you couldn't really help in any other way, and there was no great originality, certainly no vision or perception, in that.

MacGregor continued on his way to the dining-room for his cottage pie and rice pudding. He had done his morale boosting for the day and he was not minded to talk shop, so when he had collected his plate of evil-looking cottage pie, he didn't sit on the usual aircrew table but found himself a place among the penguins, the SHQ and other ground officers. One of the engineering officers had clearly been moaning about the loss of the two new aircraft, but at a frown from Pringle, he shut up.

180

Pringle passed him the salt and pepper. 'You'll need both, Angus! I suspect it's horse-meat. I think they left the saddle on, too.'

He gave him a kindly smile, but his eyes were sombre. He's as worried as I am, MacGregor thought, but doubted he was worried for the same reasons.

Pringle had finished his lunch and MacGregor was halfway through the gummy goo they called rice pudding when he heard sharp steps clicking on the polished floor behind him. A heavy hand descended on his shoulder.

Funny, MacGregor thought, how even a hand on the shoulder can convey volumes! No kindly hand-clap this. No prelude to come and have a brandy to finish off, old boy.

MacGregor turned and looked up.

He saw Wing Commander Cavendish's face looking down in tautly concealed anger.

'I'd like a word,' he said without preamble. He scowled at the half-filled bowl of rice pudding. 'Finished?' he demanded.

There could only be one answer. 'Yes, sir.'

MacGregor pushed back his chair and stood up, wondering what the hell it was all about.

'Right, then!'

Cavendish turned smartly as if on the parade ground and marched towards the door. MacGregor had no idea where they were going. He had no choice but to follow. They marched out of the dining-room — the man of authority followed by a puzzled miscreant. For although there was no doubt Cavendish considered a crime had been committed, MacGregor had not yet guessed what it was, except that someone had to suffer for Maddox's debacle. Down the corridor they continued, turning smartly into the Mess office.

The door was half-open. Sergeant Fowler was sitting at

his desk. He looked up guiltily as if he was falsifying the accounts, which he probably was.

He too jumped to his feet, and when Cavendish told him brusquely, 'I'd like the use of your office for a moment, sergeant,' he backed out grovelling, as if from the presence of royalty.

Cavendish wasted no time. 'I've a bone to pick with you, MacGregor.'

'I kenned that by the way you brought me in, sir.'

'Don't be impertinent!'

'Och, I was nae being that. I thought maybe it was a little drastic.'

'You *are* being impertinent.'

'No, sir. Maybe what you have to say is drastic.'

Cavendish's nostrils flared, his eyes narrowed. 'Serious is the word I would choose, MacGregor!'

MacGregor inclined his head.

'For I am sure we both regard morale as serious!'

Oh, God, MacGregor thought, here we go again! This is where I came in and no doubt where I'll go out. Morale! Aloud, he said, 'Yes, sir! Very serious! But what exactly has it to do with me?'

'A great deal, MacGregor.'

'You're not seriously holding me responsible for the collision, are you?'

'No.'

'Nor for young Maddox?'

'I think his training could have been better.'

'The training of us all could be better. But just let me wise you up on one thing. Three-quarters of the bombs dropped by our Command don't land on the right target. I've dropped bombs in France on the wrong target. We all have! If we've operated at all.'

He paused to let that barb go home. Then he went on, 'I'm no Maddox fan, but you can't take it out on him for that! Nor can you try to come storming after me.'

182

'I wasn't storming, as you see fit to call it, for that.'

'For what, then . . . sir?'

'For morale in general. And your contribution to the lowering of it.'

'My contribution to the lowering of morale! Christ almighty, how?'

'By spreading foolish stories.'

'About?'

'About a howling dog which you,' his voice became witheringly sarcastic, 'with your special Highland gift, can hear.'

For a moment MacGregor was shaken, not because Cavendish was angry, but because he clearly took the matter seriously.

'You're surely not serious, sir?'

'I am serious. Very serious.' He paused. 'I can quite see that when you spread these silly stories, you were not. That it was probably your idea of a joke. But surely you're sorry you ever started this? Surely you could see how this would snowball? Surely you can see now the effect these stories have on the young and foolish?'

'Sir, I didn't spread stories. I said on the odd occasion that I heard a dog howl. Other people have made more of it.'

'A good deal more,' Cavendish said drily. 'The whole Station appears to have heard of it. The gen now is that it's a ghostly dog. And presages loss.'

'I've always thought it was a real dog. I've actually looked for it. But there is a legend in Marshfield village about a howling dog. The pub has a photo of it.'

'And you conveniently matched the two together! If you match that howling dog to casualties and botched targets, then it cannot but undermine morale! I prove my point, I think. You, MacGregor, have helped 13 to regard themselves as unlucky. You are clearly bad for morale!'

Bad for morale! God, Macgregor had heard that convenient condemnation before. For chaps who got their tail out of line or questioned Authority. Bad for morale. The rotten apple in the barrel. Get rid of him!

Stung by anxiety, he snapped back, 'If anyone's bad for morale, sir, it's you!'

'How dare you say that?'

'Because it's true! You don't stick up for your squadron. You don't bat for them with Group. We've got inadequate aircraft with inadequate bomb sights and armament.'

'And when I manage to get us new ones, you let the youngsters write them off, MacGregor!'

'And write themselves off, too, don't forget! They don't do it because they want to! And, Christ, you can't blame me for that!'

'No. But perhaps your leadership on the operation could have been better.'

'Och, leadership! I'm glad you mentioned that, sir. Because,' he thrust his face forward into Cavendish's, 'that's where 13 is bloody unlucky! In its leadership. *Your* leadership! We're led by an inadequate, operationally inexperienced Wing Commander, who has never,' he separated each word to give it maximum velocity, ' . . . done . . . a . . . single . . . op!'

That felled Cavendish like an ox, sliced him down the middle, unmanned him. The crimson glow of anger drained from his face, leaving it as white as a sprog pilot's mopping up his gunner's spattered brains.

'A commander who has never once done what he's asking his men to do. Who doesn't know what it's like to bomb in anger. In cloud! In opposition! Who doesn't know how easy it is to miss. God in heaven, Maddox's mistake was understandable! I hold no brief for Maddox. But it could happen to any crew. Experienced Wingcos know that! Chairborne sprogs don't.'

Now he had plunged the fatal knife into his superior officer, MacGregor couldn't help going on turning it.

Partly because he couldn't stop himself, partly because he was goaded by the Wing Commander's manifest pain. There was another reason, too: besting Cavendish, getting him as it were on the floor, eased some of his deepest doubts about his own courage and manhood.

And yet when Cavendish turned and, without another word, opened the door and stalked out without bothering to close it behind him, MacGregor almost ran after him and apologised.

But he didn't.

After a moment, Sergeant Fowler crept back in, eyes nervously darting all over as if he expected to see blood on the floor. 'Is it all right if I come in now, sir?' he asked a pale-faced MacGregor.

MacGregor nodded wordlessly.

Sergeant Fowler looked at him closely. 'Are you OK, sir?'

'Never better.'

He was thinking he had come to a pretty parlous state when he was actually sorry for Cavendish. But his common sense told him that he had merely downed him. That was always his fatal flaw, to wound but not to kill. He would probably regret this argument. The Wing Commander was in a far stronger position than he was, and infinitely more ruthless. Vengeance would be his.

But first, fate or the gods, or whatever myopic creatures were running the war, dealt Cavendish and 13 Squadron a strange card.

The following day, the AOC was on the scrambler telephone to Wing Commander Cavendish. His enthusiasm was clearly audible across the room. Cavendish had to hold the instrument away from his ear.

'Just had the PRU reports in, Charles! On 13's factory op! Bloody good show! Bloody marvellous! Hardly a stone standing!'

It took some little time to cut through that froth of

exaggerated enthusiasm to discover that it was in fact Maddox's target that had been the right one. The other, the one bombed by the rest of the squadron, was a decoy hastily erected by the Hun.

'You have to hand it to them, Charles! Cunning bastards, the Hun! But luckily you and me and 13 Squadron are just that much more cunning than they are, eh, Charles?'

* * *

The AOC's praises ran round the Station like reinvigorating wildfire. The last had become first again. A suitable sermon for Simon, Pringle thought, when he heard about it. Once again, Maddox was on top of the world and, in the light of his demolition of the target, the fact that the rest of them had bombed the decoy was no bad thing.

However, the day's good news did not make MacGregor's insolence any the less, nor did it change Wing Commander Cavendish's view on MacGregor's effect on squadron morale.

Although he was aware that no doubt MacGregor would feel that whatever action he took was prompted by the man's taunts and the effect of those on his personal vanity, such was not the case.

Cavendish was a good deal more mature and observant than MacGregor realised. He studied his men more closely than anyone knew. MacGregor's response to his squadron commander's reproof had, in Cavendish's opinion, been not only insolent but exaggerated and disturbingly over-emotional. It had shown signs of acute stress and anxiety.

So Cavendish, when he lifted the telephone and asked to be put through to the Medical Officer, had exonerated himself from any personal vindictiveness.

'Lesley,' he said when she answered, 'I'd like a word.'

186

'A word,' she repeated, sounding wary. 'What about? My replacement?'

'Good heavens, no! Group have kept quite mum about that. And frankly, Marshfield isn't going to jog their elbow.'

'You surprise me, sir.'

'I don't see why. We don't want to lose you. You're fitting in.'

'Am I?'

'Indeed you are. You're an asset. In fact, I'm ringing you now to ask for your help.'

'Times are changing,' she said and gave a little pleased laugh.

'It's about one of our pilots. I'd like you to run the ruler over him. If I could just fill you in with his background . . .'

She was remarkably co-operative. She still remembered Bates. She wasn't going to make the same mistake, if mistake it was, twice.

As a result of their conversation, two days later, as Mac-Gregor made his way to the Mess dining-room for a spot of lunch, checking the letter rack on the way, he found a note in the his pigeonhole. It bade him tersely to report immediately to Sick Quarters.

A wry smile spread over MacGregor's face when he read it. A *tete-a-tete* with the Luscious Lesley, her of the dark, shiny bobbed hair and wide blue eyes, would have been welcomed by any red-blooded lad on the squadron. And yet . . .

As he walked the few hundred yards to Sick Quarters, MacGregor's nostrils held a hint of rat smell.

Reaching Sick Quarters, he was immediately whisked inside her office.

'VIP treatment,' MacGregor said, making himself comfortable in the chair she waved him to, and giving her his best innocent smile.

187

She gave a nice enough, but slightly uncomfortable smile in return, took a packet of Gold Flake from her desk drawer and offered it to him.

He extracted one and brought out his lighter.

'I didn't know you smoked,' he said, as she also helped herself from the packet.

'I do. But just occasionally.'

He spun the wheel of his lighter. 'This being an occasion?'

She laughed uncertainly, and when he leaned across the desk to light her cigarette, her fingers trembled.

She drew in a lungful of smoke as if it were oxygen, narrowed her eyes and began, 'You've never reported sick, Flight Lieutenant?'

'True. Ought I to have done?'

'No, no! Of course not!'

She paused, made some vague remark about liking to keep an eye on everyone's health, then continued. 'Yet you went through the Battle of France.'

'True.'

'When 13 Squadron casualties were terrific.'

'True.'

'It must have been a shattering experience for you.'

There the penny finally dropped. The rat smell became unignorable. The poor lass was as good as reading off a check-list of questions. She'd been through this before with Cavendish, the bastard! Cavendish distrusted him. Worse still, he, MacGregor, had insulted Cavendish's manhood. So Cavendish had decided there wasn't room for both of them on the squadron. Therefore he was going to do what they did to Siegfried Sassoon in the last war. Mentally unstable. Flak-happy. Bordering on the deranged. The attitude was the same, only in this war the label was different — Lack of Moral Fibre this time round.

'Not true!' MacGregor answered loudly.

188

She frowned. 'But you did a lot of ops.'

'So?'

'You must need a break.'

'When I've finished the tour, I'll get one. When. And not before.'

She ground out her cigarette.

'Well, I do think you need a medical examination.'

'If you say so, doctor.' MacGregor took off his jacket with exaggerated alacrity and began unbelting his trousers.

She said hastily, 'Waist upwards. Jacket and shirt will do.'

'Och, lassie! That's only half a job.'

She frowned. 'On the couch, please.'

Now that he was sure of her complicity with Cavendish, he made it hard for her, watching her with exaggeratedly wide eyes as she went about her job with sphygmomanometer, stethoscope, thermometer, spatula and hammer. He saw an uncomfortable blush creep up under her pale, fine skin.

When she tested his reflexes, he gave great international footballer kicks, and when she took his blood pressure, he gazed soulfully up into her eyes and said hoarsely, 'If it's up, it's because you . . .'

'It's not up,' she snapped.

When she enquired about his bowels and waterworks, he so phrased his replies and assumed such facial expressions that she didn't know whether to laugh or cry.

He held his hands out for her to see their steadiness, and then invited her to do the same to have a dekko at hers.

When she asked him if he ever suffered from headaches, he said, 'I have this constant one.'

'Tell me about it.'

'It's called Cavendish.'

189

It was not very gallant of him, but he was pleased to see her flush.

She asked him how he felt about operational flying.

'There's only one thing I like better.'

And the silly lass fell into the elephant trap and asked him what that was.

'Sex.' He said loudly. 'Sex and flying are very similar.' Then he paused and, when she said nothing, went on, 'Aren't you going to ask me about my sex life? Or didn't Cavendish tell you to do that? Don't you know that if you'd been a male doctor that would have been the first thing you'd have asked?'

And then, just as he was thinking those were unbecoming remarks for a MacGregor, the silly wee lass pinched the end of her pretty nose with her fingers in a vain attempt to stop her tears.

'Oh, Christ!' MacGregor let out his breath in a long exasperated sigh. 'Oh, Christ!'

He felt an outsize heel. Come to that, he *was* an outsize heel.

'I'm sorry,' he said, and in his own defence, 'it's not fair posting women as MOs!'

But that made her weep all the more.

'You sound like Cavendish,' she said in muffled reproach.

'Christ, now you are insulting me!'

She gave a tiny tearful laugh, and then he was up and out of his chair and round the desk and putting his arm round her shoulders.

His arm worked wonders. It was the first time in her life that she had felt a man's comforting arm, and warmed by it, out came all her fears and frustrations, her feelings of guilt, how she felt she had been inadequate, especially with Bates.

'Listen, lassie! We're all inadequate,' he said, smelling

190

the sweetness of her newly washed hair. 'We just don't dare to admit it. We wouldn't be able to go on if we did.'

He had always got on well with women, but today he was surprised at his own flow of easy wisdom and philosophy. In no time at all he had forgotten her collusion with Cavendish, or if he hadn't forgotten, had made it understandable in the light of her guilt about Bates.

In another few minutes he was prescribing a drink and, to his surprise, she was accepting. Plans were forming in his head. Ryan had a part share in an old jalopy, which he would lend his Skipper.

By twenty hundred hours, they were rattling along the road to the village, and now darker, more delectable plans were forming in MacGregor's mind.

* * *

They headed straight for the Stars and Stripes. Not that MacGregor thought much of the place, but there was nowhere else unless you went into Hythe, and Ryan hadn't got much juice in the old jalopy.

The bar was only half full because most of the airmen came in later after they'd tanked up a bit at the Sergeants' or Officers' Messes or at the NAAFI.

There was quite a decent fire, and in the corner MacGregor found a rickety sofa just big enough for two, which he drew up beside it.

'What are you drinking, Lesley?'

'A brandy, if they've got any.'

'Bad as that, is it?'

'It's been that sort of day,' she agreed.

It struck him she was wondering what on earth Cavendish would say when she told him MacGregor was as fit as a flea.

'Brandy's under the counter,' Wilf told him. 'But,' he winked, 'seeing it's you . . .' He brought out a bottle and

191

poured a generous tot. 'Funny you knowing the name of the Yanks' dog, sir. And do you see? I've pinned up their photo again.'

'So you have! Good for you!'

'D'you see, sir? Their names underneath. Each one signed. All of them, from Captain Shea to little Lieutenant Robinson.'

'What was all that about?' Lesley asked when he returned with the drinks and set them on another rickety piece of furniture, a small table with a tiled top.

'Just the Yanks that used to be here.'

'When?'

'The last war.'

'I must have a look.'

She got to her feet, walked over to the bar and peered up at the photograph above the hatch.

'Nice-looking lads,' she smiled, returning to sit down. 'Plus dog. Is that where you got your story?'

'My story? Which one?'

'The one that the Wingco's so browned off about.'

MacGregor frowned. 'Jesus, he didn't bat your ear with that as well, did he?'

'It was peripheral.' She smiled again.

'Stupid bastard!' MacGregor said with feeling, and took a long swig of his beer. 'So what's he going to say when you give him your verdict?'

'Which one?'

'On me.'

She pulled a wry face and shrugged.

A terrible thought struck him. Women were indeed the weaker sex. They had a built-in desire to please authority. 'You're not going to let me down, are you? You are going to tell him I'm A1.'

'That's an awful thing to suggest,' she exclaimed. 'Of course I'm going to tell him you're A1. Why did you think I mightn't? D'you reckon I'm frightened of him or something?'

'You wouldn't be the only one.'

'Well, I'm not.' She paused. 'No, that's not true. I am. But not enough to let him interfere with my medical opinion. He overpowers me, but not altogether. My father is exactly like him. My father's a surgeon in the Navy. Very tight-lipped. Autocratic. Unapproachable. Distant. I always wanted to please him. But at the same time I always wanted to have the guts to stand up to him.'

'And did you?'

'No. Never.'

'Do you love him? Your father.'

'Of course.'

A wry thought occurred to him. 'And how about Cavendish? D'you fancy him?'

Her reply was immediate. Too immediate. 'I loathe him.'

'The two can be confused sometimes, lassie. Attraction and repulsion.'

'You being a bit of an expert?' she laughed teasingly and, reaching out, lightly touched his hand as it rested on the table. 'So why not tell me about your girlfriend? Seeing I didn't ask you this afternoon.'

He told her as much as he considered it prudent to tell her. Yes, he'd met a girl when he was at agricultural college. He liked her, but everyone knew the war was coming. He'd had a brief affair with a young Frenchwoman. No one since he came to Marshfield.

'That situation is vacant,' he said, raising his eyebrows several times in humorous invitation.

In fact, he wouldn't have minded offering her that vacant situation. Except that she was the serious kind and with life, his life, hanging on a thread, he wasn't going to get serious with any girl. But as the evening wore on he liked her better and fancied her more, and he began

193

to forge unworthy plans for bringing the evening to its triumphant conclusion.

She told him about her schooldays, her young brother, her family's devastation when he was killed.

'The flower of the flock, as they say. My father would much rather it had been me.'

'That's a silly thing to say!'

She shrugged. 'You don't know my father.'

'True. But I know Cavendish and therefore you have my deepest sympathy.'

She smiled faintly. 'Now you tell me about your family.'

So he told her about the farm, his walks in the mountains, his father, whom he had to confess he liked, their intense pride in their clan. He almost mentioned that intermittent, fleeting second sight, but he didn't. To mention it was to admit it, so instead he told her about his younger sister, her pony, their dogs.

It was all very cosy, very encouraging. Some of the sergeants and the younger P/Os in the squadron came in. They eyed MacGregor enviously, but they played the game and kept their distance.

Wilf brought out the brandy bottle from under the counter whenever requested, and it wasn't until Wilf called, 'Time! Time, gentlemen, please!' that MacGregor realised the evening was over.

And it wasn't until the MO tried to rise to her feet that he realised she was pie-eyed.

MacGregor put his arm round her and they made a reasonably dignified exit. But the shock of cold moonlit air almost knocked her out.

In the car, he opened the window wide, saying her breath smelled like a distillery.

'You bought me it,' she pointed out.

'So I did! Do I get anything in return?'

She clasped her hands on her knee and said nothing.

MacGregor had been considering stopping the car in

194

a convenient field gateway. After all, she was very fanci-able. A nice bit of crackling. But instead he drove straight and steady through the main gates of the camp and round to the Officers' Mess. He stopped the car by the side entrance, the one that opened onto the corridor and which thereby bypassed the bar. It was frequently left unlocked.

Flying Officer Stamford's head was sunk on her chest. He could hear by her regular breathing that trustingly she was asleep.

'Lesley! Which is your room?'

She jerked awake, blinked, and then slowly, as if it was a difficult question to answer, 'Upstairs. Room 7.'

MacGregor swore under his breath. Upstairs! Jesus! He glanced up at the blacked-out windows. God knew who was moving around in the corridors. Getting unobserved to Room 7 with one drunken MO in tow would have foxed an SOE agent, might well result in one not over-popular Flight Lieutenant being delivered for discipline to Cavendish.

Luck was with them. The door was unlocked, the down-stairs corridor empty. MacGregor guided her towards the stairs. She kept catching her shoe on the treads, stumbling and giggling.

'Ssh!' he put his finger to his lips.

'Ssh!' she echoed twenty times louder.

They reached the first floor.

'Left or right?' he asked her.

'Right.'

From behind a closed door, he could hear a radio playing, laughter, music.

'Which is the Queen Bee's room?' he whispered.

'That one.'

The next door was labelled 'Bathroom'. Water gurgled and a sweet, overpowering scent of bath salts leaked out. Behind the next, a lavatory chain was pulled. And just as

195

the bolt on the door was snapping back, he saw the blessed number seven.

He opened the door and shoved her inside.

'You'd better go,' she said, 'you'd get shot if you were found here.'

'Court-martialled,' he replied cheerfully.

And then, as if her right hand didn't know what her left hand was doing, she put her arms round him and held up her face for him to kiss her. 'You're a good man, Angus MacGregor.'

Then she began unbuttoning his jacket.

'You've got it wrong, lassie! It's you that needs to get undressed.'

He began unbuttoning hers.

After that, she unfastened the buckle of her skirt and let it swish down round her ankles. He stared wide-eyed for a moment at her black silk knickers, the dainty suspenders spanning the soft silky flesh above her stocking tops, and thought, This is it, after all. What the evening was all about!

Suddenly a voice deep inside MacGregor called, 'Stop!' Some ghostly chieftain intoned something bloody foolish about a MacGregor not taking advantage of an inebriated woman. So as she removed her shirt and disclosed a tiny bra half-cupping beautiful rounded breasts, MacGregor demanded sternly, 'Lesley! Where is your nightie?'

Averting his eyes as she unclipped those tiny suspenders and rolled down her stockings, he repeated sternly, 'Your nightie!'

When she appeared not to hear, he dived towards the bed, rolled back the white counterpane, lifted a pillow and found another froth of nonsense, this time in snowy white with blue ribbons, which made him feel sick with missing such a chance.

He dropped the thing over her head. 'You're a bonny

wee lass,' he said almost apologetically. 'Pity you're not sober!'

Then he pulled back the bedclothes. 'Get in!'

She seemed at that point to sober. 'I'm not going to bed with you.'

'Of course you're not!'

He pulled the covers up round her. He turned her head to one side.

'What are you doing?' she asked.

'Just in case you're sick.'

She seemed to go to sleep as soon as her head touched the pillow.

But he doubted she was. He felt she was watching him through half-closed lids as he tiptoed to the door, opened it, made sure the corridor was still empty, and glided out.

What a missed opportunity, he told himself again. But he knew it wasn't, not just because a MacGregor didn't behave like that, but because she really was a poor lass.

Deep down she fancied Cavendish. There could be few worse fates for any woman than that.

13

And now fate was catching up again with Marshfield.

Thirteen Squadron was high in Group's favour and once again chosen for what Group said was a highly important operation. Pringle had already guessed what that might be.

On the Battle Order were five names — MacGregor leading, Saville, Owen, Rawcliffe and Maddox.

At briefing, sure enough, the target was the *Derflinger.*

The ship had been sighted leaving the Skagerrak and was estimated to be two miles west of Esbjerg at twelve noon that day, on a southerly course.

'And I bet it's going to Flushing,' Pringle thought as he briefed the crews.

Met were giving a clear sky with some patches of low stratus. But Pringle had to stress that the ship was likely to be heavily defended.

MacGregor was minded to point out that if the opposition was expected to be that strong, in clear weather, there were bound to be considerable casualties amongst such a small force, and to hint at the connection with the disappearance of the previous five Blenheims on 13 Squadron's first op.

But in the end, he held his wheesht as Pringle emphasised Group's message that this was another most important target for which 13 Squadron had been specially chosen.

Pringle watched them take off one after the other, waved upward and away by the Waafs and poor perplexed

Simon. Over the hedge, the beach and off on an easterly course to find the *Derflinger.*

The formation found the *Derflinger* all right. But they also found two *Staffeln* of Me 109s flying an impenetrable escort umbrella over her.

MacGregor took a decision that no MacGregor should ever be asked to take. It was alien to his nature, or at least it was alien to his nature as he'd known it till he came to Marshfield. But it was also inevitable. No sane commander would have taken any other. To attack would have been suicidal.

Gritting his teeth, MacGregor ordered the whole formation to return to base. Pursued by Me 109s, they were lucky to make it to a band of stratus which for once Flanagan had forecast accurately, and which, thank God, extended almost to the coast.

Seated within sight of the coast, at his desk in Marshfield Station Chapel, Simon Wetherby was writing out the order of service for next week's church parade. He had barely finished when the air raid warning sounded. The whole works this time, shattering the empty quiet that always held the Station when the squadron was airborne and away — first the terse tannoy announcement, 'Enemy aircraft in the vicinity', then the banshee wail of the siren on top of the hangar, and from far away Marshfield's civilian warning joining in.

Warnings were so common that he had almost learnt to disregard them, the same as anyone else. But today he heard the throb of engines. He got up and walked over to the window. Through the lattice of the tapes, like evil flies in a useless web, swept three Me 109s.

He knew them to be 109s because Mark Pringle had taught him how to recognise them during one of his visits to the Intelligence hut. There they hung from the ceiling, those black-crossed aircraft, under the large label YOUR ENEMY.

The three disappeared from sight. But he could hear them, the zoom of their engines, their cannons. And now the Bofors guns round the airfield had started up. The floor shook. In rapid succession, three bombs!

God almighty!

It was a prayer, he told God, not an imprecation, as the heavy crumps were followed by three more.

A proper raid this time. And on the airfield. He gabbled a few words, part of him wanting desperately to dive under the table, under the chair, under the altar even.

But the other part won. He opened the door and went outside. The half-clouded sky was full of little white dandelion puffs. He saw the Mes wheeling and diving, their engines screaming, saw bombs actually falling, felt them through the soles of his feet, smelled them. Smelled the dust, the cordite, the smoke, the funeral smell of upheaved earth. And all the time as he watched, he felt quite detached as if he were a child at the cinema watching a splendidly entertaining film. And even though the German bombers were having it all their own way, it hadn't anything to do with him.

Then he saw from the south-east, emerging from cloud low over the horizon, 13 Squadron's returning Blenheims. Bigger and bigger they grew, approaching fast.

The Me 109s fell eagerly upon them. The battle began.

And now the padre was up there with the boys. He was jumping up and down, urging 13 Squadron on. He knew they would be getting short of fuel, would be tired, knew it was the worst possible time to engage the enemy.

And for himself, he had never felt so excited before or since. Then he saw one of the Mes fastened like a black panther on the tail of a Blenheim. He saw the Blenheim desperately trying to snake around, heard the stutter of cannon fire, shook his fists. 'For Christ's sake, somebody! Do something! Help him!'

Suddenly he saw a strange silvery winglike shadow that

seemed to slice between the two battling aircraft. And then that dreadful scream of an aircraft in its last fatal dive.

He closed his eyes, and then opened them quickly again. Then widely and disbelievingly. It wasn't the Blenheim that was crashing. Miraculously, it was the Me spinning down, round and round and round, and then vertically down.

When it hit the ground and he felt the earth quake under his feet, he laughed with relief. He even yelled at the top of his voice, he the padre, the Anointed of Christ, the Peacemaker, 'Serve you right, you bastard!'

Those words would haunt and reproach him through the years, but then they didn't.

He might well have spoken them for the whole Station. What a boost to morale that was. The sneaky bastards thinking they could attack on home ground! Marshfield was like a football crowd. Against the odds, their team was winning.

So Britain was alone. So Marshfield was that much too close to the Continent. So the aircraft weren't adequate, the crews green. So what?

When the other Mes had beaten a hasty retreat and the All Clear had sounded, Bicycle Clips cycled to the Admin block to get his order of service roneoed in the orderly room. He was asking himself if he might add a footnote to his sermon claiming a minor miracle, and in the orderly room he joined in the conversation of the clerks, some of whom had witnessed that swift and marvellous turnabout of the event, and who were loud in the praise of the pilot, young Maddox.

Maddox was in the Officers' Mess at that moment, lapping up the congratulatory pints everyone insisted on buying him. Horner went down to Flights, ostensibly to inspect the damage to Sugar, but really to see Pip. He had recognised for some weeks that he had become very

201

fond of the girl, but today he had been astonished by his own anguish at the sight of the Mes bombing the airfield, knowing that she was there, imagining her dead or injured or buried under a mound of rubble. He couldn't wait to see Pip, to put his arms round her, feel her solid, competent little body pressed close to him.

Of course Ginger, the real hero, shooting from the rear turret, must have been the chap who'd downed the Me, and he'd gone off to meet Pam in the hope he would find her generous in more than praise.

'Well done, Jack Horner! You pulled out a plum there all right!' Chiefie Chalmers was standing in the door of the Flights office, demolishing a sandwich. 'I've just been down to have a look at your kill.'

'Wasn't mine. I didn't do anything. Ginger got him.'

'Did he now?' Chiefie Chalmers wiped the crumbs off his mouth with the back of his hand. 'Well, mebbe you're right. And mebbe you're not. It's the funniest wreck I've ever seen. Just looked like the nose was sliced off clean as a whistle. More like a collision than a shoot-down.'

'Ginger's a real dead-eye dick.'

'Bullet didn't do it. No bullet in the fuselage. Was like another wing sliced through him. But none of our kites had collision marks.'

'A fast sustained burst, that's what Ginger says did it. Was the pilot dead?'

'Not quite. Soon will be.'

'Poor bugger!'

'Aye. You're all poor buggers. But you wouldn't've said that if he'd got young Pip.'

'Where is she?'

'Up where she should be, mending what he did to you!' Chiefie Chalmers put his fingers to his lips and whistled. Pip's head appeared at the top of Sugar's ladder.

'Don't keep her off her work too long,' Chiefie grumbled and went inside.

'He won't!' Pip called, bounding down the steps and into Horner's wide-open arms. 'Oh, God,' she half-laughed, half-cried, 'I was so afraid. I saw him after you . . . I thought . . . I mean I thought you couldn't get away . . . I've never prayed so hard . . . then I lost sight of you . . . and I thought . . .'

She buried her face in his jacket. He almost wept with her, almost told her how afraid he had been for her, told her how much she meant to him, had begun to clear his throat in preparation to do so when at that crucial moment she seemed to become aware that someone was watching them. Pulling round, still in Horner's arms, they both saw Maddox. A diffident, almost forlorn Maddox.

'Peter!' she called out. 'Come over here! Congratulations! You capped the lot. Thanks! You were wonderful!'

And then, as he came up close, not diffident now but smiling, lapping up her praise, she freed herself from Horner and flung her arms round both of them, squashing them together in her sturdy little arms.

It was just a girlish hug, just an emotional release from unbearable tension, and yet Horner couldn't get it out of his mind. It was, he thought, as if he was going to be saddled with the little bugger for the rest of his life.

* * *

'I have a little job for you, padre.'

At twenty hundred hours, just as Simon Wetherby was about to cycle up to the Mess for dinner, the SAdO telephoned. An amiable and breezy man, he was in an especially amiable and breezy mood. There is nothing like surviving a raid to make life seem good.

'I'm delighted to hear you have a job for me. Always happy to be of use,' Simon Wetherby replied, leaving the rest of the SAdO's remark to be clarified in that officer's own good time.

'It's *a propos* Jerry. Seems the bastard's still breathing.'

'Bastard? Which bastard, sir?'

'Why the one Maddox shot down, of course. The Me 109 pilot.'

'Oh, I see.'

'They've carted him off to Hythe Memorial Hospital.'

'Is he badly hurt?'

'He's had it, of course.'

'Of course,' the padre repeated.

'But it seems he wants to see a padre. We thought it should be you. Under the circs, it should certainly be you. I've organised it with MT. They are sending a car round to you. Should arrive any minute. So pack your clobber and just go.'

Instinctively, the padre made a protest, an unfortunately feeble protest. He murmured he was just about to go up to the Mess for dinner. He could have bitten off his tongue. What a stupid, inept thing to say!

The SAdO sounded disgusted. Contemptuously he said, 'I'll get the Mess to save something for you.'

And hung up.

Ten minutes later, Simon Wetherby was seated in the back of the Station Humber, clutching his mobile sacrament case in one hand and his vestment bag in the other. He was shivering. His mouth felt dry. He couldn't get his mind round all this. Part of him was still up there in the sky with the battling aircraft. Fear, and its bedfellow, hatred, still gripped him.

'Bloody Hun!' the corporal driver threw back at him over his shoulder. 'Why the bloody hell do we bother with the bastard? Shove a pillow over his face, I say!'

The padre tried desperately to think of some Christian but noncontroversial reply. But none suggested itself. Besides, the hyped-up part of him wanted to say, 'Yes! Why not! Why not a pillow over his bloody head?'

As if aware of this, the corporal added in the silence, 'The bastard wanted to kill us, didn't he?'

'I suppose so.'

'Course he did! What did he bring his bombs for? Didn't drop in for tea, did he?'

'True.'

'He damaged the decontam. No one in it, luckily. And he missed the WAAF site by a whisker. Someone up there was looking after them, you'd say, wouldn't you, padre?'

He didn't give the padre time to confirm or deny. He went on furiously, 'I've a popsie down there at the site. A lovely lass. If he'd killed her, I'd've torn him apart with my bare hands!'

Momentarily he took both of his big meaty hands off the steering wheel, their thick fingers spread to show their murderous capability. And to the padre's terror, the Humber wobbled dangerously to the slippery edge of the ditch.

He brought out his handkerchief and wiped his forehead.

'Sorry, padre. Very sorry.' But whether the apology was for his sentiments or his fearful driving, he didn't make clear. The padre was relieved, but not glad to arrive at the little cottage hospital, the war memorial for the 1914–18 conflict.

In the shadowy hall two small furled flags, a Union Jack and a Stars and Stripes, were propped against a brass plaque. The walls were tiled in a hideous pattern of green and brown. The whole place reeked of pungent disinfectant.

'Padre!' A middle-aged VAD advanced and beckoned.

'A pillow over his face,' the corporal driver muttered to her by way of greeting.

'You might as well wait in your vehicle,' she told him curtly. 'The padre will not be long.'

She didn't take issue with his sentiments. She simply

205

rustled ahead of the padre in her red, white and blue uniform, leading the way down a short, cheerless corridor to the ward. The ward that for ever afterwards he would think of as his white crucible. White walls, white bedsteads, white counterpanes, white sheets, white pillows, white curtains screening the bed to which she led him.

She parted those white curtains. The padre saw a white bandaged head above a white face, a pallid mouth, slack and dribbling, heavy lidded eyes, only half open.

For the first time, the padre saw a German face. The hated Hun.

Only it wasn't a Hun's face. It was Bates. It was Butterworth. It was Maddox. It was any of the young boys on the squadron.

Simon Wetherby put down the vestments bag and had began to open it when the VAD snapped, 'There's no time for dressing up, padre! Just give him what he needs!'

What he needs! For Chrissake, how could he give that! He needed life. He needed the years of his youth back again. He needed to love, to marry, to have a family, to make his contribution to life, to mature, to grow wiser, to know peace.

The VAD stepped back and pulled the curtains sharply closed. With painful slowness, the padre saw the boy raise his cupped hands towards his mouth. He wanted the Sacraments.

With trembling, clumsy fingers, Bicycle Clips brought out the wafers and the phial of communion wine.

He had seen death. He knew the boy was close to it. He poured a little wine into the silver chalice. The phial chattered against the rim like frightened teeth. The boy was too far gone to accept the wafer. The padre tried with the chalice, but the wine simply dribbled down his chin.

The pilot's half-open eyes were fixed on the padre's face, as if willing him to do something. The padre dipped his finger in the wine and spread it gently over the boy's lips. Slowly, the tip of his tongue licked in a few drops.

The padre knew no German, so he whispered in English, hoping it wasn't too hateful to him. 'The Blood of our Lord Jesus Christ which was shed for thee, preserve thy body and soul . . .'

And before he had time or voice to finish, he heard the boy whisper in perfect English, 'Unto everlasting life.'

Then he gave a long sigh. A shadow like a cloud crossed his face. And he died.

The padre leaned over and kissed his forehead. He felt something in himself had died, too.

He packed up the pathetic little sacrament case. The VAD offered him a cup of tea, but he declined. Sensing his mood, the corporal driver remained silent all the way back to the camp.

He went straight to bed. He woke in the night to hear the sirens going again, and although the All Clear sounded almost immediately after that interruption, he couldn't sleep. He spent the rest of the night composing in his mind a letter to the Group padre, requesting he be allowed to resign his commission on the ground that he now found it impossible to reconcile the Christian doctrine with the prosecution of the war, and that therefore he must consider himself a pacifist.

He wrote the letter out in his office at the chapel, and then, hoping to catch Mark in the ante-room before lunch, cycled early to the Mess.

'What's all this about, then?' Mark asked, as they settled themselves down with their half pints in their usual corner and Simon Wetherby handed him his letter to read.

'The RAF and I,' the padre said, 'have come to the parting of our ways.'

'I see.' Mark Pringle read the letter slowly, folded it up and handed it back. 'Last night I suppose? The German? Seeing him face to face? Seeing him die?'

207

'Oh, more than that, Mark! Much more!' He wanted to describe to his friend that this was his personal crucible, his baptism of fire. 'It was seeing me face to face. Me! Seeing my ideas, my so-called principles, my so-called beliefs, my so-called faith.'

'Mmm, well, having no faith, I can't go down that road with you.'

'And all the better for that, you'd say!'

'Indeed I would.'

'But you think I'm doing the right thing?'

'I don't know what you're doing exactly.' Pringle stabbed a finger towards the letter the padre still held in his hand. 'Do you intend sending that to Group?'

'Yes.'

'Leaving Marshfield? Leaving the RAF?'

'Yes.'

'Walking out on us?'

'I suppose so.'

Pringle put the tips of his fingers together and half-closed his eyes thoughtfully. 'Then no, I don't think you are doing the right thing.'

'You surprise me.'

'You shouldn't be surprised.'

'Well, I am. I expected you to sympathise. To understand. You've always gone on about the waste of young lives.'

'So I have. So I do. But will your resignation lessen the waste?'

'Possibly not.'

'Then consider the other likely results.'

'I have. Or at least some of them.'

'First of all, you would be pilloried.'

'I am quite prepared for that.'

'Oh, for God's sake, Simon! Stop trying to play the martyr! You're not even sure of the beliefs for which you want to be martyred. For which you would be labelled.'

208

'I shall be labelled as a conscientious objector. What's wrong with that?'

'Your timing's what's wrong with that! You can't declare yourself that now! Not at this stage. This vital stage! You're part of the scene, part of the fabric, part of Marshfield, part of the RAF, part of our war effort. You're known to the squadron and to all the Station personnel!'

'But it's for them that I feel I should do it. And you're the one who's always gone on about the waste of young lives. I've seen it now. Seen the waste. From both sides!'

'Listen, Simon.' Mark Pringle spoke slowly and weightily. 'I have modified some of my ideas. I've had new and unwelcome insights. I've come to the reluctant conclusion that in some cases lives have to be imperilled. Sometimes it's worth it. Sometimes it isn't. In war, we're all compromised. We're all interdependent. We all want to survive.'

'But with our principles intact.'

'God in heaven, Simon! How can you say that? What principles? Turn the other cheek? Love your Nazi neighbours? Bombard the Hun with roses? You took the decision to join the RAF, because you thought Munich was a betrayal. So it was. You didn't have to join up. Nobody forced you. But when you did, you joined a fighting force. You took on responsibilities. And you abnegated others. You've got to think clearly now how your apostasy would affect other people, if you do decide to give up. It's a kind of LMF.' And then, leaning forward to pat the padre's arm apologetically, 'No, forget I said that. I shouldn't have. Nevertheless your going will be seen as desertion. And that is bound to affect morale.'

'You sound like Cavendish.'

'Yes, well, perhaps he isn't quite as unreasonable as he's painted.'

'I thought you didn't like him.'

'I still don't. But he has a job to do. The squadron has to be on the top line and he has to get it there.'

'That's a turn-round. Mark.'

'Maybe. Maybe not.' Pringle sighed wearily and rubbed his eyes. For the first time Wetherby noticed how gaunt and strained his friend looked. Perhaps the Intelligence Officer's secrets, his inside knowledge, were as disturbing as his own muddled Christian conscience.

'I'm betraying no secrets,' Pringle went on gravely, 'when I tell you, Simon, that shortly Marshfield and 13 Squadron will have a very important role to play. A crucial role. I can't tell you more than that.' Then he stood up and drained his glass. 'And right now, I don't want your belated conscience to lower their morale in any way. Or for that matter, to lower mine.'

14

Pringle immediately regretted his brusqueness to the padre but he had no opportunity to smooth his ruffled feathers, and indeed he doubted he would have the sophistry so to do. A Christian conscience was such a superstitious luxury at this moment. He doubted he would know the right words to span the divide between it and the emerging nuclear world.

For here it was taking shape in front of his very eyes. As a student, cycling in Italy and Greece during the long vac at Cambridge, he remembered seeing distantly out on the horizon over the Aegean the eerie black funnel of a sea trumpet taking swift shape. He had barely time to reach shelter before it struck the coast, sucking everything up in its path — waves, trees, tables, tents, chairs, cars, bicycles.

That had been a brief meteorological interruption. But this thing that was as certainly taking shape might be the end of everything.

Three days after his conversation with Simon, 13 Squadron was placed on the Battle Order again. Although no op was yet on the cards, that in itself argued some urgency. Maintenance were working flat out to repair the damage sustained during the raids, the equipment officer was going mad in his search for spare parts from maintenance units all over the country, and the low-level gunnery practice was still continuing.

Not that the crews minded the practice. As MacGregor remarked, it was better than sitting on their bottoms waiting for what Group would dream up next, but it played ducks and drakes with getting the aircraft on top line.

The weather was still moist and heavy. November mists had given way to cold December sleet and rain. And with the typical muddle-headedness of the RAF, the penguins, that is the chairborne brigade, led by the SAdO, decided that since December was here, Christmas should now be on the Station menu. There was nothing, the SAdO declared, like Christmas preparations to raise morale.

He set about badgering a morose and unenthusiastic Simon Wetherby to suggest something especially Christmassy. The padre's suggestions were dolefully unenlightening. In fact ever since the shooting down of the Me 109 the padre had been especially doleful and unenlightening. So the SAdO had perforce to dream up most of the Christmas programme himself, with the help of the Queen Bee, who was an overgrown schoolgirl at heart and liked that sort of thing.

There would have to be a Christmas service of course, but best not to make it a compulsory parade. A crib in the chapel and others in the various Messes. That would give the chippies and the wallahs in the paint shop something to keep them out of mischief. Dances in all the Messes too, and a tree beside the flagpole, with decorations on the grass beside it, each Section being told to make a contribution for it.

'Why so keen all of a sudden for a walk?' Jack Horner asked Pip in a mixture of suspicion and hope after Maddox had landed them brutally and bouncily at the end of a low flying practice at fifteen hundred hours that December afternoon. 'I've hardly got an unbroken bone left in my body.'

'Well, lots of reasons why,' she answered, 'and your

212

bones look all right to me.' She seized his hand. 'Feel all right, too. It wasn't that bad a landing. I saw it.'

'Landings, like beauty, are in the eye of the beholder. You're biased towards the little bastard.'

'No, I'm not.'

'So why d'you want to walk?'

'Goodness!' she sighed, putting her hands to her waist and stretching her muscles. 'Why do I want to walk, eh lad? I've been bent double over S-Sugar all day. Since seven hundred hours. I'm off shift now. I just waited to see you in. I need a change. I need to stretch my legs. Besides, I want to collect things.'

'All right. Such as what?' Jack asked, deciding not to look a gift horse in the mouth. If she'd got around to suggesting walks, who knew where that might lead? And though his pragmatic self told him, not far, he repeated less suspiciously, 'Such as what?'

'Such as materials for Christmas.'

'Jesus!' he turned his eyes up to heaven. 'Women!'

'No, not women,' she told him, wriggling out of her overalls. 'The SAdO! Chiefie just this minute told me. We're having a tree by the flagpole outside SHQ.'

'Lit up, I suppose, so that the Hun can get a better aim.'

'No. Not lit up. But decorated by each Section. I'll enjoy that. I'm a dab hand at making stuff out of nothing.'

'I believe you are,' he told her fervently, as they set off together to walk towards the Napoleonic canals. 'I believe you could even make something out of me.'

She eyed him sideways, frowning. 'Are you trying to tell me you're nothing, Jack Horner?'

'As good as.'

'Then you're stupider than I thought!' She sounded monstrously angry. 'Don't you ever dare say that to me again! And don't dare think it! Mind,' her brows smoothed, 'I know you don't really think it.'

213

'Not always,' he admitted, smiling.

'Sometimes you reckon you're a hell of a navigator.'

'Not very often.'

'A dead eye on the guns when you get the chance.'

'Possibly.'

'That you'd make a really good pilot.'

'Not really good. Just about a hundred times better than Maddox.'

'Oh, shut up about Maddox!' she said. 'Let's forget him for now. I want to enjoy the walk.' She breathed deeply of the mossy, marshy smell of the dykes. 'There are so many things you're good at, Jack.'

'Tell me one,' he said, catching her hand and slipping it through his arm.

'Well, you told me one yourself,' she laughed. 'You make a perfect iron hexagon!'

She turned and held up her face for him to kiss her.

'And I have,' he said, 'a near-perfect way with women.'

Alas, too perfect! Too perfectly gentlemanly. It was a kiss and no more, and there was no way walking along the dykes, outlined against the fading sky, that anything more exciting or intimate than a kiss could take place. Besides, the ground was soggy, the dykes full of black water, hazardous enough for gathering the materials for Pip's Christmas creativity without bringing in sex.

The greatest hazard was snatching the bulrushes, the ones with the great brown torpedo-like heads which could be made into marvellous displays, Pip said, using silver aircraft paint. Some of the fitters had already begun on making stars out of broken bits of Perspex and angels from Duralumin.

'I can't wait to see all this,' he said. 'Roll on Christmas!'

They returned to camp via the Waafery with an armful of the bulrushes and branches of hazel which already showed next spring's tiny pinky-green catkins. Those catkins were like seeing the rainbow, a promise of better times to come.

And why not? Why not better times this very evening? Before whatever tomorrow might bring. 'How about us going in on the Liberty bus to Marshfield?' he suggested.

'Tonight?'

'Why not? We're free tonight. But they've just pinned up a warning we're on ops tomorrow.'

'OK,' she said. 'Give me time to clean up.'

'All right. We can just do it. See you at the guardroom. Seven-thirty.'

He stood at the gate of the Waafery, watching her disappear with her armful of rushes and hazel branches.

She turned at the corner of one of the Nissens and waved. Then the semi-darkness swallowed her up.

* * *

Thankfully Pip saw that Pam had made down her bed for her. She laid her harvest carefully on the topmost brown hairy blanket, and turned to Bronwen, the only other occupant of the hut at that moment.

'Be a love will you, Bronwen, and see no one swipes it.'

'I will if you'll win me a bit of Perspex from the hangar.'

'OK. What're you going to make?' she asked, busily unlacing her shoes, and taking off her jacket.

'It's not me. It's Johnny. He's going to make me a ring.'

'Oh, that's lovely! Really romantic. Have you two clicked?'

'Yes. He's ever so keen. He's making plans. The Wingco says he might give him a job as a footman come the end of the war.'

'Lucky you! Nice work if you can get it, eh? Roll on civvy street!'

'Amen to that.' Bronwen sighed, and then offered,

215

'Want me to rub up your buttons while you're getting ready?'

'Oh, please!' Pip threw her jacket to Bronwen, and fled out of the hut, across the soggy grassy field to the ablutions block. The bath-water was just off cold, but bearable. She had managed to buy a cake of Imperial Leather soap from the NAAFI and she had also queued for another tiny bottle of Evening in Paris perfume. Those aids to feminine appeal, plus her parachute knickers and her cochineal lipstick, made her feel quite close to the million dollars of the movies.

'Hope you have fun!' Bronwen wished her, as she watched Pip carefully brushing and arranging her short, springy hair.

But what was called the Exigencies of the Service dictated otherwise. At that moment, the door of the hut burst open. In came one of the SHQ runners, the message carriers, red-faced with the exertion of cycling up from Flights. 'LACW Armitage?'

'That's me!'

'You're wanted at Flights! At the double!'

'Did Chiefie say why?'

'No. Just to come. Bring your overalls.'

'Oh, no!' Pip folded up the man's boiler suit that did duty for overalls, stuffed it in her respirator case, and set off.

At the main guardroom she left a message for Jack Horner and just past the guardroom she managed to flag down a petrol bowser going towards Flights.

'Looks to me like tomorrow's a maximum effort,' the driver told her as she climbed up into the passenger seat. 'Bags of hundred octane on the indents. A bit of a flap on.'

'There's always a bit of a flap on.'

'You're right there.'

'Sorry to drag you back, hinny!' Chiefie Chalmers

216

apologised when the bowser dropped her off at Flights. 'The Wingco now reckons he needs S-Sugar as well.'

Pip blew out her cheeks in an exasperated sigh.

'It's a big do. The bugger said we were to work all night if necessary.'

'Well, it won't be, I don't suppose.'

'No. But I didn't tell him that. He likes to think the great unwashed are suffering.'

'I'll say he does! And so we are!' She looked at her watch as she rolled up her sleeves. Jack would just about now be arriving at the guardroom, no doubt wondering if she'd changed her mind or had spent too long luxuriating in the half-cold bath. She hoped the corporal SP gave him the message, but SPs couldn't always be relied upon.

However, he and Maddox and Ginger would probably be glad they'd have S-Sugar for tomorrow's op. Though not the newest of aircraft, she was an old and familiar friend. Tonight, especially tonight, it gave her a funny feeling to be working on the rest of S-Sugar's damage. There was a suspicious little pool of hydraulic fluid on the concrete. There were bullet holes on the port fuselage, perilously close to the pilot's seat, and then there was a half-inch fracture inside a bend in a pipe leading to the starboard engine. Although she didn't need it, everywhere under her hands was proof of how close to death Jack and Ginger and Maddox had been. The overwhelming feeling of thankfulness that they had survived so far gave way to overwhelming apprehension that tomorrow they had to go through it all again. And tomorrow, maybe the opposition would be worse. And would their luck hold for that?

'What's all this about a maximum effort, Chiefie?' she asked him as he came up and stood watching her struggling with the unions.

217

But he just shrugged and walked away to look at the new tyres they'd put on yesterday.

It took half an hour to undo the wretched unions and do them up again after she had dealt with the pipe. When she'd finished, something made her look down and there was Jack, all done up in his best blue, with trousers pressed and untidy hair slicked down with Brylcreem.

She scrambled down. He caught her and they threw their arms round each other. Then she lifted his forage cap and ruffled his hair, and threw her arms round him again. 'I mistook you for Ronald Colman,' she said, 'with your hair like that!'

Chiefie coughed loudly to show he was in earshot, but she didn't care. All she could think was that here she was working on the proof that Jack had been within an inch or less of death. and here he was with her, till tomorrow at least, so wonderfully alive.

After a moment, Chiefie came up again, wiping his hands. 'I gotta go over to L-London, have a dekko at how Corporal Lumb is working out. You can cope here, can't you?'

It was his way of being nice to them.

Jack took off his tunic and got ready to work in his shirtsleeves. 'Might as well see you do a proper job,' he said, climbing up onto the Blenheim wing beside her.

With the beetle-backs, the engine cowlings, off, she was meticulously examining the long lengths of alloy tubing, hoping the tiny leak of fluid she had spotted on the concrete was from no more than a loose union.

After a long silence, she looked across at him and said, smiling apologetically, 'Not much of a night out for you.'

For several minutes, he watched her as she concentrated on the lengths of alloy, testing the integrity of every union.

Then he said, slowly and weightily and with painful

218

sincerity, 'There's nothing I'd rather be doing. Nowhere I'd rather be. No one else I'd rather be with.'

She had found the guilty union and was apparently totally absorbed in tightening it. She didn't trust herself to say anything in case she spoiled that most precious moment.

Then he went on, 'Pip, I've got very fond of you. Very, very fond.'

She nodded and made a rough little noise in her throat, and then said thickly, 'And I'm very fond of you.'

'When we've finished on the kite, let's go and have a coffee and a bite in the Sally Ann. Then we can talk, can't we?'

'About?'

'About us.'

She felt a great lurch of excitement. She thought he was probably going to ask her to marry him, or perhaps because aircrew were funny about marrying in case they got the chop, to ask her to be engaged till the end of the war.

She nodded, reached across and squeezed his fingers. He took her hand in both of his. That in itself was a bit like an engagement, their hands solemnly joined over the wing of his aircraft.

It was nearly twenty-two hundred hours when they finished work on the aircraft. Just early enough to get coffee at the Sally Ann and maybe one of their doughnuts.

'Back in two shakes.' Pip jumped down onto the concrete and went into the Flights hut to take off her overall, wash her hands and face, take her comb and lipstick out of her respirator case and repair her appearance.

When she came out, she heard voices. Angry voices. And there was Maddox talking, if it could be called talking, to Jack Horner. They were both shouting and swearing and gesticulating at each other.

Jack was demanding to know why Maddox had

219

appeared, why he was always bloody well appearing. He had been standing bemused under the wing, going over in his mind what he was going to say to Pip. He knew what he wanted to say, but talk of love and whatnot was alien to him, and he didn't know how to put his very real sentiments into words.

Then he had heard Maddox trotting around, calling, 'Pip? Are you there, Pip?'

And immediately his blood and his suspicions boiled over.

'So why the hell have you come down here?' Jack was yelling.

Maddox at first didn't reply. He must have taken on a load in the Mess bar. His breath smelled like a glycol leak. He couldn't keep steady on his feet.

Then he muttered, 'I came because Pip asked me to. Didn't you, darling?'

'No!' Pip said.

'Yessh, you did!'

Maddox turned to her. As he did so he swayed and stumbled. To steady himself, he grabbed Pip's arm.

And that did it.

Horner sprang forward with his fist clenched and with every intention of landing it on Maddox's nose, officer or no officer. But faster than he, Pip grabbed his wrist.

'No!' she shrieked. 'No, don't hit him! Please don't hit him!'

All she could think of was, strike an officer and you were finished. You were dead. Or as good as. Court-martialled. Discharged with ignominy. Probably imprisoned.

Stoutly, she stood between them, her arms outspread, like a bloody mother hen, it looked to Horner, protecting her favourite chick.

'You bloody rat!' Horner shouted at Maddox. 'That's right! Hide behind a girl! I'd make mincemeat of you!'

'Don't you dare lay a finger on me, Flight Sergeant! I

am an off... issher. And I have more right than you down here. Thissh issh my aircraft. I am your Ssshkipper.'

The slurring of his S's might have been funny under any other circumstances. But not these.

'You're not a Skipper! You'll never be a Skipper! You're a bloody liability!'

Once he'd started, Horner couldn't stop. Out it all came, all the frustrations and angers of the past months.

Oh, God, don't let Jack go too far! Don't let him get put on a charge for insubordination. And don't let him destroy Maddox's confidence. For then Maddox's famous luck really will drain away. So will Jack's. And so will mine.

'You're the worst pilot on the squadron. The worst Skipper!'

'How come I bagged the Me, then? You insubordinate, uneducated, ignorant bastard!'

'You didn't bag it, you clueless clot! Ginger did! It was Ginger's shooting! You did fuck all, except go green! You whining miserable rat!'

They both tried to push Pip aside, to get at each other. They looked as if they could kill. Pip lifted her foot and landed the heel of her good heavy WAAF-issue shoe on Maddox's shin, and with both her hands shoved hard against Jack's chest.

'Stop it!' she shouted, swinging her foot forward now to land a hefty kick on Horner's shin.

He looked at her aghast, disbelieving, as if she had suddenly turned into an alien and unrecognisable monster. 'Are you taking his side?'

'Of course she is,' Maddox shouted. 'She always has done. She's mad about me!'

That really got through to Horner. Suddenly he remembered things about her attitude to Maddox that he would rather forget.

'I'm not! I don't! Oh, just break it up! Just go!' she babbled, wondering how long she could keep them apart, wishing Chiefie would come back and then immediately wishing he wouldn't, because then Jack really would be for the high jump. Officers always won in the end.

'Are you telling me to go?' Jack asked her in a suddenly deadly-cold voice.

'Yes, yes,' she gabbled, 'go!'

'You're sure?'

'Yes! Go! Just go!'

And at that, without a word, he turned on his heel, his jacket over his shoulder, and walked away, his feet hard and angry on the concrete, then disappearing softly over the grass.

When he was at a safe distance from Maddox, she called after him, 'See you in a moment!'

But he threw over his shoulder, 'Like hell!' and quickened his step.

For a moment, she was bereft of speech. For several seconds, she considered running after Jack, or shouting after him again that she would come in a moment to the Sally Ann. But the Sally Ann by now would be shutting. If she ran after Jack, Maddox would come with her and the row would start up again, and if Jack was foolish enough to lay a finger on Maddox, the little clot would have him court-martialled.

It was Maddox who broke the silence. 'What on earth do you see in him?' he asked scornfully, not in his usual voice. She began to glimpse a different Maddox from the eager blue-eyed boy. But then, she told herself, it was common knowledge drunken men often reverse their characters completely. The feckless Irishman was quite different, her mother said, drunk from sober.

In reply she said coldly, 'I think you've had too much to drink,' and added, 'sir,' in a derisory manner.

'Maybe I have. Maybe I haven't.' His mood teetered between apology and aggression. 'Maybe I haven't had enough of that wonderful stuff.' He suddenly laughed.

'You should go back to the Mess, Peter. Go to bed. Get some rest. Otherwise you won't be fit for anything tomorrow.'

Tomorrow. That was a daft remark to make, a daft reminder.

'Tomorrow! Yep, tomorrow!' his face seemed to crumple. 'Christ, tomorrow I got to fly with those bastards again!'

Pip opened her mouth to say something and then prudently shut it again.

'You heard what he called me,' Maddox went on, breathing now on the embers of his anger. 'You were a witness to his...' he tried to say the word 'insubordination', couldn't quite get his tongue round it and gave up.

'Where's their team spirit, Pip? Where's loyalty to their captain?'

'You've done all right so far.'

'I have! I've done all right! But have they?'

'Yes, you've all done all right.'

He swayed on his feet staring at her, a bit like a cobra about to strike, she suddenly thought. But that was a very fanciful thought indeed because there was no one less cobra-like than clumsy clueless harmless Maddox. And yet his eyes seemed to glitter with malice as if he hated her. As if she were suddenly the source of all his troubles, and the one thing she wanted at that moment above all else was to get away from him and make him go safely back to bed. Then she would leave a little note for Jack at the Sergeants' Mess, or else she'd see him tomorrow before the op and all would be well.

'Look, Peter,' she said reasonably, 'I'm going back to the WAAF site now. I'll walk with you as far as the Mess.'

As they were leaving Flights and turning towards the main road, he said, 'Let's cut across the airfield. Cavendish doesn't like officers fratting with other ranks.'

223

It was certainly a Station Standing Order that officers and airwomen shouldn't have dates, and if seen out together it was a chargeable offence. But most aircrew didn't give a damn.

'Cavendish has more or less promised me my full ring.' He turned to her with a smirk, and lest she miss the weightiness of what he was saying, 'Flying Officer!'

'Congratulations.' She swallowed a smile.

Then suddenly, as they reached the grassy mounds on the Flights air raid shelters, he grabbed her arm. Taken off guard, she felt herself spun roughly round. He was only a few inches taller than her, but thickset, strong and desperate. Pulling her fiercely against him, he twisted one arm behind her back, as his wet mouth tried to find hers.

'You're hurting me!' she gasped and he gave an eerie, alien, childish laugh. She wriggled and kicked and squirmed, her feet slipping on the muddy grass. She tried to bite his hand. She could feel that torch in his trousers again, and remembered what Pam had told her and felt sick with fear.

Instinctively she fought. She dug in her nails. She used her feet. But the more she fought, the more did he come on, the stronger, the more desperate he got. She had a nightmare vision of him as a wild animal grunting and slobbering and snuffling, fears and tension all swept into a terrible animal aggression, no longer human, no longer reachable.

Still panting, twisting her arm behind her again, he half-dragged, half-frogmarched her into the foul-smelling shelter. Shoved her to the damp earth floor, subsided on top of her, tearing at her skirt, her silk knickers, fumbling at his trousers.

Nothing could be as bad as that again. Ever.

When it was over, she tried to get up and stagger away, but he came after her, grabbed her arms, flopped his weight round her shoulders, weeping like a baby.

She couldn't remember much after that. Only the cold and painful walk to the WAAF site, sidling past the blacked-out WAAF guardroom, making straight for the ablutions block. The need to cleanse herself was the only driving force she was immediately conscious of.

It was there that Pam found her, took one aghast look at her friend on the concrete floor beside the bath, and took charge.

'Oh, God!' she said, putting her arms round Pip's shoulders. 'Jack didn't . . .? It wasn't Jack? Jack couldn't have . . . wouldn't have . . . not Jack . . .'

'No. No. It wasn't Jack.'

'Thank God! Ginger would have killed him. So would I. Who was it? Tell me! Let me get my hands on him!'

But Pip wouldn't say. 'Not now. Maybe some time. Not now.'

Thank God for small mercies, the bath-water bordered on hot. Pam streaked back to the hut and brought towels and some of her precious bath salts. She took the knickers and stockings and bust bodice along to the incinerator and burned them. Then she sat on the edge of the bath and they wept it out of their systems.

Pam had stowed away the twigs and rushes and put a hot-water bottle in her bed. She had put on an extra blanket from her own bed, and she made her take a couple of aspirin because Pip couldn't stop shivering.

She couldn't get off to sleep. Her mind was full of nightmare pictures, feelings, fears. She didn't feel angry. She felt soiled, dirty, lost and desolate and immensely sad. She couldn't hate Maddox. She knew it was the terrible inhuman strain aircrew were under. That Maddox had finally cracked. That he was done for. That Jack would probably now get his way and that Maddox's name wouldn't be on the Battle Order again.

She woke late in an empty hut, with the black-outs down and a cold, shimmering snowy light streaming in.

All the other girls except Pam had gone off to their duties. Pam was standing next to her holding a mug of tea she had brought over from the cookhouse. Her cheeks and nose were bright red with the cold. There were flakes of snow on her cap. 'I've phoned in to Chiefie and told him you're sick. He said not to worry about coming in. Stay in bed. Keep warm. It's bloody cold out there. Snow. Christ! We could do without that! So you just rest yourself. I'll wave the boys off for you! Shall I give Jack your love?'

Pip shook her head,

'Why not?'

'Because.'

'Just that? Just because?' She leaned forward and whispered, 'Not because of what happened last night? You're not going to let that come between you, are you?'

Pip didn't answer. She bit her lip. How could she explain that the world had changed overnight, wobbled off its axis? She wasn't the same person any more. Would never be it again.

'You mustn't!' Pam urged, her face contorted with anxiety. 'You really mustn't! You and him are made for each other! He won't let it come between you, so don't you!'

Pip shook her head wordlessly. Then she gritted her teeth and asked, 'What time are they due back, have you heard?'

'Sixteen hundred.'

'Is it a maximum effort?'

'Yep. So long as they can get them all airborne with the snow.' Pam took off her cap and shook the melting flakes from it, eyeing her friend anxiously. 'So what shall I say to Jack?'

'Tell him to take care.'

'Is that all?'

'That's all.'

226

'I don't have to tell him that. Ginge'll take care of him.'
'I know.'

Under the pile of blankets, she crossed her fingers. There was nothing else she could think to do.

15

There were a number of fingers being crossed as, watched by Pringle, the ten crews filed into Intelligence.

There was a surprise in store for them. Not the target — the fact that the target was the dreaded *Derflinger* again. But another surprise which Cavendish waited to deliver until the thirty men had digested Pringle's measured and sombre briefing.

'I cannot overemphasise,' Pringle said, 'the importance Command attach to the sinking of this ship.'

He wondered what they would all say if just for one wild moment he told them not only what he knew, but also what he suspected: that they were being asked to nip in the bud Hitler's nascent atomic bomb programme. That would chill their young bones to the marrow. For there could be nothing more terrifying than nuclear weapons in Hitler's hands.

Einstein had fled to America warning that just such a programme was under way. Martin Klaproth had identified uranium and its powers two centuries ago. All over the world, in small secret laboratories, experiments were going on. And now Germany had the whole of European expertise and raw materials to draw on. Heavy water, deuterium oxide, was being made in that Norwegian plant, and God knew what other components assembled, and collected and transported by the *Derflinger* to the new factory at Steinheim, which was likely to be their research establishment too.

They'd got the factory. The factory was in ruins. They

must get the ship. Delay was all they could hope for. But delay it must be.

None of this showed on Pringle's face as he tapped the ribbon of their route with his pointer. 'The *Derflinger* was last seen by HM submarine *Upholder* on a southerly heading. She is expected to hug the Dutch and German coasts, passing between the islands. At 15.05 hours her route should take her to 51.30N 03.20E. There you will intercept and sink her.'

No ifs or buts or try tos. Sink.

He glanced round. No one spoke. They stared at him with a strange, distant attention, their cigarettes glued to their lower lips. A pall of smoke hung over their heads. In the silence, he could hear the grinding of the bomb trolleys as they trundled along the perimeter track.

Then he pulled down the blown-up picture of the *Derflinger* and a little gasp riffled the silence, as if they were focusing their anger, summoning up the blood.

'An ugly ship, gentlemen! A sinister ship. Take another very good look. You've studied her in your ship recognition classes. A formidable foe.'

The crews groaned. Someone blew a raspberry.

Pringle tapped her superstructure with his pointer. 'Very little of that. Funnel mid-aft.' He moved his pointer to the hull, outlining it. 'In that bulging hull is a very important cargo.' He paused. 'Any questions so far?'

Lennox put up his hand. 'What is this very important cargo? Is it aircraft spares? Or gold? Or art treasures, or what?'

'Group don't specify. Only that it is regarded as of the highest possible importance.'

Then he went on with what exactly was known of the *Derflinger*'s armament, or at least what Group were going to disclose of it. Then on to the call signs, codes and colours and IFF recognition.

Pringle was followed by Flanagan, always good for a

229

laugh, who promised them just the right amount of cloud cover and got howled down for his pains.

Then, a pleased smile momentarily softening his face, Wing Commander Cavendish took over and announced his surprise.

'After making myself a considerable nuisance to Group,' he said, 'I am being allowed to lead today's attack.'

If he had been hoping for a standing ovation he was certainly disappointed.

A groan, quickly suppressed, after a fierce look from MacGregor, travelled round the room. The raspberry-blower performed again. Even Maddox, who usually tried to butter up the big boys, remained silent with his arms folded and his head sunk on his chest.

In fact, taking a second look, MacGregor reckoned the lad looked sick. Oh, God, he thought, not another last-minute scrub!

But he hadn't the time to worry then about Maddox. Instead he politely began the clapping and, sluggishly at first, the rest of the boys loyally joined in. At least Cavendish was trying to break his duck.

'Thank you all. And thank you, Mark, for putting us so clearly in the picture. I will be leading A-Flight. Angus,' he tried to smile cordially at MacGregor,' will be leading B-Flight. In both flights, I want you tucked up tight under your leader. It has to be done with the utmost speed. And believe me, gentlemen, it has to be done.' And then, bastard that he was, he took a sideways swipe at Mac-Gregor. 'We shall not abort this time, no matter the opposition,' adding as a postscript which somehow accen-tuated rather than alleviated the hidden insult, 'though you were absolutely right so to do before, Angus!'

For a few minutes MacGregor seethed. There could be no greater insult to a MacGregor than accusing him of turning away in the face of overwhelming odds. But he didn't allow that remark to faze him. He knew he had been right not to attack, that these boys wouldn't be here today if he had decided otherwise. But he hated Cavendish just that little bit more for making that remark. And it doubled his determination to get that ship somehow.

'Before we conclude the briefing,' Wing Commander Cavendish was now saying, 'Group Captain Hurst would like a few words.'

This time Cavendish led the polite clapping to welcome the dapper little Station Commander as he jumped onto the dais.

He was frequently at the briefings, but rarely spoke above wishing the crews good luck. Pringle raised his brows questioningly to Cavendish. 'He wanted to,' Cavendish whispered. 'His own suggestion. He has an interesting point to make.'

'A relevant point?' Pringle whispered back in disbelief. For the Group Captain, with only his World War One experience, tended to be regarded as a has-been, or indeed on occasion, a never-was-er.

'In fact, yes. For once. Perfectly relevant.'

The Group Captain cleared his throat. He began by congratulating the squadron on being chosen for this special operation and emphasising its importance. He ended,

'When I was flying, at the very end of the last war, there was a band of pilots who did more in a day than most of us did in a lifetime. They were the American 96th, who destroyed the fortifications on the Ramilly Heights, thus allowing our troops to pour through. They, gentlemen, were your predecessors here at Marshfield. You are the inheritors of their proud tradition. May their spirit of service go with you. I wish you all good hunting and Godspeed!'

Then, to MacGregor's relief, it was all over. He could

now occupy himself with the preparations before becoming airborne. The suspense before a trip was always the worst part. Once you were on your way and doing things, all your thoughts fell into their proper perspective.

Outside, it was still snowing — softly, slowly the flakes falling like white feathers from the dark sky. The airfield had been transformed into a Christmas card, the ugly wooden buildings turned into sugar cottages, the lorries into sleighs, the ground crew throwing snowballs at each other while they de-iced the wings of the Blenheims, all standing like big toys waiting for children to come out and play with them. Someone had built a snowman and put a red woollen cap on his head, a muffler round his neck and a clay pipe in his mouth.

No one spoke in the lorry that took them over to Dispersal, stopping at each Blenheim for a crew to jump off before scrunching over the snow to the next one. Maddox still looked ill. He'd got a long scratch on his face, which stood out red and bloody against the pallor of his skin. A few too many last night, most likely.

Nevertheless, MacGregor leaned across, tapped his knee and for some reason lapsing into Gaelic murmured, '*De tha coarr?*' Then louder, 'Are you OK, Peter?'

'Me? Bang-on! Top line! Never better!'

Horner raised his eyes to heaven.

MacGregor's crew were the last to be dropped off. Lyttle and Ryan had gone ahead and were already climbing into J-Jig when MacGregor suddenly realised they were being followed.

Turning his head, a few yards to the right, he saw him — his thick brown coat speckled with snow.

MacGregor stopped. The dog stopped too, looking directly at him, his long tongue hanging out of his red mouth.

MacGregor took two steps forward, leaving deep footprints. The brown dog took four steps forward. But no

232

paw-marks appeared behind him, no breath steamed out into the cold air. He stayed still as stone, silently waiting, watching MacGregor.

MacGregor knew now — but the knowledge did not frighten him. Rather it elevated and excited him. He walked to the Blenheim conscious all the time that the dog was following him.

Before getting into the aircraft, he stopped and looked behind him. There the dog stood, his head raised, his brown eyes looking straight at MacGregor as though he had found his master.

Slowly, MacGregor began climbing the ladder onto the port wing with the dog jumping up the steps behind him. But when he settled down into the pilot's seat and looked around he could see no sign of the dog. All he could see was Lyttle, and, in the turret, Ryan swivelling his guns. And all he could hear was Lyttle moving about in the nose. Yet he knew the dog was on board.

He leaned out of the window. He put up his thumb to the waiting ground crew. He pressed the starter on Number One engine, listened to its reassuring sound, watched its propeller slowly turning. Then he pressed Number Two starter button.

All ready to move now, on the intercom he called out, 'Good to be on our way, eh?' and Lyttle and Ryan dutifully called back, 'Too right, sir!'

The green flare flashed on the platform of Flying Control. MacGregor opened the throttles and led his five to take them to join the queue behind Cavendish's. All ten Blenheims were now slowly moving towards the black strips of cleared grass on which they would take off.

Cavendish turned into wind, opened up his throttles, hurtled over the grass and up into the air. Harris followed in N. One by one the queue shuffled forward, continually getting smaller until J-Jig took up a position opposite the band of snow-covered Waafs, waving and cheering.

233

Turning into position, he opened up to full power.

The ground fell away behind them as J climbed. Circling the field, he waited for the others to join him — Maddox in S next to him to port, with F beyond. To starboard G and C. MacGregor led the formation round one circuit of Marshfield before joining Cavendish on a north-easterly course.

Then down to the water went all ten Blenheims — engines at rated power, in rich mixture, +1.5 boost, twenty-four hundred revs, at maximum cruising speed towards Flushing.

Now they were on their way, MacGregor felt calmer than he had ever felt — his eyes sweeping over the well-behaved instruments, his ears pleased by the rhythmic thunder of the engines.

Below he could see the pattern of the sea formed by the slipstreams of the low-flying formation in front. Above was the blanket of stratus promised by Flanagan, shutting out the rest of the sky like a black lid. He glanced to port. To his surprise he saw S-Sugar was yards away from him. Far too far away. So unlike Maddox who had always before eagerly pressed in on him, almost touching his wing-tip. He saw Maddox's profile — intent, serious. Finally, he caught his eye, waved him closer.

Sugar moved a short distance nearer, but Maddox neither smiled nor waved.

Now the coast of Belgium appeared on the right, chalky white in the snow. No sign of activity there. No guns, no searchlights. Long may it continue, he thought, edging the formation closer to Cavendish's five ahead.

He glanced down at his watch. There was a nice westerly wind hurrying them along. Only another fifteen minutes to ETA.

Still no sign of enemy opposition. Not even a trawler was hugging the Belgian coast.

234

Behind him, Ryan was swinging the turret, moving his guns up and down, searching the sky.

Still no sign of fighters — and there ahead was the gaping mouth of the Scheldt. With luck, low as they were, the whole formation could sneak right up to Flushing without being observed.

Then the lid of stratus above them suddenly cracked. Five yellow spinners whirled down on Cavendish's formation and the air was filled with the red beads of cannon fire.

From the rear, he could hear Ryan opening up, calling out, 'Three fighters, Skipper! Six o'clock high!' The whole aircraft shuddered as the Brownings fired. And then, 'Got him, Skipper! Got him! The others are turning away!'

But ahead he saw a blaze of yellow on the water from a crashed Blenheim. There was no sign of the other four. Presumably they had dived into the stratus for cloud cover.

Both formations had now been broken up. No question now of the one big attack. MacGregor still kept J-Jig on course towards Flushing. Entering the Scheldt with no sign of the other Blenheims, he reached Flushing and an intense barrage of anti-aircraft.

Not a trace of the *Derflinger*.

Turning away to port, he went up the narrow creek between Walcheren Island and the mainland. Looking from side to side, he saw no sign of any ship, and was just deciding which way to turn when abruptly the whole sky darkened into pitch-black night.

He began coughing violently, half-suffocated by smoke.

'Smoke screen!' he called out. 'Mike . . . open the bomb doors! Arm the bombs! She'll be hiding in there somewhere!'

Somehow he had to find her. He wasn't going to return

to Marshfield empty-handed. Cavendish's words still rankled.

Then he felt a weird sensation. It was as if hands other than his own were on the controls, other eyes than his were guiding the Blenheim through the dense darkness. It was something like Maddox had described, coming into land at Marshfield through thick fog.

Suddenly, dead ahead, the wraiths of smoke solidified into a ghostly hull, topped by that thick funnel.

'*Derflinger*!' He called out triumphantly. 'It's the —'

His voice was drowned as a storm of yellow, white and red flak burst from the towering steel hull. Exploding shells began ripping the Blenheim apart.

Immediately Lyttle began firing the forward gun, followed by Ryan opening up from the turret.

J-Jig swerved violently to the left as the port engine exploded in a shower of red-hot fragments. The windscreen shattered. The cockpit was filled with the reek of cordite. A cannon shell ripped through the shoulder of his jacket.

Suddenly he realised that all the Brownings had stopped firing.

'Mike!' he yelled. 'Ken!'

Struggling to keep the juddering aircraft straight, he turned his head and saw the navigator's body, half-in, half-out of the nose, covered in blood, his head shattered, his dead hand still clenched on the Browning's trigger.

'Ken!'

No answer.

Quickly he glanced backwards.

A moment of utter horror. The whole turret blister had been blown clean away. Only the air-gunner's legs dangling grotesquely.

MacGregor pressed one hand to his mouth as a wave of sickness almost overwhelmed him. His vision blurred.

His body shook uncontrollably. He was filled with a terrible feeling of utter helplessness.

He was alone in this eruption of lethal fire.

Then he saw a shape beyond his wing-tip. He was conscious of other shapes moving with him.

On the starboard, seven DH 4s — with his new awareness he could even remember the names of the pilots from that photograph in the Stars and Stripes: Kingsland, Rex, Gallagher, Mitchell, Virgin, Bateman and Womack.

And to port, seven more DH 4s formating — nearest was Captain Shea waving him on, with young Robinson tucked in beside him and, beyond, Hollingsworth, Grodecki, Hartman, Mackay and Martin.

And now, towering above them, were the iron sides of the *Derflinger*, dead ahead.

The whole formation never hesitated. Led by MacGregor in J, the fourteen American DH 4s of the 96th crashed into the ship as one.

There was an immediate white-hot flash. The whole sky became alight — killing the black smoke, illuminating everything in an uncanny shimmering light as the *Derflinger* and the fifteen aircraft sank below the sea.

* * *

Twenty-five miles south-west, all that remained of the battle that had raged ferociously between the Mes and the Blenheims were six fires burning on the sea. Bits of grey-green fuselage, a tailplane with a black cross on it, two floating tyres, a smouldering wing with a roundel just distinguishable, a bright yellow blob bobbing up and down on the water.

One Blenheim, S-Sugar, with half a tailplane and its fuselage riddled with cannon fire, emerged out of the low cloud, pursued by an Me 109, and dived down on the water towards that bright yellow blob.

237

Standing at the open window, Horner adjusted his binoculars to bring the blob into focus.

'It's one of ours. It's —'

A burst of cannon fire interrupted him. Maddox pulled back the stick sharply and plunged into the safety of the overcast.

'Who is it?' Maddox called.

'Cavendish, I think.'

'Any sign of the crew?'

'None.'

'Is he alive?'

'Can't see.'

'Better find out, then.'

The nose dipped sharply as Maddox descended. He began a steep turn round the Mae West, right on the water, then round again.

'Cavendish all right,' Horner reported.

'Better keep him company, then,' said Maddox.

He continued to circle till two Me 109s forced him back into the stratus layer.

But within minutes S-Sugar was back again, soon joined by pursuing fighters. And so the dangerous merry-go-round went on.

Cocooned in cloud, S-Sugar kept vanishing, emerging now and again before plunging back into the overcast.

Maddox was keeping an eye on the tiny yellow smudge, as Ginger pounded out SOS on the W/T emergency frequency while Maddox was sending Mayday on the TR9. 'Circling survivor in Mae West 51.15 North, 02.40 East. Send ASR launch.'

No reply. Nothing but the crackle of static. On the intercom, Ginger called out, 'They're not receiving us! We're too low.'

But back went S-Sugar down to the sea. At least the yellow blob was still there. So were the Me 109s. Again and again, led by one with a bright orange spinner, the fighters came in to attack, while Horner could hear the sound of flak ripping into the Blenheim's metal skin.

Just ahead, a burst of crimson and yellow flared as an Me 109 burst into flames.

'Got one!' Ginger called. 'Got the bastard! Hell! Another coming in nine o'clock!'

Maddox was throwing the Blenheim this way and that with gut-wrenching zigzag up-and-down evasive action.

For the three of them time stood still. Still no response had come from the ground.

And then on the SOS frequency just one letter came through the squealing and crackling of the static — R. Received.

Ginger left the W/T and got back into the turret. Now for Maddox and his crew there remained the agonised suspense.

When was the launch coming? Would it arrive in time? The man down there was in icy water. And what would the Mes do when the ASR launch did arrive?

And all the time Maddox, the schoolboy who boasted he had looped a Blenheim, was executing his famous wiggly stuff just above the water, yelling with terrifying exhilaration, while Horner and Ginger kept their eyes on the Mes and fired.

But he was no longer a schoolboy. Breath-taking, audacious, inspired, every manoeuvre brilliantly judged, diving like a thunderbolt, then climbing like a rocket, wings vertical one moment, then swinging the aircraft purposefully towards the attacking Mes the next.

Maddox had entered his element. He and the Blenheim had become fused into one fantastic bird. A lethal bird, spitting out continuous fire now from the forward gun.

Smoke began pouring from an Me on the left. Then the aircraft beside it exploded into a mass of falling debris.

No longer was Sugar a bomber, wary of opposition,

fleeing from fighters. Dizzy with Maddox's gyrations, his mouth dry with the stench of ammo, ears and hands aching with constantly firing broadsides into the fast-moving Huns, Horner had a sudden vivid memory of their affiliation exercise when Maddox had lunatically tried to snatch the fighter role from the Hurricane.

He was doing it now, only this time he was succeeding. He was making the Blenheim a better fighter than the Me.

And all the time, with the plates of her fuselage shivering, the growl of her engines drowned by the chatter of the Brownings, S-Sugar kept watch over the yellow blob bobbing up and down on the sea, turning ferociously head-on if any of the Mes threatened to approach.

'You just try!' he seemed to be saying. 'You just try getting under my protective wing!'

None of them did. From a distance, they hosed streams of cannon fire.

Maddox hardly seemed to notice that every now and again they got a lucky shot into S-Sugar's fuselage. But for the most part, the fighters were having difficulty with such a dodgy, unpredictable target so close to the water. Prudently, they held off lest they dive too close and slip into the waves.

And then suddenly, ahead on the horizon of the sea, Horner saw an arrow of white streaking towards them.

'They're coming. Skipper! Look! At twelve o'clock. Look!'

'I can see them.'

Horner said, 'The household cavalry at last!'

Ginger called out, 'What's been keeping you, boys?'

But now the Mes had also seen the launch. With a revived show of strength, the leading one with the orange spinner made a sudden darting dive towards the man in the water.

240

Maddox dived too. Made a lightning turn. For one mad moment Horner thought he was going to ram the bastard.

Almost he did. Then a quick pull out. A rapid burst from the forward firing gun, and down the fighter screamed.

A great plume of water. Beads of sea-spray on their windscreen.

Then nothing.

Horner pressed Maddox's shoulder. 'Great stuff, Skipper!'

And from the rear turret, Ginger called out, 'Terrific, sir!'

Meanwhile, as though scalded, the Mes retreated to a safer distance from this mad, whirling dervish

But not before the rearmost fired a parting salvo. A cannon shell whistled uncomfortably close to Horner's left ear.

'Bastards!' he shouted, watching as though in slow motion the white streak of the ASR wash getting bigger and bigger as it closed on the yellow blob in the water, till finally it was directly underneath the circling Blenheim.

The white wash disappeared. Men reached down, hauled the Mae West-clad body on board.

And abruptly, the white wash started up again, this time heading westwards.

Then, and only then, did Maddox swing the nose of S-Sugar round to follow them, while the Mes left together on a southerly course, presumably for their Belgian bases.

But S-Sugar had been badly hit. There were jagged holes down the port fuselage close to the wing root.

But not just the fuselage had taken heavy punishment. Now the port engine began backfiring — stuttering, falling mournfully silent, then starting up again, roaring to a crescendo.

The speed began dropping, the needle on the airspeed

indicator inched backwards on the dial — 140 — 120 — 105 — 90.

Shivering and shuddering, drunkenly swinging left and right, S-Sugar made for home.

Leaving the turret, Ginger prayed that Maddox's luck would hold.

Then, with a noise like thunder, the port engine exploded in a guttering mass of orange flames.

Immediately Maddox pushed the fire extinguisher button, then started to climb to just below the cloud.

Standing behind him, Ginger peered anxiously ahead. He could see farther at this height, but still there was nothing except the sea steaming with wisps of mist.

And then a wave of relief shot through him.

Ahead now were white English cliffs, yellow English sand, green English grass. Then an English house and the tower of an English church, under a blue and white unmenacing sky.

And then he dropped his eyes and saw blood.

Blood all over Maddox's uniform. Blood pouring down onto the floor.

He turned to the navigator. 'Jack!' He pulled at his arm. 'Jack! Quick!'

Horner left the navigation table, grabbed the first aid box and rushed up front.

Maddox was bleeding from a chest wound, and arterial blood was spurting from his neck. But with his hands still clutching the control column, Maddox was trying to talk.

He moved the stick up and down and sideways. 'See!'

'Wires to the controls severed,' Jack said.

'We've had it!' Ginger muttered.

Slowly, painfully, Maddox nodded. Then he turned his head and pointed to the navigator. 'Jump!'

'Like hell! I'm staying!' Horner turned to the air gunner. 'You go, Ginger!'

'Not bloody likely! I'm staying too!'

'Go on! Jump!' Horner attempted a grin. 'Give Pam and the parachute girls a thrill.'

'Balls!' said Ginger. 'We're not leaving our Skipper. We're a crew. We stay together.'

So the three of them huddled round the stick as S-Sugar staggered nearer and nearer to the coast.

'Mayday, Marigold Control!' Jack reported, while Ginger fired off the red Very light, Injured Man Aboard. 'We need an ambulance.'

'S-Sugar, ambulance and fire engines waiting!'

But by the time they reached the field, the blood had ceased spurting and Maddox was dead. Hands still gripping the control column, but dead.

Try as they did they couldn't shift him, so Ginger moved the seat back and Horner sat on top of Maddox, prising the pilot's hands off the controls and gripping them with his own.

With one engine out, no ailerons, S-Sugar's fuselage riddled with holes, somehow Horner managed to line up for the approach. There was only a light wind, and the clouds were broken.

Beside him, Ginger was about to pump the wheels down.

Horner began easing back the bit of engine they had.

Lower and lower S-Sugar sank, nicely positioned but wobbling badly.

Ginger was calling out height and speed as they approached the field.

'Three hundred feet . . . 200 . . . Speed 72.'

That was only two mph above stalling. The wings lurched to the left and downwards.

'That's better. Height 100 feet. Speed good.'

The nose dropped farther. 'Steady . . . steady!'

Just in front of them, above the sand dunes and the marram-grass, loomed the airfield hedge.

'You're too low, Jack! Higher, man . . . higher!'

243

Horner pulled back on the stick. Immediately the Blenheim began shivering on the stall.

'Speed . . . speed!'

Horner pushed the nose down again.

'Seventy-one . . . seventy-two . . . seventy-three!   Good! Good!'

Just below them, the ground was scudding past.

'Height ninety . . . eighty . . . seventy . . . climb . . . climb! Airfield hedge ahead!'

Feebly the aircraft staggered up a few more feet.

'Good! Good!' Then an agonised pause. 'Speed, man . . . speed!'

The wings practically brushed the hedge.

'Great! Pull back! Pull back!'

'Cut the engine.'

The port wheel touched the ground.

Then suddenly, the sound of rupturing, tortured metal. A huge slewing lurch to the left.

The port wing had broken off. Within seconds, the Blenheim had turned turtle.

Skidding over the grass upside down, it came to a shuddering stop.

Immediately smoke filled the cockpit.

Ginger saw a great billowing sheet of red and yellow fire shoot upwards.

Frantically, he pushed his way up against burning-hot metal, seeing Jack and a dead Maddox pitifully locked together.

He put out his arms and tried to get them out.

Jack looked up, put out a hand.

'No good, Ginger! Go, man, go, before she blows up! We're OK. We're OK!'

And then a cloud of white foam burst all round them and firemen were trying to climb up through the smoke. Ginger heard an explosion that shook the earth.

The sky went black — and the next thing he remembered he was in a hospital bed and a nurse was bending over him.

* * *

'Then the tumult and the shouting died away,' Simon Wetherby whispered to himself as he walked from the chapel to the Mess, and he felt the unnatural silence all around him.

Anywhere else, with thirteen aircrew killed, two badly injured, four aircraft lost, and a fifth a write-off, that silence would have been one of sorrow. But this was an RAF station, one of the most unnatural places on earth.

The silence was because it was the morning after the night before. The squadron was stood down. Basking in its success and the AOC's congratulation, they had given their fallen comrades the wake they deserved, drinking and singing the night away.

The padre, still in a state of indecision, had been wakened through the night by snatches of ribald songs: 'Roll me over in the clover/Roll me over, lay me down, and do it again!' and another parodied dirge, beginning 'An airman told me before he died/I do not think the bastard lied'.

Finally he had put his head under the white counterpane and managed to drift off to sleep.

Now the next item on the agenda, as Wing Commander Cavendish, back at his desk yesterday within twelve hours of his ditching, had announced, was 'Christmas, boys!'

And tonight was Christmas Eve. A garishly decorated tree stood by the flagpole. All the sections had put up their decorations.

The Officers' Mess, when Simon Wetherby reached it, was hung with holly and tinsel and interesting baubles that looked as if they had come from an aircraft's inner workings.

245

As the padre was about to pass the bar, Mark Pringle hailed him. 'I've been waiting for you, Simon,' he said. 'I've got your drink! It's a Scotch. We're going to down it for Angus.'

They were also, Simon Wetherby knew, downing it to mend the slight crack that had appeared in their friendship.

The padre slipped into the chair opposite the Intelligence Officer at a table in the far corner.

'*Deoch slainte*, as Angus would say!' Mark raised his glass. '*Deoch slainte*! Come on! Drink! It won't bite you! Warm you up!'

Simon raised his glass and clinked it with Mark's. '*Deoch slainte*!' He took a sip. 'And thanks. I'm glad I didn't resign. At least not then. There might well come a time,' he sighed, 'when I resign the whole lot.'

'You mean,' Mark smiled, 'earn an honest living?'

Simon gave him a small smile in return.

'You realise that sinking the *Derflinger* was vital. To our survival. Maybe to the whole world's survival?'

'If you say so, Mark. I accept that.'

'It was vital for the squadron, too.'

'I find that harder to accept.'

'It was the turning-point for them. You'll see.'

He put his hand on the padre's arm. 'I'm sorry I was so snappy with you the other day.'

'My fault. I bring out the snappy in people.'

He drained his glass. 'Let's have the other wing?' he suggested and fought his way to the bar. He found himself standing next to the Wing Commander.

'No! These are on me!' Cavendish turned and saw the padre about to bring out his Mess chit. 'Put that away! Damn it, man, you're the only poor sod who has to work over Christmas.'

The Wing Commander had recovered from his ordeal

with remarkable resilience. It had been a needed baptism of fire. He had done what he asked his men to do.

Standing beside him was Lesley. 'I wondered,' the padre asked her, 'if you'd any news of the injured?'

'Not a subject to discuss in the Mess,' the Wing Commander interjected sharply, climbing back onto his usual high horse. 'Close the hangar doors!'

The MO flushed, but she ignored him. 'Very little, I'm afraid,' she answered gently. 'Both are badly injured. Flight Sergeant Horner is still unconscious.'

And perhaps to keep the Wing Commander in his place, she added as Simon Wetherby began to move away with his drinks, 'I'll let you know, Simon, if I hear any more.'

She rang him at the chapel shortly before the Christmas morning service. 'I heard just half an hour ago, Simon. The chances of F/Sergeant Horner regaining consciousness are small. F/Sergeant Johnson is progressing. Have you spoken to his parents?'

'Yes. They've telephoned me twice.'

'And shortly,' he told himself, peeping at the congregation through the slit in the curtain behind the altar, 'I shall be talking again to his girlfriend.'

She had been to see him three times since that dreadful crash. Now he could spot her in the front row of chairs beside the airwoman called Pip whom she had dragged along with her on all three occasions. They were both regular members of his congregation and Pip had always struck him as a bright, competent little thing. But now all the spunk and stuffing seemed to have gone out of her. She looked a waif, her uniform still pressed, her buttons shining, her shoes polished, but a waif.

For once the chapel was healthily full. The congregation shuffled to its feet as he emerged singing, for he had a good tenor voice, the opening stanzas of 'O Come, All Ye Faithful'.

247

He had intended to include 'Silent Night', but Cavendish, dropping in to tell him the first news about the casualties, had vetoed it on account of its Germanic origin.

Hymns were followed by a short address and then the Confession and prayers for the taking of the Sacraments.

It was the first time that he had administered the Sacraments since he had done so to the German pilot, and his voice shook. But any disturbing memory was doused by a very present disturbance.

At his words, 'Draw near with faith, and take this holy Sacrament to your comfort . . .' the girl with the blonde hair and the pillar-box lips got to her feet and advanced a pace. Then she became aware her companion was not accompanying her. She turned and seized Pip's hand, pulling her to her feet. Pip resisted.

'I can't.'

'Course you can!'

A tug-of-war ensued, until the distressing argument seemed to be resolved by Pip giving in, coming forward and kneeling beside her friend at the altar rail. But when the padre proffered her first the wafer and then the wine, she waved them both away.

Neither of them referred to the incident when they stayed behind to enquire about their boyfriends. Simon gave the news about Johnson almost verbatim, the news about Horner he ameliorated.

He saw the two girls again when he and Mark joined the others in the Airmen's Mess where, as part of RAF tradition, the officers served the other ranks with their Christmas dinner.

Huge helpings of turkey and sausages, puddings and mince pies and barrel-loads of beer were downed. The two girls sat at the end of a table. He didn't see either of them put a forkful in their mouths.

He was thinking he might go over and offer them some

248

more pudding, a mince pie, even to pull a cracker with them, and then give perhaps some words of comfort.

But what words did he know, let alone feel able to bring out?

Then the Group Captain appeared, and such was the power of Christmas or the strength of the beer that all the other ranks got to their feet and cheered this unpopular little Commanding Officer.

He jumped onto a table and stood amidst the ruins of turkey and pudding to deliver his Christmas message.

This was a special Christmas, he told them. Marshfield and 13 Squadron were on the up-and-up. All men here today, and those men who had not returned, had distinguished themselves in the spirit of the fighter pilots of the Battle of Britain and their Yankee predecessors of the 96th. A spirit that never dies.

'As some of you know,' he ended, 'there is a poem about the 96th. I give you its last three lines:

'Spirits that must come back;
And I hail them then, who have died like *men*,
The Ghosts of the Eighth Attack!'

A slow clap showed the beer and the Christmas spirit were beginning to wear off. An old man's sentimentality was not for them.

'I sometimes wonder if they did come back,' the padre allowed himself to whisper to Mark Pringle, receiving only a derisory raising of one eyebrow in return.

Then the SAdO cut the slow clap short by calling, 'Three cheers for the Group Captain! Hip! Hip! Hooray!'

When the cheers had died away and glasses were recharged, the padre saw to his relief that the chairs where the two girls had been sitting were empty.

And it was only in the early hours, after the officers' Christmas dinner, when too much rich food and too fre-

quent passing of the port, and the bawdy songs from
the aircrew in the bar below, kept him awake, that the
revelation came to him.

Yes, they did. They did come back!

THE PRESENT

22nd December

Leading Aircraftwoman Pip Armitage

I hate Christmas. Ever since that Christmas of 1940 I vowed I would never put up a piece of holly or fir or ivy, and certainly never silvered bulrushes or silvered branches. That Christmas was the bottom of the pit for me. And yet here I was, decades later, sitting in the front pew at Marshfield Church under a canopy of holly and ivy and yes, silvered bulrushes.

I had come because of Simon Wetherby. I had come early for the dedication of the memorial window to give Simon support. Over the years I had become very fond of him. He hadn't changed much and yet I wondered how many of the congregation would recognise him in his white monk's habit. That was a send-up for the book. And yet it wasn't. It was in him all the time, just as most things are in most of us all the time.

And I hadn't kept my vow over Christmas. Since Christmas is primarily for children, you can't deny it to them. And I can remember several Christmasses I enjoyed.

I had kept in touch with Simon Wetherby since those dark winter days at Marshfield. Pam had kept dragging me along to the padre to find out what news there was on Ginger and Jack. I think Simon got pretty browned off with us, but he did his best.

I only wanted to know that Jack had lived. I couldn't bear to think of him not being somewhere in the world. But I knew I would never get in touch with him. During

253

those awful days of mourning for the lost boys, including Maddox, and the injured like Jack and Ginger, I wept also for the loss of me — the loss of what I thought of as my cleanliness and decency. I was unworthy even to weep for Jack and the others. Before I left the Station I went through a period of trying to scrub myself clean. I made myself my own bath-plug, because it's a well-known practice in WAAF camps for girls to remove the plugs to discourage others from using the hot water. I became very unpopular because I was always doing just that. Running the meagre hot water away, scrub-scrub-scrubbing, like those pictures of a little piccaninny trying to be white.

I wouldn't take Communion and I never have done since. Apart from Simon — and he isn't typical of the Church, indeed no longer really belongs to it — I haven't much time for that organisation.

After a few weeks, mid-February 1941 in fact, I began to suspect I was pregnant. There was no testing in those days, but I suppose the best indication is that somehow you know. Pam suggested all sorts of remedies for getting rid of it — hot gin, boiled parsley, Syrup of Figs. I didn't try any of them. But I didn't know what to do. I couldn't tell my mother/grandmother because that would kill her, I thought. She would think 'like mother like daughter', and I couldn't tell my real mother because she had enough problems coping with the feckless Irishman, and anyway she had wisely stayed in Eire.

I didn't at first go to the Medical Officer, because she would have had to tell the WAAF Queen Bee and I would have been discharged under Clause 11, and sent packing with a railway warrant and a packet of Spam sandwiches. So Pam persuaded me to go and see Simon.

For a while we talked about Ginger who, Pam told me, was making good progress in a Manchester hospital, and he told me that Jack had been moved to some special

254

place in Scotland, but he didn't know where, and he still hadn't regained consciousness.

I told Simon I thought I was pregnant, and then I wished I hadn't. He clearly knew nothing about women and such a physical condition clearly embarrassed him. He was fair mithered, as my mam would have said. He asked if I knew who the father was and I said of course I did. But I didn't want to say.

He looked even more embarrassed and the interview ended up with me feeling sorry for him. I became certain that he was a lame dog. He was the last one I was ever going to help over a stile, but because I'd decided he was that, we kept in touch over the years.

Chiefie Chalmers guessed. He became very protective, wouldn't let me up ladders or lift anything heavy, which took a bit of doing because now, as the silly old Group Captain had said, 13 Squadron really was on the up-and-up. There was talk of converting to Beaufighters and before I left that's what happened. I could see even then that the ship-sinking operation had been the turning-point for them. But at what a cost!

One morning, I was violently sick in the hangar. It reminded me of the time Peter Maddox had been sick, and being sick had saved the crew going on that first fatal operation.

Being sick didn't save me. Chiefie took me into the office, put his arm round my shoulders and told me I'd have to face up to things. Get myself discharged and sorted out.

I would have delayed longer had I not had a telegram from our next-door neighbour to say my mother/grandmother had died of a stroke. I was shattered. I went up to Leeds on two days' compassionate leave for the funeral, and sitting in the train coming back, I thought it all out.

First I had to see the Medical Officer, Flying Officer Stamford. Although in January a young male medical officer had been posted in, he wasn't much liked, and her clinics were always better attended than his. I was glad to see a woman and she was kind. She asked me if I had family to go to and I lied and said that I had. She asked me if I wanted the baby and I said no, but I would look after it and love it when it came, and that at least was true.

'What's your relationship with the baby's father?' she asked me.

'He's dead.'

'I'm sorry.' She took my hand in both hers. I saw she was wearing a diamond engagement ring. As she saw me looking at it, she blushed, slipped it off her finger and threaded it through a chain round her neck, tucking it out of sight under her collar.

'I've only just got it,' she said, apologising to me of all people. Or maybe she was just apologising for her happiness. 'I shan't wear it for a while. People talk.'

I wondered who it was she was engaged to. But as I was coming out, I saw the Squadron Humber drive up. Out got Wing Commander Cavendish, walking sprightlily and actually smiling, so I drew my own conclusions. I remember thinking, That's life! Someone's on the up-and-up. Someone else is on the down-and-down. But I didn't begrudge her her happiness. If she could find it with him, if she could humanise him, good luck to her!

And now, as I sat in a pew waiting for the memorial window service to start, I looked across the aisle of Marsh-field Church at a smart and handsome couple being shown by the verger to their seats, and there they were. Charles and Lesley Cavendish. They looked happy enough. They didn't recognise me.

I had had one more talk with Simon Wetherby before I left Marshfield. The RAF in its wisdom makes every single person who leaves a station go round to every Section with what's called a clearance chit. I suppose this is in case they leave with a library book or an unpaid Mess bill or something more valuable in their kit-bags. The aircrew never have these filled in properly. They sign the clearance chits themselves with names like Donald Duck and Mickey Mouse and Adolf Hitler, and nobody takes a blind bit of notice. But it's a different story for us on the ground.

So having got cleared from the orderly room and collected my railway warrant to Leeds, I went to the chapel. The padre told me there was no more news of Jack, and I knew for certain I would never see him again.

The talk on the grapevine was that Jack had been moved over these last few months to so many hospitals that all trace of him had been lost. And Ginger, when he was convalescent, had told Pam he reckoned maybe Jack wanted to be lost.

The padre didn't tell me this, but maybe he knew. He gave me the address of a home for mothers and babies in Leeds, actually in Headingley, quite near our house in Alma Terrace. He said the home was run by the Church of England, was supposed to be large and comfortable with a big garden, and I should go there some weeks before the baby was born and stay on for several weeks afterwards.

He gave me a leaflet with a picture on it, and it looked quite nice and he told me to keep in touch with him.

On the day I was discharged from the Service, I had eaten all my Spam sandwiches by the time I was halfway to Leeds. It looked filthy and smelled sooty after the sweet-smelling fields and hedgerows, the soft mists of Marshfield, and the house was cold and unwelcoming without the presence of my mother/grandmother.

I had been told that I could keep the tenancy of the house for a while at least, and she had left me her furniture, including her sewing machine. Pam had given me two u/s parachutes as a farewell present, and as soon as I got home I started sewing them into underwear and little girls' dresses which I sold in the market.

I went through the house and made pretty clothes of any-

257

thing that wasn't too worn and faded. My efforts sold like hot cakes. They were just what people wanted in wartime.

Before I got too big and clumsy, I decorated the house and made some covers for the chairs. I took down the picture of the yellow-haired girl and the lame collie. From now on he would have to stay in the same field he was in, or get himself over the stile.

In its place I bought a cheap print of marsh birds in flight. They carried me back to those walks along the dykes with Jack and our last one looking for Christmas bulrushes.

The neighbours kept their distance, though I could feel they disapproved. And round about that time I began to understand my real mother a little.

What I will never understand is the Church of England home. I know now that Simon didn't realise what it was like. It was an enormous decayed house in the semi-suburbs, surrounded by a high brick wall. There was a garden but it was now all overgrown with sooty laurels that kept all the light from the windows. There was a large dining-room full of dark Victorian furniture where we ate our meals. There was one huge picture above the empty marble fireplace: Jesus on the Cross wearing his crown of thorns, dribbling the only bright colour — his drops of crimson blood.

The food was minimal and we were all hungry. The kitchen quarters of the house were given over to a laundry and by day and all day we worked in it, boiling sheets in overflowing coppers, scrubbing dirty collars and cuffs on drubbing boards, our feet in water up to our ankles.

But I survived it, and there I gave birth to John.

They say that a woman can never love the child of a rape. But I did. I do. He was the one compensation for losing Jack Horner. After he was born I did ask Simon to make what would be, for me, one last attempt to find out what had happened to Jack.

Even if he had found him, I wouldn't have contacted him. I was too ashamed. Too unclean. Any doubts I might have had about my uncleanliness the Church of England removed. All us girls were unclean.

Simon sent me a card for John's birth, with guardian angels joined over a crib, which I threw into the waste-paper basket, and he never found out what happened to Jack.

My life became a lot of nevers. I never fell in love with anyone else. And to this day, sitting in this church, watching half-familiar faces fill it with sad, sad memories, I had never been to church. I had fallen out with the Church over that home, for the mental mistreatment exceeded the physical, and the Church should never have allowed it to happen.

When I got back to my own little house, Simon came to see me. His disenchantment with the Church went hand in hand with mine. He told me then how well 13 were doing. They were now the leading pin-point bombing squadron of the RAF. Wing Commander Cavendish had been awarded a DSO for that famous ship-sinking op. There was some talk about an award for Mac-Gregor and someone wrote a citation, but apparently it never got beyond 13 Squadron's orderly room.

'Cavendish always blamed him for the dog,' Simon said. 'D'you remember that story? The dog that haunted the airfield?'

'Yes, I remember.'

'Supposed to be the dog that belonged to the 96th.'

'That's right. But people said it was a real dog and one of the cooks in our hut used to put out old meat for it.'

'I must say it was never heard again after MacGregor died.'

'D'you believe in that sort of thing, Simon?' I asked him as I handed him a cup of tea, and young John played on the floor.

I thought he gave young John a strange look. 'I believe,'

he said, stirring his tea, 'that there's a pattern and purpose to our lives. That something watches over us. Some "divinity that shapes our ends/Rough-hew them how we will." '

He finished his tea and set down the cup. 'I'll tell you something, Pip. Something I've never told anyone else. I watched the Me shot down. I saw something flash between it and the Blenheim.'

'Bullets,' I said and laughed, suddenly thinking Jack would have said something that sounded like that but was much ruder. But I remembered Chiefie saying he and the Maintenance Officer had examined the wreck, and it had been a bit of a puzzle, seeming to have been brought down by what appeared to be a collision with another aircraft — but there was no sign of collision on any of 13 Squadron's Blenheims.

And then I also remembered Peter Maddox babbling about the old-fashioned aeroplane, the DH 4, that had guided him in, and for a second I wished I could believe. But only for a second, and then I thought what strange things we believe, what crutches we use in order to get ourselves through life.

And yet I had no cause to grumble. Not all my nevers were bad nevers. After John was born, financially I never looked back. I suppose he provided the incentive. While he played around my feet, I sewed at my machine. I designed my own styles, cut them out and made them up. I established quite a clientele. An up-market clientele. I opened a shop which had a big flat over it, and a garden at the back for John to play in. I moved away from my disapproving neighbours.

When the war was over, I didn't join in the celebrations. But I did take John to see his grandmother and his feck-less step-grandfather and we had a reconciliation of sorts. I bought a lot of Irish tweeds and linens when I was there, and some lace. The tweeds were heavy to work on, but my ladies loved them.

I had a letter shortly afterwards from Simon, saying he was going into retreat to try to discover what he was meant to do. 'I so want a sign,' he wrote. 'I so earnestly want to believe. I feel my life should have a purpose. That I have something to give, something special to do.' He asked for news of John and of me.

John did well at school. He passed the 11-plus and went to Leeds Grammar School. Then, as I knew he would, he joined the RAF. But only on a short service commission. After that, he went into civil flying.

Shortly after that, Simon wrote to tell me he had decided to become a monk. Not just any old monk. He was to join an independent working order that bore only very loose Anglican allegiance. Their vows were the usual ones of poverty, chastity and obedience.

He would find most difficulty, he said, with obedience. The monastery was on the edge of the Yorkshire Moors near a village called Ruswarp behind Whitby. It was a private foundation and each monk followed his chosen job and gave to the community his own particular skill. He had not yet found his.

But John had. Aircraft and flying were in his blood. Were and are his life. He never misses an air show. He's a real gen man on all types of aircraft, old and new. He's a good-looking fellow with fair hair, a bit untidy, but lovably so. And thoughtful.

When Simon eventually found that his metier was stained glass-making, and when some time later he conceived this project of a memorial to Marshfield and 13 Squadron, John insisted on making a financial contribution, and on coming with me to the service. He wasn't married, but he lived with a nice young woman.

I knew John would always look after me if I needed looking after, which I hoped I never would. He loved me, which I certainly needed. But my one great need was the same as it was when I was eighteen: to love Jack Horner and to have him love me, and that was something nobody could do anything about.

I glanced around the church just once, as the standard-bearers brought in the flags, all dubbined boots and white gloves and military precision. I used to like the Squadron flag — the phoenix rising out of the ashes — and the Squadron motto, 'Out of the Fire'. But now the sentiment was too painful because my phoenix perished in the ashes, could never rise.

Then the clergy, all dressed up in embroidered satin and silk and silly hats, processed in, and Simon — I was proud of his simple white habit — came to sit beside John and me. John liked him. Over the years Simon had been to our house several times. As John got older he asked why I didn't marry Simon, and I said because neither of us was the marrying sort. We're friends. Indeed we are.

In his letter to me about the window Simon had said, 'I hope in it to capture what I didn't know I knew.'

I thought that was very profound. I was tremendously eager to see it. But first we had the hymns, the usual ones, 'Oh, God our help in ages past', and 'Guide me, O Thou great Jehovah', and the address by the retired Chaplain-General, who was dressed in the most colourful robes of all.

It was when the Chaplain-General had come forward and bade us all sit down that I spied Pam. She suddenly leaned forward and I saw a flash of yellow hair, and below it a pillar-box mouth. But she didn't see me. We'd kept in touch for several years. Until after she'd married Ginger and become an Air Force wife and gone to live in Hong Kong. From then on, they went to various postings and fewer and fewer letters came my way.

I listened to the Chaplain-General going on about the courage that never dies, the love, the tradition, the sacri-

fice which inspires generations from First World War to Second World War to Korea, to you name it. I gave all that an invisible curl of my lip. But John drank it in.

After the service was over, I would treat him to a slap-up meal in Hythe — not in that run-down pink hotel where Jack had taken me, that would have been too painful, but in a new place on the front where there was no barbed wire any more. Then it might be appropriate to tell him a bit more about his father.

Now the Chaplain-General was finishing and he was inviting Simon to unveil his window. I could see that Simon's hands were trembling so much that he could hardly pull the cord. I felt quite giddy myself. It was the combination of the melting waxy smell of flickering candles, the heavy scent of pine needles mixing with expensive perfumes and after-shave and incense.

Then the curtain swished back. The window was revealed in its glistening beauty and I was truly amazed.

Simon had indeed captured what he didn't know. Maybe what none of us really knew. But what all of us knew a little. Somehow he had captured the beauty of the air, so that one felt one was high up there, floating safely in ever-changing, delicately clouded heavenly blues and whites.

The main figure was St Michael, the Captain of the Heavenly Host, his wings shimmering, each feather delicately picked out, edged in silver, bending down to receive two airmen, one in the khaki of the First World War Yanks, the second in RAF blue. Both were young. The faces of both might have been modelled on John.

And as one looked, as in a great picture, one saw more and more. A brown retriever dog in the left-hand corner, and as a large candle guttered, and another was lit and infinitesmally the light changed, the window also shimmered and changed.

263

A rustle of interest and approval ran round the congregation. But it was John who pointed it out first.

'That's a wonderful effect!' He turned and spoke across me to Simon. 'How did you get just that suggestion of the DH 4?'

He was pointing to a white cumulus cloud below which, yes, now I saw it, and almost immediately now I didn't, a shadowy, ghostly, perfectly formed DH 4!

Now everyone was pressing forward to congratulate Simon, shaking his hand. As the crowd moved forward, I saw Pam who waved eagerly. I saw a prosperous, plump Ginger. And then I saw a figure getting up to leave in haste. In such haste that he was caught full in the light of the wall sconces and I saw the wreckage of his face.

I grabbed my son's hand. I didn't tell him anything. I just pulled him along against the tide of people pressing forward. I put my head down and burrowed. But I held onto John. John had to be with me. John was my confession. John was my past. John was how Jack Horner would have to take me, always supposing he wanted me. Always supposing he wasn't married. Always supposing . . .

I caught Jack Horner by the tail of his jacket. He spun round, and then instinctively clapped his hand to the ruined side of his face.

I pulled his hand down. I stood on tiptoe and kissed it.

Then I did nothing. I just stood in front of him, saying nothing. I don't know what my son thought. I don't know what Jack thought either. Jack Horner looked at me almost in awe. Certainly in total disbelief. Then he looked at John and then at me again.

Then he flung his big long arms wide, threw them round both of us, hugging us fiercely to him, rocking us backwards and forwards, backwards and forwards as if he would never let us go.

Never, never — my last and best never!

264